FINDING YOUR ZENITH

ELIZA PAYNE

Finding Your Zenith

Copyright 2016 by Eliza Payne

Cover art by theillustratedcat@gmail.com

To my one and only penguin, Scott

Acknowledgments

I would be remiss if I didn't take a moment to stop and thank the folks that made this book possible. First and foremost, I need to send out a special thank you to my husband, Scott. He is my soulmate and that place where I find my true zenith. Without him cheering me on, this book would have never seen the light of day. Also to my children, without whom I would not have full meaning of life and what it means to love someone unconditionally. Also, for my extended family, you are each and all special to me. Familial bonds are also central to the theme of this book and it is because of my family that I have such a well of knowledge to draw from on this subject. Love to you all.

I also would like to take the time to thank my online family, the people I met through Tumblr fandom and some of whom I can call real friends now. Without you and without this work that started out as a fanfiction and became something else entirely, this book would not be possible.

I also need to take a moment and send a big thank you to the two characters that inspired my own characters; this book is a tribute to that pairing. Those who have been there since this story's birth, you know what it means to me to have this tale out there for the world to read. It is because of these characters and the ones who became Jake and Lexi to me that inspired me to believe all the more that mythic love exists and that everyone has a right to find their true zenith, that highest place of being.

Finally, I need to thank the great state of North Carolina. I may not have been born here, but I am proud to call this state home. I fell in love in the Triad and that love has carried me from the mountains all the way to the sandy shores of the Outer Banks where this beloved tale is set back to good old K-Vegas where I hang my hat.

If home is where the heart is, then mine resides here, amongst family and friends.

Chapter 1

Lexi Green put her car in gear and pulled back out into traffic. She had just gotten her assignment and it was definitely going to be a tough one. She knew the name: Julian Belfast. His file was clear. Class III threat, considered armed and dangerous.

Her mission was very clear in her job as a U.S. Marshal. Orders had come down from top brass; she was to bring him in unscathed. She needed this job more than she needed to breathe. Her sister's very life depended on it. She had gotten herself involved with the worst kind of man and Lexi shuddered every time she thought about Laurel living in the same house with that psycho.

Thomas had been so sweet at first and Laurel had fallen hard for him. They had a whirlwind romance, marrying in a matter of weeks. Laurel was a school teacher at their hometown elementary school. Thomas was a cop and had come to her kindergarten class as a volunteer for the kids, teaching them about the danger of strangers.

Laurel had fallen for his sweet southern charm and boyishly handsome looks. Lexi had been so happy for her until that first night when Laurel had called her in the middle of the night, sobbing and telling her to meet her at the hospital. She had felt a cold dagger of fear pierce her heart at the sound of Laurel's voice. The only other time in her life she had ever sounded that broken was when their mama had passed.

Later that night, after she'd been properly looked over at the hospital, Laurel had told her that Thomas had been getting increasingly more violent. Lexi had listened in horror as her sister relayed the tale of the latest evening of horror.

Laurel said she had come home and cleaned up the house and made Thomas his favorite dinner. She had been planning it all week, Lexi remembered. It was their six month anniversary and Laurel had wanted to make it special. Laurel said she had opened the bottle of wine right before Thomas was supposed to arrive home. She said he had been late sometimes but never as late as he was that night.

Laurel had given her a small sad smile saying "I thought maybe he was late because he stopped to get me something for our anniversary. I had one glass before he got home just trying to calm my nerves because I was so worried. Every cop's wife knows there is a possibility her husband might not come home. It's bad enough worrying about you out there doing God knows what." Lexi had stayed silent at her remark; they had butted heads on Lexi's choice of occupation too many times to go into it now.

Laurel had told her that Thomas had finally gotten home and flew into a rage when he saw that dinner was cold. Laurel said she had tried to tell him that he had been late and she'd tried to keep it warm, but then he had thrown her against the wall screaming that if she wasn't a lazy drunk she'd have his dinners hot and ready for him.

By the time the fight was over and Thomas had finally passed out, he had broken three of her ribs, blacked her eye and broken her wrist. Lexi's heart had broken right then and there. She had taken her home with her and told her agency that she was taking the rest of the week off for a family emergency and they could go to hell if they didn't like it. There hadn't been any questions.

She had been disappointed when Laurel took him back a few days later on the promise that he would get help, but she hadn't been all that surprised. Sadly, she knew the statistics on domestic violence all too well.

But this latest fiasco of Thomas was the last straw. She had been planning on helping get her sister away from him for a long time. She knew a friend of a friend who ran an underground halfway house for battered women. It didn't cost anything; people volunteered their time, talent and resources. There was only one small problem. The halfway house was in Alaska and required a private pilot with their own plane. So Lexi had been working day and night to put extra money away to fly Laurel to safety.

It also needed to be someone they could trust. To make matters worse, Thomas was an Atlanta city cop and as such, he had connections everywhere. He was a dirty one at that, from what she could discern, and it was hard to tell who greased whose palms in Atlanta where he was currently working.

The only solution, before taking that kind of risk, was to hire a private pilot and they were certainly expensive. But she had worked hard her entire adult life and she had quite a nice nest egg set aside for a rainy day. This wasn't quite what she had in mind for its purpose, but her sister's safety trumped a trip to Jamaica hands down.

Focusing on her case now as she drove, she pondered over the information she had so far been able to glean. She had read the file at least three times before she walked out of her boss, Matt Lincoln's office. He was the one who had given her this assignment. He had wanted her to make certain that she could handle it and if it would be worth the risk overall. The back story on Julian was that he was a wanted fugitive. He had been accused of murdering thirty three people in the most horrible ways imaginable. He had gutted them and dressed them like they were deer and had evidently left pieces of them all over the state of Georgia and parts of the Carolinas.

It wasn't in the file but Matt, had told Lexi that the stomach, intestines, liver and spleen of each victim were never found. It was believed that he kept them as trophies. Some speculated that he might be eating them. Lexi hoped that the last part was some sort of urban legend from some backwater southern town. Lexi sighed as that was exactly where she was headed now. When Julian had been indicted, he had somehow managed to wrangle the smoothest and dirtiest defense attorney in the state of Georgia. He had wisely suggested change of venue and in some loophole of a technicality the bastard had ended up out on bail. Predictably, since then, he had gone off the grid.

Lexi didn't know where to start exactly, so she was heading to the rural area surrounding Charlotte, North Carolina, where the only lead she had was located. Julian had once been involved in a gang down there and she was going to go feel that out and see if she got any bites. Criminals on the run often went back to their roots. All she needed was for him to make one mistake and he was all hers.

Being a U.S. Marshal isn't exactly what every little girl dreams of, but that's exactly the path that Lexi's life had taken. She had gone to nursing school at the very young age of 20, finishing at the top of her class.

She had then worked as an emergency room nurse in the heart of inner city Atlanta while simultaneously converting her associate degree to a bachelor's degree. She started nursing as a fresh faced 20 year old and by the time she had decided to change careers at the age of 26, she felt burned out and twice her age. She had seen the worst things that human beings could do to one another.

Lexi knew that the worst thing for her was the number of rape victims she had seen. She had quickly become a forensic nurse specialist in the area of rape investigation in an attempt to help the poor girls, women and even men she saw come in night after night. The hardest part was when she went to court to advocate for her victims and to give testimony on the perpetrator's evidence, oftentimes the assailant went unpunished or received a light sentence.

But most disheartening was the number of perpetrators who jumped bail and left without a trace. Once impassioned about her work, she became increasingly unsatisfied and regretted her decision to become a nurse. She thought about changing career paths and going into a different field of nursing, but at night when she was lying in bed and supposed to be sleeping, those people's faces flashed before her eyes. They were the victims of rape, but more than that they were the faces of a horribly failing justice system.

She had stumbled upon the whole thing quite by accident. She had put in a search for one of the known assailants in the case she was supposed to testify on and she came across something about a U.S. Marshal apprehending a known serial rapist. She knew at that moment that was the career she was meant for.

She had no qualifications as a law enforcement official; like none whatsoever. But, she had wrangled herself a "meeting" with Matt Lincoln, the head of the U.S. Marshal regional office in Georgia. She had pleaded her case and provided him with a polished resume and an enthusiastic speech of how her nursing and forensic expertise could lend to her apprehension of the "bad guys".

He had sent her on her way, but from that day forward, Lexi had made herself an ever-annoying presence, waiting outside his building every day, bringing him coffee and homemade brownies.

Oh yeah, she had been shameless in her pursuit. Lexi suspected he had given her the position and slid her in under the radar just to get her off his back. She really had made his life a living hell. That had been a year ago and she knew she had more than proven herself in Matt's eyes. He pretended to give her a hard time, but she knew he was secretly proud of his protégé.

Lexi pulled into the dive bar on Peachtree Grove Boulevard on her way out of town. She was supposed to be meeting the pilot for her sister's "disappearance" to give him the deposit. That was how sure she was that she was going to nail Julian's ass to the wall. Lexi pushed all other thoughts from her mind as she pulled the handle open to the bar and squinted as her eyes adjusted to the fusion of bad lighting and swirling smoke from cigarettes and something that smelled suspiciously like marijuana to Lexi's trained nostrils. But, she didn't care one bit about who was getting high. She was here to put her plan into motion.

Scanning the dimly lit interior, she finally was able to identify him as the only one sitting at the bar.

Her earlier fears of being able to pick him out of a crowd were unfounded. The only other people in the place were a fifty-ish year old woman and an old man sitting at the opposite end of the bar. The pilot was sitting at the far end, one hand on his glass on the counter and the other dangling a cigarette between two of his fingers. She watched him as he took a draw from it, squinting his eyes slightly as he did.

He had chestnut colored hair that was shaggy with locks that fell slightly over his eyes when he glanced down into his half empty glass; whiskey unless she missed her guess. He was wearing a black t-shirt, tight blue jeans, and a black leather vest stitched with wings on the back.

He turned to see what the bartender behind the bar had been staring at and she met his gaze that seemed to appraise her carefully and his eyes flickered between what appeared to be interest and amusement.

He didn't look anything like Lexi thought a pilot should. She silently chastised herself for expecting something like those adventure movies from the eighties, lasso in hand and hat perched atop his head. Because instead it looked like she had gotten something akin to a street urchin; albeit a very good-looking street urchin. He had the bluest eyes of anyone she'd ever seen besides herself and she was instantly disarmed. *That*, she did not like at all.

Lexi took a deep breath and walked up to him, extending her hand. "Hello Mr. Jackson, my name is Lexi Green."

Chapter 2

Jake had seen her walk in; she would have been hard to miss in a place like this. He knew she didn't think he saw her, but it was his job to spy on people when they didn't know it. It was also his responsibility to know where every person and every threat was located.

His survival and sometimes the survival of others depended on his keen senses. They were overdeveloped from his years of training in Special Ops Forces. He guessed you could consider what he did as highly paid favors. He was a mercenary and while ruthless, he was known for getting the job done, but in the most tactful and expedient way possible. Jake knew that confused most people because he had the dumb redneck look going on. It was a good cover given that he was from Georgia anyway and the southern drawl came naturally.

He watched the blonde, who had just come in, carefully look him over and he almost wanted to sneer at her. She looked like a goody two shoes; like she had just walked off the cover of a fashion magazine. She was wearing black pants with heels that ended in legs that seemed to travel to the sky. Her narrow waist was accented by a tight-fitting pink sweater that fell off one shoulder to reveal porcelain skin and a black tank top with spaghetti straps that looked like they'd slide down nice and easy.

He flushed at that last errant thought, feeling slightly bad for thinking it and blamed it on the half empty glass of whiskey killing his inhibitions.

He knew he was supposed to be meeting some hotshot U.S. Marshal and he had to admit, this girl had him curious. She wasn't what he had expected at all. For one thing, she didn't look any older than 19; baby-faced, scrubbed clean of any obvious make-up, wheat-gold hair arranged in a neat up-do.

Her mouth was set in a thin hard line as she crossed the room to meet him. Her movements were graceful, yet had purpose. She was so slight with her lithe body, it didn't even look like her feet hit the floor fully before she was in stride again. It was almost as if she was floating on the air; like an angel.

An angel?

Where the hell had that come from? He'd clearly been out of commission for far too long and it was making his mind go soft at the first sight of a pretty face.

He shook his head and picked up his glass and took another long swallow of his whiskey, relishing the burn as it hit the back of his throat.

She had just introduced herself and had extended her hand and his brain seemed to be running about two steps behind. He rubbed his palms over his jeans and took her delicate hand in his much larger one. He had expected her handshake to be limp and clammy, but instead her hands were warm and soft with a firm grip.

"Jake Jackson. You can call me Jake," he finally managed.

She eyed him warily, her brows furrowed in obvious curiosity, like she was trying to figure out a puzzle etched onto his face. He had never seen anyone look at him with such open scrutiny before. He shifted in his seat, feeling slightly restless all the sudden. He took another swig of his drink and stubbed out his cigarette in the ash tray.

She looked at him with mild amusement that she was disguising as disapproval. "You planning on drinking while flying my sister?" She asked him, but she really was genuinely curious.

He ignored her question and found himself wondering if she drank. "You want anything?" He motioned to the bartender; his drink was about gone. No sense in waiting until it was done to order another, he mused.

"Just a soda please." Lexi smiled sweetly at the bartender as he walked away.

"You even old enough to drink?" Surely you had to be at least 21 to be a U.S. Marshal, but damn if he could remember the rules right now.

Something like surprise and anger flashed across her features before she answered. He could tell she was biting her tongue and it amused him for reasons he couldn't understand.

"Yes, I'm old enough to drink." Lexi drew out the last word and smoothed her hand down over her pants leg, brushing away imaginary lint. She reached into her bag for her envelope and she noticed Jake got fidgety all the sudden. She realized with a start that he had been reaching for his gun. Who did this guy think she was? The mob?

"Do I make you nervous, Mr. Jackson?" She asked him as he took the envelope from her and scanned the contents quickly before stuffing it inside his vest. She vaguely wondered how there was room for a pocket since it fit him so snugly, but then he was speaking again. She didn't know why, but she bristled every time he spoke.

He carefully appraised her as she watched him take another sip of his drink. He snorted derisively. "Nervous, nah. I don't get nervous." He paused. "You can call me Jake. Only person called Mr. Jackson was my father."

She eyed him carefully and looked over his features. "I think I'll call you Jackson. It just seems to suit you better."

She didn't want to say it but she would prefer him to call her Miss Green. She liked her name just fine, but Lexi didn't exactly sound like a badass Marshal name. It sounded like the little girl with blonde pigtails that her daddy had pushed on their tree swing summer after summer. But she wasn't that little girl anymore and hadn't been for a long time.

Jake had to admit when she put her hand in her bag, he had been afraid she was reaching and getting ready to shoot him. In his line of work, he had to be prepared for anything. Besides that, his upbringing had prepared him perfectly for this life. It was like he was made for the world they lived in today. He had learned how to track and hunt and fish early in life courtesy of his father. Survival skills, the eldest Jackson had called them.

He had taught his older brother, Jeb too, but he hadn't taken to it as well as Jake had. He thought it was probably because Jake was a loner whereas Jeb was the exact opposite; he hated to be alone. He always had to be near people.

While Jake usually stuck to one night stands, Jeb almost always had a steady girl by his side. Jake had just never found that girl he guessed. He'd never given it much thought. Getting close to people so far in life had only brought him more pain. Better to be alone than to risk the hurt.

He watched the blonde take a delicate sip of her soda. "You didn't answer my question," she said quietly.

He realized he'd never answered her question about drinking and flying. "Yeah." He paused. "I mean no. I won't be drinking when I am flying my plane." He didn't know why he was tripping up on his words. He was usually a man of few words and very succinct. He liked to keep it short and simple, but he thought he had probably spoken more words to this girl in five minutes than he had his old man his whole sorry life.

Lexi nodded. "So, I'll call you when I have everything set up on the other end. Probably be about three weeks or so. You'll be ready?"

"I'll be ready." He drained the last of his drink and set it down on the counter with a dull thud.

"Okay then. I'll be in touch. See you soon, Jackson." She finally finished and then turned on her heel and left.

"See ya soon, Green". Jake enjoyed watching her walk away about as much as he enjoyed the annoyed gleam in her eye.

He wasn't the type to ogle a woman, but he would be blind if he didn't appreciate watching her hips sway back and forth as she walked away. He swallowed hard and pulled his motorcycle helmet off the neighboring barstool and got up to leave the bar. Time for a nice long ride to clear his head and cool down his core body temperature, which was way too hot all the sudden.

🍒 🍒 🍒 🍒 🍒 🍒 🍒 🍒 🍒 🍒

Lexi got back in her car and tried to squelch the bit of nerves she had just had to swallow while in the bar paying the pilot. Something about him unnerved her and made her want to talk to him for hours simultaneously.

When she walked up on him, the first thing that she had noticed was his light crystal blue eyes that seemed to pierce her. She hadn't missed the way he had taken in the sight of her. A girl would have to be blind to not notice a guy checking her out.

She guessed he was handsome in a more rugged way with a strong jaw line and hair that fell just slightly over his eyes that added an air of mystery.

She didn't know what in the world had come over her standing there and talking to him but looking at him she had a hard time forming coherent thoughts. She had gotten used to men trying to intimidate her in her line of work but there was something else about him and the way he spoke to her.

He was very handsome and she guessed the bad boy look had its own appeal. A smile crept onto her face as she remembered how he'd watched her walk away. She realized with horror that she was attracted to him and the smile faded from her features instantly. That could not happen, she chastised herself. She would have to be in close proximity of this man in a few short weeks.

Her thoughts were interrupted by the sound of her cell phone ringing. She reached into her bag, blindly searching for it, while keeping her other hand on the wheel. Finally locating it, she swiped her thumb across the screen quickly when she saw it was Laurel.

She was crying again and Lexi's heart thudded out staccato beats all the way to her feet. Adrenaline shot through her; something bad had happened. She knew it. "What's wrong?" she rushed out.

"Lexi, can you come get me? Please?" Laurel begged. She was sobbing and nearly incoherent.

"Of course. Where are you?" Lexi tried to keep her voice calm and soothing. Laurel sounded like she was at her breaking point.

"I'm at the corner of Main and Mangrove," Laurel whispered.

"Are you someplace safe?" Lexi cringed at the thought of Thomas getting to her before she did. She wanted to know what he had done this time while at the same time she knew it was going to be painful to listen to. The episodes were getting more and more frequent. She was going to have to get her out of there quicker.

"Yeah, I'm inside a laundromat. Lexi, please hurry." Laurel started sobbing again after she rattled off the address and Lexi thought her heart was going to break. As close as the Green girls were, you couldn't hurt one without the other feeling it to their core.

Lexi hung up with her sister and quickly punched the address into her GPS and drove as fast as her car would allow.

She pressed her speed dial and got an answer on the second ring.

"Jackson." His voice was clipped and gruff.

"It's me, Green. You gonna have a problem if we move the timeline up?" she asked him.

"No, ain't got nothing else going on now. Why?" he asked her.

"Be ready to go in two hours. We'll meet you at the airport. And sober up." She hung up without further explanation. He was really her only choice right now and she wasn't going to give him a chance to say no. She thought about her job. She thought about Julian. But all that would have to wait. Hopefully she could convince Laurel it was time to make a move; a permanent one.

Lexi got to the rundown laundromat on the wrong side of downtown Atlanta in record time. She pulled up to the curb and reached over to open the door as a bedraggled Laurel crawled into the car and shut the door. Lexi's plan was to drive them straight to her apartment. She lived in a nice complex north of Atlanta. It was still midday thank God, so the beltway was pretty clear. Sometimes she wished for the simpler days on the farm. She and Laurel didn't say a word.

Lexi kept sneaking furtive glances at her sister. Her hair was slicked down over the back of her head and that's when Lexi noticed the trail of blood going down behind her ear. She almost stopped the car, it alarmed her so, but instead reached out to tentatively touch her sister's head making certain there was nothing that needed immediate medical attention. Feeling relatively satisfied it could wait the 30 minute drive to her apartment, she settled back to concentrate on her driving, sparing glances at her very quiet sister every so often.

Laurel had bruises forming all up and down her arms, the purple marks marring her olive toned complexion. She glanced finally at her face where she was sporting a sizeable black eye. Her sweatshirt was ripped at the collar and Lexi could make out faint finger-bruises under the hem.

They pulled up to her apartment and Lexi helped Laurel out of the car. They went up the walkway, a couple of curious neighbors poking about. Lexi just ignored them as she guided her sister to her door. She let out the breath she had been holding when she closed the door behind them and flipped the dead bolts into place. She removed her gun from the back waistband of her pants, placing it on the table in her entryway and led Laurel to the bathroom in the back. The lighting was better and she could really look her over and patch her up if needed.

"You want to talk about it?" Lexi gently prodded as she took gauze and blotted at the cut right above her eyebrow.

Laurel nodded. "I think I have to. Or else I'm gonna just keel over from the weight of it." Laurel looked at her miserably with tears streaming down her face, her dark hair a mess of tangles and matted blood.

Lexi's own eyes teared up at the heartbreaking picture her sister made in the harsh lighting of this bathroom. Besides, it was kind of an unspoken agreement that neither of them would ever cry alone. It had been that way since they were little and was even more so now that both their parents had died. Their mom had died when they were both teenagers. Cancer had taken her in the span of a few short months.

Then, their daddy had died just this year. He had lived a nice long life but he had lost his leg earlier the previous year due to his diabetes and after that he just seemed to go downhill. Then in January, he had gotten pneumonia and just passed in his sleep. There wasn't a day that went by that she didn't miss him.

She pushed her tears away with the backs of her hands and continued working until Laurel was ready to tell her what happened.

Laurel reached up and stilled Lexi's hand by lightly gripping her wrist. She looked Lexi in the eye, her big blue eyes boring into Lexi's. "He raped me Lexi." At that, she crumpled forward and let Lexi take her in her arms. A deep and twisting pain gnarled at her gut as she held her sister's head to her shoulder, rubbing her hand over her back as she sobbed brokenly. "He's never done that before."

Lexi didn't need to know the how or the why or the details at least not yet. The nurse in her took over. Suddenly she was grateful for the pain in the ass it had been to keep her nursing license up to date. She took call at the hospital one night a week and helped out extra when she could as a sexual assault nurse examiner. Every instinct in her said to take Laurel to the hospital, but the fact that this was Thomas made that impossible.

Fortunately, she had a couple of rape kits in her car and while they couldn't do anything with it just now, at least they would have it for later if needed. One day he was going to screw up and when he did, Lexi was going to be there to nail his ass to the wall.

She tried to be as sensitive as possible. "Don't say no until you hear me out. We don't have to do anything with it right now or, even ever, but I want to do a rape kit on you." Laurel just cried harder. But nodded her head in assent.

Lexi was shocked and heartsick at the same time. She hadn't expected her to agree so easily. Laurel's willingness to put herself through the examination and saving the evidence for possible prosecution let Lexi know that Laurel was finally finished with the whole thing.

"I want away from him, Lex." Laurel whispered in a tortured voice. "I want away from him more than I want to breathe."

"I know. We're getting you away from him. *Tonight*." Lexi promised her as she took her into her arms and she just let her cry.

So help her God, she meant what she said. She was getting her sister away from Thomas Garner and that bastard would touch her again over her own dead body.

🐝 🐝 🐝 🐝 🐝 🐝 🐝 🐝 🐝 🐝

Jake hung up the phone, a little perturbed that she had ordered him around but she was paying him, so he supposed that went with the job. He was now waiting at the airport by the plane on the tarmac. They were set to take off in twenty minutes. He hoped the broad wasn't going to be late. He knew that's usually the one thing he could count on from women: they were always late and never on time.

He had already done his pre-flight checklist. It was a small plane, a Cessna he had bought with his first paycheck when he'd first started working for Special Ops Forces or SOF, a very specialized and elite private military group.

In looking at the faded silver paint job, the old girl wasn't much to look at but she'd done him right over the years. He always meant to get another plane, but he didn't see the point since she ran just fine and always had.

Jake watched a car approach the small commuter tarmac and figured that was Green and her sister. He pushed himself away from the plane and walked over to help them with their bags. He was surprised that they were early, but that was nothing compared to how surprised they were that they only had one small bag each.

He watched as Lexi got her sister, Laura, he thought, out of the passenger side. As his gaze carefully appraised the brunette getting out of the passenger side of the small sedan the marshal was driving, his eyes narrowed and he swore to himself softly. She looked like someone had taken a baseball bat to her.

He knew her story; hated it. He knew bastards like her husband. Hell, his father had been one of them. He met Lexi's eyes and it looked like she had been crying. Her sister was *still* crying. Jake cringed; two crying women on his plane? *Ah hell no*, he thought, grumbling to himself. He already didn't know what to do with one crying female, but *two*?

Lexi helped Laurel up the steps to the plane and settled her in, making her as comfortable as possible. She had known the rape kit was uncomfortable and humiliating, but she was glad her sister had agreed to it. It may come in handy down the line.

She tried to be as sensitive as possible and kept Laurel's dignity as best as she could and still be efficient in gathering the evidence. She had taken out her camera and photographed every bruise, every handprint, and every mark on her body; sadly, there had been many.

Lexi didn't know if it was better or worse that this was her sister. It was hard to remain professionally calm when you wanted to kill the bastard that hurt your flesh and blood. It was a foreign feeling to Lexi, all this rage she was feeling. She didn't really know what to do with it all the moment, so she just pushed it down, letting it coil in her gut and fuel her adrenaline so they could get out of there.

They were just getting ready to close the door to the plane when they heard the first shots. Laurel looked to her, the terror evident in her eyes.

"Stay down." She whispered harshly to her sister as she un-holstered her gun and flipped the safety to the off position, then crept to the door to survey the situation.

Jake was still outside. She squinted to see him hunkered down behind a couple of barrels and shooting blind at the three dark figures, what looked like policemen coming out from the bushes at the edge of the tarmac. She held her gun down, confused as to what was going on. Jake was shooting at them and a bullet pierced one of the cop's shoulders and Lexi gasped as he went down hard.

Jake heard her and turned, motioning to her. "Get down, Green!" He barked.

Despite one of them having been shot, two officers were both still in pursuit and gaining ground fast. The other one was still lying unmoving on the tarmac. She almost thought she recognized them, but she couldn't be sure in all of the chaos.

Everything after that point happened both in slow motion and faster than she could process it all. She pushed down the frisson of fear in her gut and fired at the one that hadn't been shot, narrowly missing his hip and hitting his hand, his gun bouncing across the tarmac.

Jake fired his gun again from ahead of her and one of them went down. He made a run for the plane, herding Lexi ahead of him, knowing the other guy had been shot in his right hand and wouldn't be able to pull the trigger properly.

He pulled the plane door behind him, slamming it shut and climbed into his seat, quickly setting the equipment for take-off.

That's when Lexi noticed that Jake was bleeding. He had a large dark stain forming on his blue chambray shirt. It was starting to soak through the waistband of his jeans. She probed at it, checking for a bullet wound.

Jake winced when he felt her touch him. "Ow, dammit." He swatted her hand away, his expression that of a wounded animal.

"You've been shot!" She said incredulously. He was getting ready to take off in a plane and had probably just shot two men who just happened to be police officers. They were going to be fugitives. She was starting to hyperventilate.

"Calm down, half-pint. It's just a flesh wound." He was trying to block the pain so they could get off the ground and he could maybe do his job and save their sorry asses. He didn't need her fussing over him.

He took off down the runway and in seconds, they were up in the air. Checking the flight panel one last time, he turned to level his gaze at her, eyes blurring in the process. "Now don't panic, Green. I've set the plane on autopilot. But I think-." And at that, everything went dark.

Lexi gasped as she watched Jake slump over in his seat.

Now what?

They had been shot at, two cops were likely dead and the person that was supposed to be flying the plane was now slumped over in the pilot's seat. She wondered how everything had gone to hell so fast.

Chapter 3

Lexi was trying very hard not to panic, but she could feel bile rising up in her throat as she felt for Jake's pulse, thankfully steadily thrumming under her fingertips. She was pretty close to panicking, but she tried to stay calm, drawing on every bit of training she had in situations like this. Even though her job was dangerous, she had so far managed to avoid being shot at. She guessed at some point anyone's luck would run out in that avenue, especially in this line of work.

Laurel was already over the top hysterical and if one more thing happened, Lexi feared she might go into shock. Using her critical thinking skills was tough in any crisis situation and for the second time that day, she was so glad she had kept up her nursing degree in the past couple of years. It looked like her medical training was going to come in handy yet again.

Lifting his shirt hem slightly, she examined the skin along his flank where she noted a good sized chunk of flesh missing. It was definitely going to need at least a few stitches.

A couple of inches to the left and he might be missing more than just some skin and tissue, she thought. In glancing at the plane's gauges and instruments, she figured it was good that she didn't hear any alarms or see any angrily flashing lights.

She grabbed her bag and pulled out a bottle of water, opened it and poured it directly on the pilot's face. She felt he had likely had a drop in his blood pressure from the wound and the pain. He hadn't likely lost enough blood for it to be related to that. She sat back on her heels and waited as he came to.

Jake sputtered and opened his eyes to see the blonde kneeling over him and he couldn't remember for the life of him why his face was wet. She was so beautiful with those concerned blue eyes boring into him. Had they gotten caught in the rain?

Everything then came rushing back to him. He sat up quickly and checked the instrument panel. Satisfied that they were still on course, he turned back to Lexi, a bit chagrined at having lost consciousness. "How long was I out?" He asked her gruffly.

"About a minute." She replied. "Feeling better?" she asked him, her voice soothing and calm.

"Yeah, I think so." Jake rubbed his hand over his face. "Why is my face wet?" He asked her.

"*Your face?*" Lexi asked, unable to control the rising panic in her voice. Now that the fear had subsided and the danger of the plane crashing was hopefully passed, she could feel the anger building.

"You, I mean, *we* shot two people, you managed to get yourself shot, then passed out while flying an airplane, and you're worried about why your face is wet?" Her voice had risen at least two octaves. She had both hands on her hips and was standing over him, her face flushed with anger.

"Now wait just a damn minute. Why are you yellin' at me? I put my life at risk for you. I had to shoot those guys back there *because* of you. So excuse me *darlin'*, if anyone has a right to be put out by all this, it's me, not you." He spat out the words and brought his hand to his side, pressing in on it hoping to squelch some of the pain, because it hurt like a sonofabitch.

"They were cops!" Lexi yelled. "I'm going to lose my job. You do realize that, don't you?"

"They weren't cops." He said gruffly while closing his eyes against the pain and leaning his head back against the pilot's chair, willing himself to be anywhere but here. Her yelling certainly wasn't helping his aching head either.

"Wait, what?" Lexi was confused. They had sure looked like cops to her.

"I mean they were, but they're dirty. They're Garner's guys." He explained. "He probably sicked them on you."

Lexi was silent for a moment. All the pieces started clicking together in her mind. They were working with Thomas. That meant that Thomas likely knew that they were headed out of town. And that was not good.

Maybe Matt would know what to do now. He was the one who had gotten her the contact information for the shelter for Laurel. She glanced back at her latest thought and noticed that she had finally fallen asleep. Lexi had given her a sedative before they boarded the plane. She was pleased to see that it had finally taken effect.

"I'm gonna lose my job. Laurel is-." But she couldn't finish. Everything had gone to hell. She really just wanted to lay down and cry, but she knew she wouldn't even if she could.

"I'll call your boss. He owes me a favor." Jake was eyeing her carefully. He was gonna lose it if she started crying. He wasn't any good with females and ever had been. He sure as hell didn't know what to do if one of them had a case of the waterworks.

"Matt?" Lexi asked surprised. "How do you know him?"

"Don't matter. I'll call him, tell him what's up." He jerked his head in Laurel's direction. "We can't take her where we were planning to." He said, checking the instruments again and pushing a couple of buttons. He'd make the call when they landed. He knew Matt from way back. They had served in armed Special Forces together. Matt had gotten out when Vivian had gotten pregnant with Carl. He had said the job was too risky and he was right.

Jake had just never had any reason to care about dying, so this job suited him just fine. It was dangerous sure, but it was lucrative and sure as shit beat fixing cars for the rest of his life. That's what he and Jeb had done with their old man before he died.

Then Jeb had gone on a bender. He turned up from time to time, but he never stuck around for long. He hadn't seen him now going on a year.

Lexi felt the dip of the plane and looked up at Jake pushing buttons on the instrument panel. "What do you mean?" Surely he didn't mean what she thought he did. They couldn't go back to Atlanta.

"Calm down. We gotta change course. Every cop in the city has a friend of a friend all over the country. We can't go to Alaska. We need another plan. I think I know where to take her to but I'll have to make some calls when we land." He jerked his head toward Laurel.

"Where exactly are we going?" Lexi asked him.

"North Carolina," was his only reply. Lexi tried not to glare at him. She knew he was trying to protect her and make the most of their very bad situation, but it was starting to gall her that he was calling all the shots.

What the hell was in North Carolina, she wondered. Her mind was reeling over the past day's events. Too much had happened. She had been in stressful situations before. She was a trauma nurse for crying out loud. There wasn't much she hadn't seen.

But on some level she recognized the difference for what it was. The things she saw were happening to other people; strangers virtually. But the things that had happened in the last 24 hours, had happened to her or someone close to her. Lexi reached over and lifted Jake's shirt gingerly.

As Jake felt the marshal's hand go to his shirt as he changed the plane's course and involuntarily pulled away. He wasn't used to people touching him.

"Stay still." She commanded. "I gotta check and see if the bleeding has stopped." He stiffened at her touch but let her check out his aching side. Her gentle hands were probing the edges of the wound, pressing lightly and testing the delicate tissues. He winced and glanced down at where her head was bent down, her brow furrowed as she checked him over.

"Sorry." Lexi muttered. Something about touching his skin made her itch to move her hand higher. In lifting his shirt, she couldn't help but notice that he had a six pack. He was all muscle and sinew, hard planes and sharply defined lines. She swallowed hard and concentrated on the task at hand, chastising herself for thinking such thoughts. In all ways, he was a professional acquaintance and thoughts like were anything but prudent in this situation.

She pulled the shirt away from his skin. It was sticky with red-black blood. On closer examination, the wound was about four inches in diameter. She probed the edges gently with her fingers, taking care not to get too close to the opening so as to minimize the chance of infection.

She didn't like what she saw. It was still oozing and if he ever hoped for it to heal half way decent and not get infected, he was going to need stitches and she told him so.

He turned around to face her. "Ain't going to no hospital. Are you crazy? Garner's guys will have every law enforcement official in the country looking for us. It's why we're going to North Carolina. Sooner we land this plane and get to where we're going, the better off we're gonna be."

Lexi sat back a little and absorbed what he was saying. She decided that there was more to this man than met the eye.

She knew he used to be armed special forces, but now he worked for a private company, the one she had hired. He had come the highest recommended in their organization and it just worked out even better that he was local. She guessed that this was why.

It seemed like he really knew what he was doing and unless she missed her guess, he had connections too. Maybe between the two of them, they had a snowball's chance of getting out of this alive. "Well then you're gonna have to trust me to stitch it up." She announced.

He looked at her like she had just grown a horn out of her head. "I don't think so, short stuff."

Lexi was getting irritated with all his little jabs. Ever since she had met him in the bar, he took every opportunity to try to make her feel like a little kid. "Well I *do* think so. It's going to get infected if we don't stitch it up. Relax I used to be a nurse." He was still staring at her and once again she was feeling very much like an errant child.

"I promise I'll be gentle, so you don't cry." She said smartly, her eyes narrowing in silent challenge. She knew it would piss him off but, she didn't care. His macho bull crap was getting on her nerves.

Jake scoffed. "I ain't gonna cry." And it was true. He wouldn't; never did anymore.

He thought he probably stopped crying when his daddy started beating him. He had cried the first couple times, sure. But it didn't take him long to figure out that the louder he cried, the longer he got beat. It got so he didn't make a sound whenever his old man was in one of his moods and got to wailing on him. He hadn't cried a day since and wasn't planning on starting now just because he got himself shot. It wasn't the first time and likely wouldn't be the last.

"Need to go get your seatbelt on. We'll be landing soon." She nodded at him curtly and returned to her seat beside Laurel, doing as he requested.

Jake sat up straighter in his seat and got ready for the plane's descent. He had a vague idea of what they were going to do and he hoped his plan was going to work. He didn't have to question his motives on why he was doing this for her. He had read her file and had done his homework. He always did. He imagined he knew more about Lexi Green than she knew about him. He had researched her life right back to where she had gone to elementary school. He wasn't a stalker. It was just his job to know every possible aspect of his mission and this one was no different.

When he had seen Garner's guys coming across the tarmac, everything had clicked into place for him. He knew that Garner was a dirty cop. Those were the ones he hated the most. But he didn't think he'd go so far as to send armed men after his wife to kill her. He had been running the same outer circles with Thomas half his life, he figured.

He knew from the town grapevine that Thomas was an unsavory sort, but he didn't figure him to be a wife beater. That, to Jake, was the ultimate of low-life scum. Them and child abusers. He had no stomach for it and no tolerance either.

The way he figured it, two things could have come from his childhood. He could have turned out to be just like his old man or he could be doing what he was doing now, which was exacting justice where the legal system failed. Not exactly legal, but not against the law either. He thought if anybody deserved to die, it was Thomas Garner and he couldn't wait to do the honors.

Lexi's head was still spinning and she swear she felt a migraine coming on. It was all just too much. Laurel was worrying her to death. Jake had made a phone call as soon as they landed. He had taxied the plane into a hangar far off the tarmac. It had been big enough to house his plane and a conveniently placed non-descript black SUV with tinted windows. The air was warm in Charlotte as they had stepped off the plane, almost more sweltering than Georgia which Lexi found odd. It was only June and it had already been so hot, it was almost unbearable.

They were now in the SUV heading down the highway to a so-far undisclosed location. Lexi had asked twice and was met was stony silence. She figured it was one of those situations where the less she knew, the better.

She had never been to Charlotte before; she hadn't ever been anywhere in North Carolina before actually. She was so tired that she could probably fall asleep if it weren't for the big ball of tension in her neck and the throbbing behind her eyes. Laurel was sitting in the back, staring out the window. She had barely said two words since they had gotten off the plane. Every once in a while Lexi would hear a stifled sob and her heart clenched in her chest each time. She wished there was something else she could do.

She glanced over at Jake who was leaning back in his seat, driving with his left hand and holding a cigarette with his other one. Lexi had never been a fan of cigarette smoke but at the moment she had better things to worry about.

Besides, for some odd reason, she thought distractedly, it looked pretty sexy on him. She flushed at the intrusive thought. Sure, he was handsome, but she didn't even know if she could really trust him. Right now she was going solely on her friend's word that he was good people. She wasn't just entrusting him with her own life; she also had Laurel to think about.

Then again, when she considered the alternative of staying around in Atlanta to find out what other atrocities Thomas might be capable of was not an option either. No, this situation they were currently in, Jackson was about their only choice at the moment and she just had to pray that he was the right one.

Jake pulled off the highway and made a left at the intersection. He had driven this road so many times, he could drive it blindfolded with one hand tied behind his back. The day's fatigue was starting to wear on him. He was used to a certain amount of drama in his line of work, but it had been a while since he had been shot at. Been even longer since he had actually taken a hit, he thought, as his side throbbed something awful. He knew Lexi was going to have to stitch it and he didn't relish the thought, but he knew she was right, although he'd never tell her so.

She was beautiful, that was for damn sure, and had the most striking eyes he'd ever seen. They reminded him of staring into the pool at his beach house after the movement of the water was down to just a small ripple across the surface.

He got the feeling those baby blues got Lexi Green any desire imaginable. But telling her she was right in any fashion wasn't something Jake was willing to entertain. She seemed like the type that might enjoy it too much.

He sighed inwardly as he pulled into the long drive that was partially obscured by the forest that surrounded the entire property. He steered the SUV around the curves up the winding path until he reached the wrought iron gates, keying in his pin before pulling through them.

He automatically checked his rear view mirror to make sure no one was trying to sneak in under the cover of their vehicle. It was an old habit really; they had cameras and guards for that stuff here, but he knew it was better to be safe than sorry. He let out his breath and slumped in the seat a little as he saw the gates close behind them.

He pulled further down the driveway, guiding the vehicle along the curvy path to the main house. It was a small compound for the Special Ops Forces. When he had called Matt and explained the situation to him, his long-time friend had suggested they come here. He was the liaison between the US Marshals office and Special Ops. They didn't often work together, but this was just deemed a special case after Garner's stunt back on that tarmac.

Garner was directly involved with a known prostitution ring. To make matters worse, he was also suspected of money laundering, embezzlement, and there was even talk that he might be involved in a child pornography ring.

That last part was only a rumor but just the fact that it was floating around, it set Jake's teeth on edge and made him want to kill the guy with his bare hands; sick bastard. He wouldn't doubt if in the course of the Internal Affairs investigation, they found the proof they needed to nail his ass to the wall on that charge too.

When Laurel had called Lexi and they had moved their timeline up, Garner had released a shit storm the likes of which Georgia SBI had never seen. He had called in his goons; also known as the fuckers who had shot him. Now a chain of events had been launched that couldn't be reeled in, not even by the Governor of Georgia himself. Matt had filled him in when he had called. Jake was now a wanted fugitive thanks to that prick.

He knew they would eventually clear his name, but it galled him to think that his reputation was on the line right now. He had worked damn hard to earn the respect of men like Matt Lincoln and Gibbs Martin and he knew that they didn't believe anything they had been told. But it still pissed him off to even have to deal with something like this.

Matt had said that Lexi was wanted for conspiracy to murder since the guy Jake had shot had died at the hospital a short while ago. Thomas had covered all the bases, he thought bitterly. He hadn't told Lexi yet; he didn't imagine that it was going to go over well. And they couldn't all stay here; this was actually considered private property. It had changed hands several times so it was very hard to trace, but the property technically belonged Special Ops Forces and it could possibly be traced to Jake and thereby make Lexi automatically in danger of being apprehended. That was to say nothing of the danger it would put Laurel in.

The way Matt had told it, if they were arrested, they would both go away for a very long time and the questions sorting it all out would get asked later if they even lived that long.

No one liked a cop killer. Thomas had plenty of money that he had set up through several accounts overseas and he wasn't afraid to throw it around. He knew Matt was right too, considering Jake himself knew of at least five law officials and two judges that would turn their head the other way given the right incentive. Jake knew he would do fine in prison. He would be pissed as hell, but he would survive. However, in looking at Lexi he wasn't sure she would survive one night in a prison setting.

Lexi smoothed her hands over her pants, although she wasn't sure why. They were so badly wrinkled from the crazy day she had, it was hopeless and she really didn't think anyone was going to care if her pants weren't pressed and starched, she thought tiredly. All she wanted to do right now was crawl under the covers and not come out for at least a week. They had pulled up outside a very large house. It was starting to get dark by the time they pulled onto the property.

There were several smaller buildings out behind the main house, which looked like a mansion from the outside. She had no idea what Jake had planned but that was a situation she was planning to remedy very soon. She had to stitch him up still yet. She figured they had about another two hours before it would be past the point of being able to stitch up the wound. After that, it would be no use; any viable tissue for suture would have died off by then.

She was hoping that he might divulge at least half his plan while she was stitching him up. Her mind was reeling; she wondered how Laurel was going to stay safe. She wondered how she was going to get her job done. She wondered if she could trust any of this situation. She had too many damn questions and not enough answers, she sighed. She helped Laurel out of the car and walked with her to the front door.

She moved to get their bags out of the car, but Jake reached out and grabbed her hand to stop her. She looked up at him, startled at the action.

"I'll get it. Go on and get her inside. Thad will tell you where to take her." Lexi nodded and moved away from the trunk of the car.

Jake spoke in short clipped sentences, directing one of the discreetly armed men to grab Laurel's bags. Lexi could tell that once he got in his familiar surroundings, he was all business. This was where he was in his element, she noted. His attitude boasted confidence and for that she breathed a sigh of relief, as that was a good sign that he was good at his job and could indeed get them to safety as he had been paid to do. Furthermore, she had not failed to notice that since their arrival mere moments ago, the men below his rank treated him with utmost respect.

She walked up to the door, steering Laurel in what she perceived to be the right direction. Her sister's movements were robotic and calculated and Lexi looked away sadly. She couldn't help but draw a parallel that it seemed like the whole day had been on autopilot. From the time Lexi's phone had rang with a sobbing Laurel on the other end, she had been on edge and going through the motions.

If she felt that way, she could only imagine how Laurel was feeling. She had known plenty of women who had been raped before; it was literally in her job description, but she had never known someone on this personal level to be attacked in that way. She knew, as a health care professional and a law enforcement official, all the things she had been trained to do and all the things she was supposed to say to a rape victim, but this was her sister; her flesh and blood. It wasn't even remotely the same thing. All she really wanted to do was make sure that Thomas suffered for what he had done to her sister.

They were greeted at the door by an Asian guy in his mid to late twenties, fresh-faced, boyish good looks. He extended his hand, which Lexi accepted. "I'm Thad Lee. I've been assigned to your sister's detail."

Lexi shook his hand firmly and then released it. He had a warm smile that reached his eyes and Lexi took an instant liking to him. She had found in both her career paths that you could tell a lot about a person by their eyes. Thad Lee's eyes exuded warmth and it reassured her faith that they would be safe here. She glanced around to find Jake coming in the door carrying Laurel's bag. She moved to take it from him, relieved that she would finally be able to get her sister settled.

A woman came into the room. She was wearing a light pink track suit but was carrying a medical bag. The two images blended in Lexi's mind and she wondered if she was imagining things.

"I'm Melinda. I'm the psychiatrist here at The Compound." Lexi just nodded her head. She was still confused about why they were there. "I'm going to be taking care of Laurel." She said and extended her hand to touch Laurel's shoulder, trying to get her attention. "Laurel, you want to come with me. I'm sure you're exhausted. We can try to make sense of all this tomorrow. Right now, you need sleep."

Melinda was pretty, her hair done in a short pixie hairstyle, her hair a rich auburn color with streaks of mahogany that framed her delicate face. She had bright green eyes, just like Laurel. Her tone in speaking to Laurel was gentle, yet Lexi got the feeling that she wasn't giving any wiggle room in regards to her instructions.

Laurel just nodded and followed the woman up the grand staircase. Jake handed Laurel's bag off to Thad who followed behind the ladies. Lexi watched them ascend the stairs and turned to face Jake.

"Why are we here, Jackson?" It made her nervous, all the security in this place. She had seen places like it before, but they usually belonged to some drug lord. She had heard of Special Ops Force and she had read Jake's file but nowhere was there any mention of this place. She supposed that was the point. It would be hard to find Laurel here, even with Thomas's resources.

Jake sighed. He had known this was coming and he was not looking forward to telling her there was a warrant out for her arrest. With her sunshine and daisies good looks, she didn't look like she had ever gotten so much as a parking ticket. In fact, he'd be willing to bet on it.

"We, you and me, aren't stayin' here," he started. He held up his hand as he saw the flare of red firing up in her cheeks, a look he was becoming quite accustomed to. "Now just hear me out."

Lexi was starting to panic. She wanted to be with her sister. Laurel needed her now more than she ever had. And if Lexi was going to be honest, she needed to be near her sister right now. She had to be sure she was okay. To her horror and frustration, she felt the sting of impending tears in the corners of her eyes.

Jake tried to pretend like he didn't notice that she was getting ready to cry; he led her into the front sitting room and gestured for her to sit in one of the big overstuffed arm chairs. She sat primly on the edge of the seat and looking at Lexi's slight form, the chair seemed about to swallow her whole. He pulled out the ottoman from the matching chair on the other side of the fire place and sat down in front of her. He took a breath and began telling her everything that Matt had relayed to him.

She sat there, her expression a mixture of shock and horror as the tears slide down her face. Jake didn't know why but in that moment she reminded him of an injured bird, its wing broken. Damn he had to be tired if he was sitting here comparing this broad to a bird. "So we can't stay here. It ain't safe for the two of us. I ain't worried about myself but I can't have you getting arrested. So after you stitch me up, we have to hit the road again."

Lexi waited until he was done, furiously swiping at her face with the backs of her hands. She hated crying and especially in front of other people. "We're leaving? This is my sister we're talking about here. She needs me," Lexi insisted, trying to appeal to his diplomatic side, *if he had a diplomatic side*. She couldn't help feeling cross under the circumstances even if she was sort of literally attacking the messenger.

He was here to help, she reminded herself.

"She is going to be okay, Green." He assured her. "Thad is one of our best guys. And Mel will make sure she gets everything she needs to heal from this." Jake knew it was a hard pill to swallow what he was telling her, but he also knew that the longer they stayed here at The Compound, the more danger they were in of being arrested or worse, caught by Garner's goons. Thomas was nothing if not a ruthless asshole. If he or his guys caught up to them, it would be all kinds of fucked up.

He was sitting close to her now and he thought he caught the vague scent of vanilla and something else he couldn't identify. Her hair been neatly put up earlier at the bar in Atlanta, but now that it was coming loose, she had tendrils of curly blonde hair wisping about her face. His hand moved to brush her hair back behind her ear and he caught himself just in time.

This was a foreign feeling to Jake. He had never been one for that touchy feely crap, he thought. But there was something about her that made him want to be the person who made her stop crying. He distracted himself with pulling a cigarette out of his pocket and putting it to his mouth, fully intending to light it. If there was ever a day he needed his vice, it was today, he thought.

Lexi reached up and took the cigarette out of his mouth and held it away from him as Jake sat back in surprise. "And what if I don't want to go with you?" She said smartly, her eyes sparking white hot anger in flashes behind her light blue irises.

"You don't have a choice." He shrugged. Jake looked at her darkly and pulled another smoke from his pack.

She had pluck, he'd give her that. Taking a man's vice from him was pretty ballsy, even for a chick that looked like her.

She was a U.S. Marshal though and Jake reminded himself that she must be one tough broad to be able to swing that job. He figured there might be more to Lexi Green than met the eye and it should make the trip they were about to take even more interesting if not make his job a bit easier.

A seasoned pro like her should understand the logic behind it all. He knew she was only balking because she was too close to the situation. He guessed if Jeb were in bodily danger, he would do everything in his power to save him too.

"Can you at least tell me where we are going?" Lexi implored, her eyes glassy from all the tears she had shed recently.

Jake just shook his head. "Believe me, you're better off not knowing. No one knows where we are going, not even Matt." He told her.

Lexi couldn't keep the surprise out of her voice. "What about my job? Did Matt happen to mention how the hell I'm going to do that?" She said hotly. This man was really starting to get on her nerves. He was just so gruff and bossy, she thought.

"Matt said not to worry, to take care of your sister. And yourself." He added. "Now you wanna get me stitched up so we can get back on the road? We've already been here longer than I care to be."

Lexi nodded her head in agreement and followed Jake into a room off the front sitting room. It looked like a conference room. Someone had been kind enough to set up a mini operating suite. It wasn't sterile, but it was at least clean, she thought.

She looked over the supplies laid out and saw that everything was there that she needed. She had only put in stitches a handful of times. It was usually just assisting in the process in the emergency room but she knew the basics and while she wasn't technically qualified to do this, they didn't have much choice. Especially since Jake refused to go to a hospital.

If he was right about them being wanted, it was definitely smart for them to stay away from any heavily populated areas, and especially hospitals where a gunshot wound was bound to attract the police and questions that they couldn't answer right now.

Lexi instructed him to take off his shirt and lie back on the table. He looked at her blankly as if she had just asked him to strip completely naked.

She looked at him, amused by his expression. She hadn't taken him for one with a weak stomach. She couldn't quite place the look on his face, but she thought if she was pressed to describe it, he looked a little like an animal that had just been caught in a trap. She drew on her training and coaxed him into lying on the table so she could hurry up and get it done. Her plan was to work from the side while he lay flat on his back. It seemed the easiest approach.

Jake looked at the woman. He knew he was being stupid for refusing to take off his shirt. This was precisely why he tried to avoid these situations.

He had always been ashamed of the scars on his back. Too many people asked too many damn questions that he would never be ready to answer. It was a part of his life that he would rather forget. Or rather a person he'd rather forget that put them there. His father.

He woodenly moved to unbutton his shirt, feeling vaguely self-conscious for undressing in front of her. It was just a shirt, he reminded himself firmly. *Wasn't that big of a fuckin' deal*. He hurriedly slid the garment from his shoulders and laid it across the chair.

He'd have to pull another one from his bag, this one was past the point of salvation, he thought, as he laid back on the cool, hard surface. He felt absolutely ridiculous laid out on the conference table like some kind of freak on display.

Lexi worked quickly, getting everything ready for the hopefully simple procedure. She was pleased to see that there was some Lidocaine there to numb the skin. It would make stitching him up much easier. She quickly drew up the correct amount and told him that he would feel a slight pinch. She got the sutures and needle ready while she waited for the numbing medicine to take effect.

She tested the efficiency of the medication and being satisfied, set to work on him. "You shouldn't feel this, maybe some pressure and tugging from the needle, but you shouldn't feel pain, so tell me if you do," she explained as he nodded in agreement.

Lexi chanced a look at Jake before she started sewing up the gaping wound on his side. He was staring up at the ceiling as she worked to patch him up, his face impassive. Sighing inwardly, she set to work on placing the stitches, being careful to keep them as even and as straight as she could. Her thoughts wandered while she worked. She thought he had behaved strangely when she asked him to take off his shirt. Maybe he was one of those guys who was shy in the bedroom.

She flushed thinking about her own visceral reaction to him removing his shirt. She had gotten more than just the glimpse she had gotten earlier in the plane. He was all hardness and muscle, his skin tan like someone who spent a lot of time outdoors. She concentrated on her stitches and was almost done when he finally broke his gaze with the ceiling. She met his eyes as she was getting the bandage ready. Instead of the bright blue from earlier, they were now dark and unreadable.

"You're almost good as new now," she said, nervously placing another piece of tape over the bandage and admiring her handiwork. It wasn't perfect, but it also wasn't the worst she'd ever seen.

Lexi met Jake's gaze again and he still had the same expression on his face. She turned to clean up the mess she'd made stitching him up. Her mouth felt dry all the sudden. Something about the way he was looking at her, made her feel oddly exposed and yet he was the one in a state of undress.

Ignoring her misplaced thoughts, blaming them on exhaustion, she turned back to him as he was buttoning up his shirt again. "Are we ready to go?" she asked him as he got down off the table and he nodded at her. She started to finish cleaning up the mess that had been made by all the blood that had been on his back before she cleaned the wound up.

"Leave it. Thad will clean it up." His voice was clipped, but not angry. Still, it smarted a little that he was being so gruff. The least he could do was be grateful that she patched him up.

He was just a patient right now, she reminded herself. She had spotted a bottle of antibiotics on the table earlier and she grabbed them and shook one out into her palm, handing it to him. "Here you need to take this. It will hopefully keep you from getting an infection." He picked up the pill from her hand, his finger and thumb grazing her palm as he did so.

Jake had been silent the entire time she stitched him up, not trusting himself to speak. She had worked quickly and efficiently, her fingers ghosting over his skin. He wasn't used to people touching him. Something about her working to close his wound made him feel antsy. Even with the anesthetic, he could feel the warmth of her fingers and wondered briefly what it would feel like if her fingers drifted further south. He had flushed a little at the thought and cursed himself mentally, acting like some stupid high school kid getting all worked up.

"Think I should go up and tell Laurel goodbye?" She asked him.

He just shook his head. "Probably not a good idea. Melinda is really good with stuff like this. She is probably getting her settled. If she knows you are leaving, she might get upset. It's better if we just call her later with our regular check in."

Without saying anything further, he walked back to the door where Thad was waiting for them. Lexi was disappointed, but she couldn't argue with his logical explanation. Still, she followed him with a heavy heart knowing she was leaving her sister behind.

"You all be safe out there. Call in 24 hours. Here's the number." Thad said as he handed Jake a small piece of paper. Jake glanced at it quickly, committing the number to memory. The less paper trail, the better in his chosen profession.

Jake and Lexi walked out the door, hearing Thad close it behind them. Lexi felt like she was deserting her sister. Despite the men's reassurances, she felt like she needed to be there. But she also knew that if they stayed, she and Jake were as good as dead. They each got back in the SUV and after the doors were closed, Jake turned to look at her.

"I know you don't have no cause to believe me, but I'll keep you safe. You have my word," Jake offered, looking at her through the strands of hair that were hanging down over his eyes.

Lexi looked at the man beside her and she didn't know why, but she trusted him. Her Daddy had always said you could tell a lot about a person just by looking in their eyes and looking into his now, she didn't think anything bad could ever happen to her as long as she was with him. Which was crazy; she hardly knew him.

She was going on her gut alone as she nodded at him. "I believe you," She whispered.

They pulled onto the highway a few minutes later. Lexi was curious as to where they were going, but darkness had settled over the countryside they were driving through and her eyes kept closing of their own free will. As she drifted off to sleep, her last thought was that she hoped her gut was right. She had just placed her life in the hands of a mercenary.

Jake drove while his travel companion slept and stole occasional glimpses of the petite blonde riding next to him. In sleep, she looked even younger and more vulnerable and he felt an overwhelming protective impulse take over him. He had been all over the world and had assignments much more dangerous than this. But there was something about this girl that made him desperate to keep his promise to her. He decided then and there that nothing was going to happen to Lexi Green; not on his watch.

Chapter 4

They had been driving for several hours and Jake was tired. His legs had that restless ache from too little activity and his backside had long since gone numb. He had quit searching for a place to stop to stretch about 18 miles back.

They were too close now and there was no sense in stopping. He wished like hell he could have brought his bike on this trip, but he knew it was not possible. He longed to stop right now but his desire to distance themselves as much as possible from Atlanta was greater so he kept driving. He knew he probably wasn't going the speed limit but he was just anxious to get where they were going.

He glanced over at his passenger, smiling slightly at the indelicate snores coming from the other side of the car. The sounds just didn't match the package they came from, he mused.

She was turned towards him with her seat slightly reclined. She had taken a jacket out of her bag and rolled it into a makeshift pillow a couple of hours ago, which had been a damn shame in his opinion. He had been rather enjoying her head drooping forward and watching it do that head bob that always came from an impromptu nap while riding in a car. She had offered to drive, but she looked so miserably exhausted he had refused. He was wide awake anyways.

She had just looked so impossibly cute with her eyes drifting shut every few minutes and being unable to fight the sleep any longer. Jake chuckled to himself thinking about the picture she had made. Her hair was still pulled up in the up-do that she had had that morning and she had those curly tendrils wisping about, framing her small face. It had been nearly midnight when they finally left Charlotte and the sun was starting to come up as he made the turn onto the road that would take them to their destination. He had thought about taking the ferry over but he didn't want to be stuck on the boat that long. The ferry ride was at least two hours long to where they were headed.

Turning onto the last road that stood between them and their sanctuary, Jake could swear that he felt some of the tension leaving his shoulders. He hoped she wasn't too pissed when she realized how remote they were going to be. Cell phones worked but only certain carriers. In checking her files, he realized that hers would not be working which was just as well. She had it in her lap on the way there and he had taken the liberty of reaching over and shutting it off. He didn't want to take a chance that anyone could track them by GPS. He had disposed of his outside of Charlotte so at least there was nothing to worry about there. He had several disposable phones in the trunk and he guessed they would be using those frequently. He also had a fat stack of cash and several changes of clothes. It would only be about 45 minutes more now and he sat back to enjoy the ride, wondering what Lexi was going to think about it all.

He realized suddenly that he hoped she woke up on her own. Ever since she had patched him up, he had been itching to touch her again. And when his fingers had grazed hers when taken the antibiotic he had felt a jolt of electricity, which was crazy when he thought about it. She was just a girl, he told himself.

Jake didn't have a lot of female friends. He had never really had many steady girlfriends either. Sure there had been a couple here and there but no certain one that he could see spending his life with. He was no stranger to sex. He enjoyed a good romp just like any other red-blooded American male, but it wasn't something he had to have. In his training, he had learned a wealth of strategies in self-control. Women had always been a take it or leave it kind of thing for Jake.

There had only been one woman who had ever come close to making him rethink his old ways. Maria. Just thinking her name made his heart seize with pain in his chest. He had been on a mission in Mexico, his target a drug lord, Manuel Velasquez, who had a hit out on him and Jake was to be the one exacting the justice.

He had been smack in the middle of Mexico in the armpit of nowhere. He was alone; that was usually how he worked best. The guy had a huge compound and Jake easily took out the guards. He had gone in guns blazing, young and stupid, and got his target on the first hit. And then he had seen *her*.

She was a vision of night, her long dark hair in soft waves that framed her perfectly unflawed olive complexion. She had the deepest brown eyes that he had ever seen. She was the only woman there, frankly the only person left alive, and from his very rusty Spanish he had gathered that she had been Velasquez's sister.

From his intel there weren't supposed to be any civilians in the house at the time of the hit. His intel had clearly been wrong. He couldn't just leave her to whatever fate the Mexican government would decide for her. It would be obvious that she hadn't killed all those men and especially her own brother, but Jake hadn't been willing to chance it. He wasn't the kind of guy that just cut out and didn't finish the job. He knew his boss would be pissed at the extra time it was going to take to get her someplace safe, but he would have been angrier if he had left her there.

So Jake had taken a very frightened Maria with him that day they left the compound. They had holed up overnight a few miles up the coast in a run-down hut in the middle of the rain forest.

They hadn't known if they would live through the night and they didn't fight their mutual attraction.

He had been unsure at the time what he had felt for Maria but she was the first person that Jake had been with that he actually stayed the night with. He had barely had any time to even contemplate what he felt for her when she was taken from him.

They had woken up the next morning to the sounds of approaching gunfire. They had dressed quickly and run as fast as they could. He would never forget the next few moments for as long as he lived. He had been caught by surprise, literally with his pants down. It was unlike him to be so careless and he cursed himself all the way through the edge of the rainforest that let out onto a field full of wildflowers.

The men chasing them, his target's men unless he missed his guess, had caught up to them by now and were firing rapidly. Jake was pulling Maria behind him and trying to get her ahead of him when he heard her scream and he felt the sharp tug on his hand as she hit the ground. She had gone down hard, falling among the flowers. Jake turned and got down on the ground, firing his gun rapidly. The gunfight lasted for nearly five minutes when he finally was able to take down one and then the other. One by one, he felled each of his opponents and still had ammunition to spare. But it was all for nothing, in his opinion.

He crawled over to Maria who was hovering on the edge of consciousness. She had her hands clutched over her abdomen, as if she could hold back all the blood that was spurting from the hole the bullet left. She was losing way too much blood, Jake had thought. He had whispered that it would be okay, knowing in his gut that was a lie. He had told her that they were going to get her help, but he knew they were a half a day's drive from any medical facility.

He pulled her body into his lap, cradling her head in his hands as she died and for the first time in a long time, he had broken down and cried, the sobs racking his large frame. He hadn't cried when his Mama had died. He hadn't cried all those times that he got the shit beat out of him by his old man. He hadn't cried the dozens of times he had been shot at, stabbed, kicked, punched and damn near killed. But that day in that field, he had cried for Maria.

He was wracked with guilt and he had never felt so damn helpless in his whole life. He had asked himself later why he had gotten himself worked up so much about a girl he had just met and shouldn't have even had a chance to meet. He had finally decided that it was a fluke. Something that happened once in a lifetime. That was some kind of fucked up serendipity if you asked him.

No matter what had happened or what they might have had, Jake vowed that he would never be that careless again. He had no idea what had come over him now, reminiscing about Maria. He hadn't thought about her in years. He suspected that it had something to do with the petite blonde next to him.

This situation was incredibly similar to the one in Mexico all those years ago. They were on the run and, like Maria, Lexi was depending on him for safety. It wasn't like he could have just left her in Charlotte. He had taken on this job and he intended to finish the mission just like always. He stole another glance at her as she was starting to stir. He braced himself for what he was sure was going to be a big argument with her.

Lexi stretched and for one tiny moment, one millisecond, she didn't know where she was and the memory of yesterday was hovering on the edge of her mind while she got herself awake. Her subconscious told her that she was riding in a car but she couldn't wrap her mind around why she was asleep and who was driving.

When she opened her eyes and looked over to the driver's seat, she saw Jake and it all came back to her. She was still tired but she felt a lot better after that nice nap. She glanced out the window to their surroundings. The sun was coming up on their left although she couldn't exactly see it; the view was completely obscured by sand dunes on the left. To the right was a large body of water, its expanse vast, and the surface rippling slightly by early boaters out on the water.

She rubbed at her eyes, knowing she probably had mascara smeared over her face, however it would be surprising given all the crying she had done in the past 24 hours. Had it really only been that long since she had gotten that ill-fated phone call from Laurel? With a start, she realized that it hadn't even been a full day. Her sleep-addled brain was having a hard time wrapping itself around each new set of circumstances as they occurred.

"Where are we?" She finally asked Jake, taking her hair down and trying to rearrange it into some semblance of order. She would give about anything for a shower. Her only request at the moment would be a large cup of coffee, a phone call to Mags, and a shower; in that order.

She looked out at the scenery again, realizing that they were somewhere coastal and she couldn't help but be a little bit happy about it. She felt guilty instantly, thinking of her sister. She shouldn't be happy to be anywhere but Laurel's side right now. It had been ages since she had been to the beach though and the world always seemed different when she was there.

"We are about 5 miles north of Hatteras, North Carolina." He could tell her now that they were finally there. He hadn't been able to before, not wanting to risk her telling her sister. After they had gotten in the car, she had pretty much fallen asleep up until now, except for the brief moments she had taken to get more comfortable.

He had let her sleep, not wanting to disturb her. It was better that she sleep and also he really enjoyed the peace and quiet. He was half afraid she would start crying if she woke up again and he honestly didn't know if he could handle it, especially in a closed up vehicle for so many hours.

Lexi nodded thoughtfully and looked out the window, taking in the scenery. The sun was now starting to rise above the dunes and the early morning orange-yellow glow of the sun over the sun-bleached sand made everything appear much brighter. They were passing some houses now; beautiful big beach houses lining the left side of the road, all in pastel colors of green, yellow, turquoise and even pink. It amused Lexi to see the many colors of housing, their glass windows sparkling off the rising sun, pretty speckled panes against a backdrop of white sand and blue morning sky.

She thought only at the beach could one get away with such outlandish colors for a house. There were other dwellings sporadically on the right here and there as the road widened and the sound got farther away. She had never been to Hatteras before. Had never been anywhere on the North Carolina coast and she wondered briefly how she had lived her twenty some years without visiting this place. It was simply gorgeous.

Jake slowed the vehicle to make a left turn on the last street that she could see. The SUV bumped along on the sand covered road and moments later, Jake pulled into the driveway of a huge beige house and Lexi had the thought that it could have been pink and that almost made her want to laugh, but she stopped herself just in time, smiling softly instead. It was just that the thought of a big masculine guy like Jake Jackson living in a pink beach house tickled her to no end.

She looked up at the house as Jake pulled into the parking space that went under the house, the first level intended to be space kept clear for hurricanes or in case of flooding. The beach house looked to be about three stories with a large double stair case that went up on either side of a big wrap around porch, leading to the front door. Jake came around and opened her door, letting her get out. She grabbed her bags and followed him out of the car and up the steps.

They walked in to an entryway that led to another set of steps up to the living area of the house. When they reached the top of the stairs, Lexi just stopped to take it all in; it was enormous with high vaulted ceilings and an open-air feel. The living area blended into the dining room and then transitioned to the kitchen. The high ceilings and lightly colored décor made the room look enormous.

The first thing that drew her gaze, of course, was the large double glass doors at the far end of the living area that led out to an enormous deck, which overlooked the blue-grey waters of the Atlantic. Lexi sat her things down on the armchair by the door and opened the sliding doors, walking out onto the deck.

Her hair wisped about her face at the rush of air as she stepped outside. She could smell the briny scent of the sea and the change in the air density was palpable out here; heavier but cleaner at the same time.

There was a soft breeze blowing and Lexi took a deep breath, inhaling the fresh air and closing her eyes, the sun's rays warming her face, even though they were far from reaching the main heat of the day. She turned to look at Jake who was watching her with an amused expression on his face; kind of like a half-smile and half-smirk.

Jake was silent as he watched Lexi take in the house and the beach. She looked pleased and he was genuinely surprised. He thought she would be upset to be here.

Some people didn't like remote islands like Hatteras, but he loved it. He had been coming here for years, had bought the place about seven years back. He rented it out sometimes in the winter but it was nothing set, because sometimes there were times when he got some free time on the spur of the moment and this was always the place he headed after a mission. It cleared his head. As he stepped out on the deck with Lexi, he could actually feel the tension leaving his shoulders and Jake finally relaxed enough to take the first deep breath since they had left Atlanta. He walked over to stand next to Lexi as she looked out over the ocean, putting his hand to his side. It was still hurting like a bitch.

"It's always a mystery to me," She said softly.

"What is?" Jake looked over at her, taking in her wistful expression.

"How the ocean can be so big and it still comes back to the waves landing on the beach. The waves have traveled miles and miles and once they hit the sand, that's it for them; they just get replaced by the next wave." She said wistfully and then sighed.

Jake hummed his response. "Mmm-hmm". He thought he knew what she meant. The ocean was so infinite and it was hard to imagine that while they were standing here on this deck, there was somebody else standing on the other side of the Atlantic doing the same thing. Jake shook his head. He normally didn't think about things so deeply, but he had to admit she had a point. It really put things in perspective, he guessed.

He rested his hands on the railing next to hers, accidentally brushing against her fingers. He moved his hand away quickly, hoping his face didn't show the surprise he felt again at touching her skin in even the most innocent of ways. He had the fleeting thought that he didn't know if he could handle being able to touch her.

He didn't know what the hell was going on with him, but he decided that he needed to get some sleep and pronto. He shouldn't be having any thoughts of touching this girl in any way, innocent or no. He had been hired to do a job and no matter what the circumstances, he meant to do it. He ran a hand over the day-old scruff on his face and sighed.

Lexi had been startled by Jake's fingers brushing against hers. It was the slightest of touches, his fingers just barely grazing hers, but there was something about the moment that made her want to inch her fingers ever closer until they were entwined with his. It was an unsolicited feeling and it left her feeling a little confused. She wasn't used to men like Jake she guessed. She knew exactly how old he was. He was 40 his last birthday, which made him significantly older than her. The guys she had known before had been her age or close to it.

Her last boyfriend had been Brandon. They had broken up after he enlisted in the Navy. She knew their relationship wouldn't last with the distance and Lexi had so much going on at the time switching careers that she just did what the best thing would be; she'd broken it off with him. They'd slept together, but it had barely had time to get serious before he got his orders and shipped out to Okinawa. He was a nice guy, but it just wasn't the right timing.

Anyone she had dated since then didn't seem worth the effort.

Besides that, after watching what Laurel had gone through, Lexi knew she held herself back a bit. She never wanted to feel as helpless as Laurel was in her relationship with Thomas.

She knew her sister couldn't help it. Thomas had portrayed himself to be something very different when Laurel had first met him. By the time she had realized what kind of man Thomas was, it was too late.

Ever since then, Lexi had kept her heart closed off and her guard up. Sure, she had a few casual dates here and there, but honestly she had been so busy lately that she hadn't had time to even have coffee with her sister, let alone set up some awkward first encounter with a blind date.

Jake leaned back from the railing. "I'm gonna go in and take a shower. Want me to show you to your room? The kitchen is stocked with most everything we need. We'll have to make a run later for some milk and eggs and stuff, but there's most likely somethin' in there to fix." He regarded her carefully. She was listening to what he was saying as she followed him back inside, but he could see her carefully appraising the house. He wondered what it was she expected.

She nodded. "Is this house yours?" She asked him, her eyes holding a curious glint, but still nothing gave away what really lie beneath those baby blues. "And yes, I'd like to see my room and I'd love a shower." She answered his questions with a smile.

"Yes it is, my house." Jake eyed her warily, but she just nodded as if she accepted his explanation and that was that.

Still, Jake had thought that question would come in the driveway, not here in the living area a good ten minutes after they got there. He had never brought anybody to the house before Lexi, so he guessed he didn't really know what to expect.

But looking at her fresh-faced interest, he realized that Lexi wasn't like other people. He knew that between the way he dressed most of the time and his Southern accent people assumed he didn't have money or good sense. It always pissed him off. But she seemed different. It was evident that she didn't find it odd at all that he owned a multi-million dollar home right on the beach. He visibly relaxed as he motioned for her to follow him down the hall.

They went up another staircase to the next floor and Lexi thought she would really be getting her exercise here with all these steps. "Is it too soon to call Laurel?" She asked him as they ascended the staircase.

"Yeah, Thad said to wait 24 hours. So we'll call tonight before bed." He said, feeling slightly uncomfortable. Her speaking of taking a shower and the mention of bedtime later had him feeling all sorts of uncomfortable things and thinking all kinds of uncomfortable thoughts.

He didn't know what the hell was the matter with him. He was a professional dammit; now it was time for him to start acting like it instead of the horny teenager he felt like. He was glad she couldn't read his mind. She would probably think him some kind of pervert if she could hear his thoughts. She was practically half his age, he thought, mentally shaking his head.

She looked disappointed, but nodded in agreement as they walked down the hall and he opened the last door on the left. It was a beautiful room, done in beige with accents of blue, colorful nautical trinkets and wall hangings dotted the room along with a beautiful beachscape print hung on canvas behind the enormous sleigh bed.

Lexi sat her bag down and walked over to the sliding glass door where a smaller deck lay beyond it. She was going to thoroughly enjoy having such easy access to the beach air. She turned around to face him, her expression turning serious. "Thank you. I don't think I have said that yet and I'm sorry. Usually, my manners are much better," Lexi remarked.

He smiled at her slightly. "It's my job, remember. I'm going to go catch a couple hours sleep. Think you'll be okay?" He asked her, then feeling bad, remembering she was trained and could likely take care of herself just fine.

"Yeah I'll be fine. Just going to get cleaned up I guess. Plus I'm starving. I don't think I ate anything yesterday," he admitted.

Jake's stomach grumbled as if answering her. He hadn't had anything either.

"Want me to make us both something? I'm sure I can whip up something at least half way edible," she said brightly.

"Sure," Jake said, mildly surprised. He had never had anyone offer to make him food before, let alone a girl.

It's just breakfast man, he chastised himself. She was just being friendly and probably thanking him for bringing her to safety, opening his home and being a good host.

"See you in the kitchen in fifteen?" He asked and she smiled and nodded. He walked out of the room and headed next door to his own.

Lexi was pleased that she had something that she could contribute to their situation. She was used to being the one in charge. This feeling of someone taking care of her and protecting her was a very foreign feeling. She watched him as he walked out of the room and turned right back out of the room.

She sat down on the bed, kicking off her pumps and rubbing her feet. When she had put them on yesterday morning, she hadn't planned on wearing them for nearly 24 hours. Her toes ached from being pinched for such a long time.

She heard the water cut on in the room next door and she reasoned that his room must be right next to hers. She found it oddly reassuring that he would be right on the other side of the wall. Lexi was tempted to lie back on the bed and just go back to sleep. Despite the long nap in the car, it had been a fitful sleep, the kind where your mind is half in a deep sleep but keeping its claws on the edges of consciousness, unwilling to relent and let go.

It would only take half an effort and the help of gravity for her body to be relaxed back on the bed, but she knew she needed a shower and if she slept now, she would never be able to rest tonight. Sighing, she pushed herself up from the bed and headed into the adjoining bathroom to start the shower.

She undressed and got under the warm spray, relishing the feel of the heat flowing down over her travel-worn body, letting the water wash all her cares down the drain. She'd fix them something good to eat and then maybe she could explore the property and set her mind at ease that she was safe here.

Chapter 5

Lexi watched Jake walk back to his bedroom and close the door. She hoped he would get the rest he clearly needed. He had almost passed out into the soup that she had heated up for them. It was a simple meal, but it was the only thing that she could come up with that would taste half way decent without fresh ingredients.

They kitchen was well stocked with basic dry goods and the freezer had plenty of food in it, however since no one lived there full time, they had no fresh foods like milk, bread and cheese.

Lexi hadn't really cared one way or the other if she ate. Her appetite had been practically nil since they had left Atlanta. She had thought she would be hungry after all that sleep in the car, but all she really wanted to do was go walk on the beach. She quickly finished cleaning up their dishes and walked back to her room to get some shoes, then thought better of it and turned on her heel walking back to the double doors that led to the deck. It had been too long since she had been able to dig her toes in the sand.

The beach was something Lexi had always loved. She could remember the week she and her family spent on the Georgia coast every summer. Daddy would always close up the practice and Oren and Elaine came and took care of their animals. Then the Green family would take off for the beach, looking forward to a week of sun and fun.

As Lexi stepped out onto the sand, already very warm from the day's sun, she was regretting the decision to leave her shoes at the house. She had forgotten how hot the summer sand could be.

She hurried down towards the water, seeking a cooler surface for her sun-scorched feet. She stood at the edge of the water, relishing the feel of the cool, wet sand between her toes. The water lapped up over her ankles as each wave came in and threatened to soak the bottom of her yoga pants. She would definitely need to go shopping. Needless to say, she had not brought a bathing suit for this trip.

The air was much cooler by the water and Lexi was suddenly glad she had opted for an oversized t-shirt instead of the fitted tank she had planned on. There was a steady breeze blowing that was whipping her hair back from her face and she wished she had remembered to bring a hair tie. To have that the most pressing thought in her mind was quite refreshing after the past day's events.

Lexi felt the past day's tension slip from her shoulders, like shedding an unwanted second skin. She looked out over the expanse of water and thought about her sister. She thought about that bastard Thomas. She thought about Jake having to shoot those men.

Jake. Her thoughts turned to him and how mysterious he was. He was so good-looking and perhaps the most attractive thing about him was the fact that he had no idea of any of it.

She hoped he was getting some sleep. He had told her to wake him up in two hours. She didn't think that would be near enough sleep, but he had been very insistent about it. She had set an alarm on her phone and wondered why she even bothered to turn it on at all. She was still a bit peeved that her phone wouldn't work out here. She had finally figured that it didn't matter anyway, it's not like she was allowed to call anyone with everything that was going on. She hoped that this island was remote enough for them to hide until everything was sorted out.

Somehow all her musings out here on the beach just didn't matter as much. It was almost as if each thought, as it came and flowed through her mind, it slipped right back out of her and into the water at her feet, being pulled out to sea by the gentle tides of the moon.

Lexi looked around at the very few people on the beach. Basically it was her, an elderly couple sitting under an umbrella and a young couple with a little boy in tow. She kept glancing back to the little boy. He looked to be about four years old and he was very busy running circles around his parents, laughing as the waves chased at his feet.

Lexi smiled as she watched him; it was always sweet to her to watch a child laugh. Besides the fact that some of her earliest memories were of being that child that laughed carefree, hopping across the dunes, chasing after Laurel while their parents walked behind them.

Lexi walked around for a few more minutes and then glanced back at the house. She guessed she better get back inside. She walked back to the stairs and boardwalk that would take her back to the house. She was getting ready to go up the second set of steps when she spotted it in the sand. It was a Beach Morning Glory; she reached down to pick it from sandy soil under the walkway.

Suddenly, Lexi was transported back to her childhood. She had been about eight that summer and Laurel was twelve. They were at that age where sisters fought constantly. Laurel had found the Beach Morning Glory and Lexi had wanted it so badly. Even though she wanted it too, Laurel had selflessly handed it over to her younger sister.

Lexi had been so surprised and had hugged her sister fiercely. She had worn it in her hair that whole day. She had cried the next morning when the flower was wilted. Laurel had smiled at her sweetly and told her she would find her another flower. Lexi remembered it like it was yesterday and she fought back the tears as they threatened to come now. She continued up the pathway, the sting of the memory still pricking at her heart.

She was almost to the top of the stairs that led to the deck. She had exited the house through the sliding glass doors. Lexi looked up to see a very angry Jake coming down the steps towards her. He reached down and grabbed her wrist, none too lightly and Lexi looked up at him surprised and angry all at the same time.

Jake's face was red but his eyes were the thing that really told the story. His light blue orbs were piercing straight into hers. His facial features said he was angry, but his gaze emanated fear. This surprised her and she was sure that her expression mirrored this emotion.

"What the hell do you think you are doing out here?" He demanded.

"I was taking a walk on the beach if it is any of your business." She replied hotly. Just who did he think he was?

"It *is* my business and you best be remembering that." He replied, half dragging her up the stairs with her wrist firmly in his grip. His hands were rough over her softer, delicate ones but Lexi didn't mind that so much.

"We haven't even got your new ID yet, girl." Suddenly, all the little jabs and barbs at her young age, him calling her half-pint, short stuff and kid all day rushed at her and she just could not take it anymore. She pulled her wrist from his grasp as they reached the deck.

"You can't tell me what to do and where to go. I am not a child, you know. I am a grown woman, a U.S. Marshal dammit." She was fuming now, her breath coming in quick heavy pants.

Jake stood back and looked at her standing in front of him, hands on both hips, her hair whipping about her face. She sure was a sight, all that anger burning so bright that Jake could feel the heat coming off of her in waves, that fire making her face pink up and her wisps of hair had come loose from her damnable ponytail.

His hands bunched into fists at his sides to prevent himself from bringing his hand up to smooth her hair back. He felt an unfamiliar clenching in his gut that he didn't know what to do with.

She was so angry she could barely see and it didn't help that the wind kept blowing her hair in her face. Moving to brush the errant strands from her eyes, she dropped the flower and it blew across the deck.

Watching the flower blow away, it was as if she was watching her hope for Laurel slip out with the tide. The tears that she had been fighting for the past hour finally spilled over her eyelids and ran down her cheeks.

She looked down at the deck to keep from having to look up at Jake. She would be damned if she would let him know he had made her cry. She was so angry with herself; she was stronger than this. But Laurel was her sister and she was so scared for her. And here she was in a strange place with a strange man and all she really wanted was the simplicity of her life back on the farm. She thought she'd even welcome the hubbub of inner city Atlanta to this isolation.

Jake was yelling at her and the last thing she needed was for someone to be mad at her. She missed her Daddy something fierce right now; she knew if there was anyone who would know what to do right now, it would be him. Then again, he'd have likely taken a shotgun to Thomas himself by now, consequences be damned.

Jake stared in disbelief as Lexi went from madder than a hornet to crying in Mach one. He unclenched his fists and let his arms dangle restlessly at his sides, not entirely sure what he was supposed to do in this situation.

He knew societal norms called for a probable hug, but Jake didn't know anything more about hugging than the man in the moon. But for whatever reason his arms came up and stretched out, almost as if moving of their own free will, a silent offering of comfort and she floated easily into his embrace.

Lexi was so shocked to see Jake's warm gesture that she didn't even think about what motivated her to do so, she just took a step forward and allowed herself to be wrapped up in his arms. His embrace was everything that she had hoped it could be and had never realized she ever even wanted. He held her somewhat awkwardly away from him until she pressed herself into him, just needing to feel the warmth of another person right now. She gradually felt his fingers come to rest against her back, his hand splayed, tentative almost.

Jake didn't know how tightly he was supposed to hold her, but with her head tucked under his chin like she was meant to be there, he inhaled the scent of her and gripped her elbow lightly. She smelled vaguely like flowers and vanilla all mixed together. He could breathe her in all day and never have enough breath in his lungs, he thought.

He couldn't quite make sense of how fast his heart was beating in time to the random thoughts he had permeating his brain.

She smells like sunshine, was only one of such intrusive thoughts.

He had no idea how to place a name on the feeling he was having. He just knew that having Lexi in his arms felt right. More right than anything had felt to him in a very long time. And it scared the hell out of him.

Lexi buried her head in Jake's chest, feeling his chin resting upon her head, not caring in that moment how weak she appeared to be. Sometimes, it was okay to cry. Or at least, it was going to have to be, because she couldn't stop herself now if she tried.

She cried until her sobbing subsided into sniffles and her eyes burned, but finally that well of seemingly endless tears dried up.

She sniffed and pulled back slightly, unsure if she could meet his gaze, but lifting her eyes to his in apology. "I'm sorry. I don't normally break down so easily. It's just the flower-." Her voice trailed off, pointing to the direction that it had blown in, knowing she sounded like an idiot. Because really, who cries over a flower blowing away in the wind?

"Morning Glory?" he asked her and Lexi nodded, surprised that he knew what she was talking about. He trotted back down the steps to the deck, leaving her standing there staring after him as he disappeared and then reappeared a moment later.

As he walked slowly back up the stairs and stood in front of her, his movements were hesitant as if he was somehow unsure of what he was doing. She looked up at him and as their eyes met, she smiled softly at him. For in his hand, was not just a single morning glory, but a whole bunch of them.

He handed her the bouquet wordlessly. "They grow all over the place. I liked 'em so I had them planted by the pool." He said, shuffling his feet back and forth. He glanced up at her, wondering what she thought of him now. He had never given a girl flowers in his life and he sure as hell hadn't ever told anyone that he liked the damn things too.

Jake looked at Lexi silently appraising him and felt his face flush lightly. He wasn't used to someone openly studying him the way she seemed to want to do. For whatever reason, it made his chest feel tight. Then without warning, she reached up and pressed her lips to his cheek in a warm, soft kiss. Before he had a chance to react, she was already pulling away.

She held up the flowers he had handed her for his inspection. "Aren't they beautiful?" She asked him, her eyes bright with her smile and the tears that she had just shed, an alluring mixture of joy and melancholy.

He smiled back at her, wondering how she managed to look so innocent and sexy all at the same time. He nodded and murmured something like yes. He couldn't really find words at the moment, which was nothing new to him. He wasn't prone to being quite this tongue-tied though.

Because what he was really thinking was *"you're beautiful."*

It made him feel an ache deep inside even thinking about her in that way. Made him feel things that he wasn't sure he recognized. It made him want Lexi Green in ways that he wasn't sure he could handle. What the hell was he supposed to do now that she had worked her way under his skin?

Chapter 6

Lexi tossed and turned as she tried again and again to get the thought of Jake and his arms around her out of her head. It was so unlike her to develop a schoolgirl crush, but she guessed that was what it was. He was saving her life right now, she supposed. Maybe she had a thing for some kind of hero complex, she mused.

She curled on her side and pulled the covers over her. She replayed the scene on the deck in her head and try as she might, it always ended in a kiss instead. She had kissed him on the cheek when he had given her the flowers. He had looked so uncertain of his actions and Lexi had thought it was so cute.

Thinking of the flowers had her thoughts straying to Laurel again. She had talked to her a couple of hours ago, just like Jake had promised. They hadn't been able to talk long; they wanted to keep calls short just in case the lines were being traced.

Laurel had sounded okay, a little sad maybe, but none the worse for wear under the circumstances. Lexi was even able to make her laugh once, which was a pretty good sign. She had insisted that she was fine several times and not to worry about her.

Jake had briefly described to her Melinda's background and she had been impressed. She had been a psychologist for the past ten years and she specialized in rape and domestic abuse survivors. Laurel was in intensive therapy with her now and even though Lexi herself couldn't be there, she felt better knowing that she was in good hands.

She sighed deeply, throwing the covers off her, knowing sleep was elusive this night and got up to go out on the deck. She walked out into the night air, the warmth from the day still not having completely seeped away with the day's sunset. Still, she was slightly chilly in her shorts and tank top. She thought again that she was definitely going to need to go shopping the next day.

She had noticed the day before that the deck leading from her room also connected with Jake's. She was right outside Jake's door and she could swear that she heard a loud noise coming from the other side of the door. Then, suddenly she heard him yell. "No!" Her hand was poised ready to knock and then she thought better of it and tested to see if it would open.

She slid it open, not knowing what to expect, but finding the room empty save for him thrashing about on the bed. She walked over to where he was laying and found that he was asleep, apparently in the throes of a nightmare.

She breathed a sigh of relief and turned to leave the room, feeling like the worst kind of stalker. She knew she would probably be angry if he woke up to find her standing over him. Just about the time that she was turning away from the bed, his eyes opened and he met hers with an uncertain gaze and Lexi just froze.

Jake was back in the fields again. He remembered what they were called. Vanilla Orchids. They only grew in certain places. He wasn't sure what recess of his mind he had pulled that information from but

he remembered hearing that they could only be pollinated from the bees indigenous to that area. That's what gave vanilla its distinctive flavor. But if the flavor was something that was distinctive, it was nothing compared to the flowers. They smelled so good to him, like a flower with a hint of spice, very woodsy. He breathed it in, taking in his surroundings.

He was alone in the field and he didn't know why he was there. Until he looked over and saw a younger version of himself running and pulling a beautiful raven-haired woman behind him, both of them looking scared for their lives and when Jake looked at what they were running from, he could see why.

He stared in horror as the men who were chasing them aimed their guns and shot Maria as she crumpled to the ground. He screamed "No" as loud as he could; as if somehow he could change his fate.

As if he could go back to that morning. He watched as his younger self took out the men and then walked over to where Maria lay, her blood spreading out on the ground beneath her. He felt so helpless watching all of it unfold and knew he had been there before; he just couldn't put his finger on it.

Suddenly he sensed something, pulling at his consciousness, and he opened his eyes, never expecting to find those blue eyes staring back at him.

"What are you doing in here?" He whispered gruffly, running a hand over his face, the tendrils of the dream still reaching out from the recesses of his mind.

"I couldn't sleep. Then-." She stopped herself before she let on that she had heard him call out in his sleep.

His hand came up, fingers lightly encircling her wrist; he had a habit of doing that it seemed. It was a much lighter grasp than before. It wasn't an angry hold borne of fear. Instead it was tender, gentle, pleading and Lexi looked into his eyes, wondering what he was torturing him so.

She could see his face in the silvery light coming from the moon outside and his eyes bored into hers, their bright hue intense, but tinged with something dark. Then, just as quickly, he pulled his hand away as if his fingers had skated across flames instead of the delicate skin of her inner wrist.

Jake shook his head trying to clear his thoughts, his dream bleeding into the night around them, tainting his actions. He wanted with everything in him to pull her down to the bed and put his lips on hers.

But after the dream he had just had, he knew that was the furthest thing that should be from his mind. He had given himself over to these kinds of feelings before and look where it had gotten him. Where it had gotten Maria. *Dead.* He quickly released her wrist and cleared his throat.

"Should get back to sleep," he said roughly and turned over and faced the wall. "Good night." He murmured.

Lexi just stared at his back wondering what the hell had just happened. He grabbed her, looked like he was about to kiss her and then he just pulled away like nothing had happened. She sighed and turned to leave, pulling the door closed behind her. She was further from sleep now than when she had headed out for a breath of fresh air.

Looks like it was going to be a very long night, she thought, as she headed back to her room.

Inside, Jake was shaken. He had almost screwed everything; *literally*, he thought sardonically. He knew better than anybody that you could not mix business with pleasure. He was here to protect

71

this girl, keep her safe, not get in her pants, he chastised himself. She was beautiful to be sure and sexy as hell. And smart as a whip.

He decided there were qualities about her that he could go on for days about. But it didn't change the fact that he was on assignment. The last time he had let himself care about another person he had gotten them killed. And he wasn't about to let that happen; ever again.

Chapter 7

Lexi awoke early, having fallen asleep in the wee hours of the morning. She sat up and stretched, and touched her hand to her wrist, remembering where Jake had grabbed it last night before he had been about to kiss her.

She had replayed the moment over and over again and what she remembered most was the expression on his face. Where at one moment he had been all passion and fire, it was like somebody flipped a switch and drew the shades, his face once again going completely impassive. Then, he had turned over like the moment meant nothing. She sighed and quickly dressed in a pair of yoga pants and T-shirt.

She ambled to the kitchen, her nose subconsciously following the aroma of freshly brewed coffee. She found an assortment of bagels and cream cheese on the table along with a note.

Went to take care of some business. Be back soon. Stay in the house!

J.

The last part was underlined four times. She crumpled up the note and threw it in the waste basket beside the refrigerator, frowning. It galled her that he felt like he could tell her to stay in the house. She thought about calling her friend and giving him a piece of her mind about this so-called "great guy" he had sold her on. So far, the only thing that Lexi had witnessed was the man acting like a total control freak that treated her like an errant child.

Part of her knew that Jake was right. She *should* stay in the house. Right now they were wanted for questioning in the murder of an

Atlanta police officer and in the disappearance of a person. It really couldn't get much worse than that, Lexi thought, as she poured herself a cup of coffee.

She slathered a bagel with cream cheese and found herself wondering what Laurel was doing right now. She wished she could talk to her more often. Jake kept insisting that the form of therapy that Melinda was doing with Laurel was very intensive and talking to anyone at this juncture, that might remind her of the trauma could set back her progress by weeks or even months.

Lexi loved her sister too much to risk that just to soothe her ego. Part of her knew that she had a bit of a savior complex. Lexi was a natural giver and it showed through both of her career paths.

It showed in her relationship with her peers and it definitely showed through the many things she did and would do for family. Lexi couldn't really remember a time when she hadn't put somebody else first before herself. But it was the way she preferred it to be. It made her feel wanted; special. Call her crazy, but it felt good to be needed.

Sourly, she wondered how long her captor was going to be keeping her under lock and key. In glancing out at the vast Atlantic, the sun was shining bright and the grey-blue waves were lapping rhythmically at the golden brown shore. She was dying to get out there and sit in the sun and let the water wash over her feet.

The door downstairs opened and shut and Lexi had the momentary thought that she didn't have her gun on her. Just about the time she was kicking herself mentally for such an oversight, Jake appeared at the top of the stairs, hefting several bags on each arm. He walked over to where she was sitting in the big arm chair by the double glass doors and dropped all the bags at her feet.

Lexi looked up at him quizzically until he finally said. "Got you some stuff to wear. Should be enough for now." He gestured to the bags as Lexi reached down to open the first one up, which contained an assortment of bras and panties, all of them lacy and in various colors of black, red and pink.

Lexi felt the blush creeping up on her face and closed the bag back up hurriedly. She hoped to God he had not picked this stuff out himself. Something about Jake holding up a pair of panties with Lexi in mind just made her heart do all sorts of weird things and other parts of her body were chiming in as well.

"How'd you know what size to get?" She questioned as she held up a pair of denim shorts that were exactly her size. She looked up to meet his gaze and was met with the top of his head as he wouldn't even meet her eyes. He didn't look to be any more comfortable with this than she was and Lexi found herself to be extremely amused.

"I guessed at most of 'em. The rest I had to get from some of your stuff." He admitted sheepishly.

Lexi didn't know whether to be angry, mortified or grateful. In looking through the clothes, he had appeared to have thought of everything. She even had two bikinis, one solid black and the other in a delicate pink and white floral print. She held up the bottoms to the black one, thinking that at least he wasn't planning on locking her away in a tower or anything. He at least was planning on spending some of their time outdoors.

"Wait. Don't you think somebody is going to be awfully suspicious of you going and buying women's lingerie?" Lexi couldn't help herself, but she put emphasis on the last word and was pleased to see the blush creep back into his cheeks again. It gave her just a thrill to realize that she had any power over him at all with her words. She wondered briefly how much power she could wield over him physically. She felt her mouth go dry at the realization that he would dominate that situation hands down.

For all of Lexi's toughness in the field, in the bedroom she knew she lacked confidence. She found herself wondering if Jake could bolster that confidence and mentally shook her head, trying to clear the images that popped unbidden into her mind. What the hell was wrong with her?

"Nah, I know the shop owner. She owed me one." Jake replied gruffly. Lexi wondered what Jake had done for all these people that they owed him, and knowing his profession, decided immediately she probably didn't want to know.

Jake watched as Lexi rifled through all the bags, holding up this item or that. When she held up the black lace panties, his mouth had gone all dry and he could feel himself actually getting hard and he had to shift to readjust, hoping to god that she didn't notice his predicament. He wasn't thinking about her *in* those panties as much as he was thinking about removing them from her body with him positioned between her thighs. He could visualize it so clearly that now he was painfully hard and he shook his head to clear his thoughts.

Not gonna happen, Jackson.

Jeb's voice then creeped into his brain, much the way it always did: completely unwanted. *"What's the matter Jakey boy? You ain't gonna tap that?"* And then that laugh that was so distinctively Jeb.

Jake swallowed hard. Tap that? He'd sure as hell like to. But he wasn't about that. Jake had never been about putting another notch on his belt or bedpost or whatever the hell they called it these days. He wasn't on a quest to sleep with as many women as he could, unlike Jeb.

Jake didn't think that he had ever really "made love" to a woman before. Sex for Jake had always been something hurried, two bodies pressed together searching for a release and then going your separate ways. But in looking down at Lexi, her golden hair spread around her as she continued to peer into the bags, pulling out one treasure at a time, he knew that Lexi wasn't that kind of girl either. She was somebody that you would have to take your time with. If the circumstances were different, Jake might have signed up for that. But, they weren't, and he'd do best by remembering that.

"Thanks for the clothes." Lexi said, looking up at him. "What are we doing today?"

"We got an appointment at 5:00 in Ocracoke." He answered, looking up at her as she replaced all the items in the bags. He bent over and picked up two of the bags to help her carry them to her room.

"We have to pick up some paperwork. You need a new I.D. at least for the time being. I talked to Matt this morning. We are no longer wanted for murder. Someone came forward and confessed to killing that cop." Jake looked to her waiting for her response.

Lexi looked up at him in surprise. "What? But I was there. I saw you shoot them." Lexi wore a puzzled expression, trying to figure it out. "Who would confess to a crime they didn't commit?"

"Somebody who got paid a lot of money by Garner and his men." Jake waited for that to sink in before he went on.

Lexi seemed to relax a little bit at that. "But, doesn't that mean we can go home now?" she said.

Jake shook his head. "Afraid not. Thomas put out a missing person report on Laurel. They won't act on it for 24 more hours but Thomas has a manhunt down in Georgia. We spread a false trail down to Savannah and another one down to Florida. That will buy us some time. He is trying to force us all out of hiding. That means you are in more danger than ever. He's desperate. He sent men after both of you and they shot at us and shot at my plane. We have to assume he wanted you both dead." He didn't think he needed to spell out the rest for her, given her occupation.

They carried the bags over to the bed and sat them down. Lexi turned to face him. "What if he finds her, Jake?" Lexi asked, looking up at him, her bright blue eyes pleading.

"He won't. I give you my word." He promised. He glanced around the room and wondered how in the hell in 24 hours she had managed to turn the guest room into such a feminine atmosphere. There was pink shit everywhere he looked.

Suddenly Jake felt like his skin was two sizes too small, much like he had when he was picking out all the stuff he had just handed her.

Without warning, Lexi reached up and put her arms around his neck, hugging him. This girl really liked to hug, he thought. His arms came up around her waist like before, his fingers splaying over her back like they were made to rest there. Like it was an old habit he'd perfected.

She turned her head and kissed him on the cheek. Okay, she liked kisses too, he thought.

"Thank you." She whispered against the shell of his ear and it was almost his undoing, her soft breath against his flesh, her voice a tiny vibrating hum against the sensitive skin of his neck.

He pulled away somewhat awkwardly, his hands dropping to his sides as if they suddenly didn't know what purpose they served. "It's no problem." He moved to go back out the door. He suddenly felt the need to put as much distance between him and Lexi as he could.

Maybe getting out of the house would do them some good. "You want to go down to the beach in a bit?" He asked her from the doorway and was met with a bright smile that lit up her whole face.

"Are you kidding?" Lexi smiled. "Yes!"

He nodded. "Alright, then. Meet me on the deck in 10, Green." He said as he walked away to head to his own room, his expression unreadable but she thought she detected a hint of a return smile before he turned away.

"Yes, Mr. Jackson." She could almost hear his scowl, but she couldn't keep the tease out of her tone. She knew he hated it, but it was almost as if she couldn't help herself. He was so easy to rile and she really didn't have anything better to do at the moment.

Lexi fished the black bikini out of the bag and wandered into the bathroom, hoping to find some sunscreen. She hoped Jake had thought of that. And when the two thoughts collided, she had the realization that Jake was going to have to put sunscreen on her back.

God help her, but the thoughts of his hands on her in even such an innocent way, had all sorts of erotic images dancing through her head. She thought about his reaction when he had handed her the bags of clothing.

If Jake Jackson came unglued about picking out women's lingerie, she had to wonder how he would react to seeing her in it.

Chapter 8

Lexi waited patiently at the end of the boardwalk that led down to the beach. Jake had to go back for the sunscreen that she had already reminded him twice that they needed. She readjusted the top tie of her bikini, a little self-conscious in the skimpy attire. She reminded herself that she was at the beach and no one even knew her here. She stuck her toes in the sand, testing the temperature. The one thing that Jake had forgotten was a pair of flip flops. She had only brought tennis shoes and pumps, neither one appropriate for the beach sand.

Jake cursed to himself as he grabbed the lotion from his bathroom. Ever since Lexi had come out of her room wearing that bikini, his thoughts had seem scattered. He had picked out the damn thing and now he was kicking himself for doing it.

The thing was, the number she had on was the most modest bathing suit in Chloe's whole shop. His friend had found it hilarious that he was picking out clothes for Lexi. He had tried to explain that there was nothing going on, but his long-time friend wasn't buying any of it.

The devil of it was that there really wasn't anything going on with him and Lexi. Nothing except a few touches that set him on fire and the damn smell of her hair that he couldn't get out of his nose. That cloying sweet vanilla and flowery smell that permeated the air of every room she entered. It was intoxicating and annoying all at the same time.

He finally got to the boardwalk and he had to stop to catch his breath. Damn, he was getting out of shape. It had been a long time since he had to trek the jungles of Central America or the Gobi desert and this beach trip was giving him a run for his money.

That was the thing about barrier islands, they served just the purpose their name suggested. The houses were built way back off the beach to allow for years of beach erosion and that, of course, meant a hell of a walk to get to the ocean, but he loved it here and wouldn't change it for anything. He figured every good place worth going to had its quirks.

He took a minute to breathe in the fresh sea air and knew that this was what he had been missing lately. He felt the tension of the past several months easing as he started down the boardwalk. He had to stop again when he spotted her at the end of it. Her back was to him and he took a moment to pause and watch her. Her hair was blowing in the wind, blonde tresses reflecting off in the golden light of the sun. She was narrow with slim hips, but curvy in all the right places. She turned to look back towards the house. *Busted.*

His face flushed slightly in the noonday sun as she smiled and waved at him and he waved back. He had never met anyone as happy as her. Her whole world had just gone to shit and here she was smiling and waving at him on the beach, like they were here on vacation together.

It seemed ridiculous to Jake and at the same time, it seemed very much *her*. He didn't know her all that well, but at the same time, he felt like he sort of did.

He finally reached her and mentally chided himself into keeping his eyes above her neckline. He would if he knew what was good for him.

"Hey, got the sunscreen." He shook the bottle in his hand for effect. Had he really just stated the beyond obvious? Yeah, *real eloquent Jackson*, he thought.

Lexi took it from his hand and led the way across the sand. They found a spot far enough from the waves and Lexi spread out the blanket she had found in the closet. She wondered briefly if he was going to think it was weird to share a blanket with her. It seemed kind of intimate, but then they had been thrust into this situation out of their control. They may as well make the best of it.

Lexi began applying the sunscreen over her legs and belly, making sure she covered every surface. She was so pale and she knew it wouldn't take long for her to burn on a day like this. She balked when she had gotten everything she could reach with her own two hands. All that was left was her back.

She turned to find that Jake was watching her intently, his expression again dark and unreadable. She shifted her eyes a bit, unsure of how to ask him to help her out. "Can you get my back?" She asked him, handing him the lotion.

Jake took the bottle from her, unable to speak. Was she serious? He set his jaw in a hard line and tried to think about anything other than the fact that he was going to be rubbing his hands all over her. Was she *trying* to kill him?

He squeezed a generous dollop onto his palm and then rubbed his hands together in an attempt to warm the lotion.

Lexi turned and held her hair out of the way, the breeze blowing and that infernal vanilla and floral scent traveling on the wind straight into his senses. He placed his hands at her shoulders and felt her jump slightly at his touch. He stilled his hands, unsure what to do at first. He worked in a grid, rubbing his hands in a circular motion down over her back, squeezing more lotion onto his palms when he ran out.

His hands were just above her ass, rubbing the lotion into the skin right above her bikini bottoms. It struck him as absurd that something as benign as suntan lotion could be so sexually charged. He stepped back, finally satisfied with his work.

Lexi had loved feeling Jake's hands on her. It was all she could do to bite back a moan when he moved his hands lower and lower until they hovered right at the hem of her bathing suit bottoms. She had imagined last night what his hands might feel like, but she had been wrong.

It was far better than any fantasy she could dream up. His hands were rough and callused, but his touch was gentle. It was easy to imagine him caressing other parts of her body and she could feel her pulse gathering intensity between her thighs.

And then all too soon, he pulled his hands away. She turned to him, unsure of what she was going to find when she did. Was it going to be surly Jake or mysterious Jake?

But his expression wasn't the brooding one she'd come to expect. Not at all. His pupils were blown wide, black bleeding into blue, and she realized with a stutter of her own breath, that he was just as turned on as she was. The heat behind his gaze practically burned her, making the rays of the sun pale in comparison.

She found she could not hold his stare for long. She lowered her eyes and reached out to take the lotion from him, her fingers brushing against his hand and she forced her eyes downward, as if looking at him again would turn her to stone. Her breath hitched in her chest again as she took a deep calming breath and finally met his gaze, now impassive, those blue eyes cold and piercing once more.

Jake cleared his throat and pulled his hand back. "We should go see what the water feels like." He said, looking out at the vast grey-blue of the Atlantic.

"Wait, it's your turn." Lexi told him.

Jake turned to her, confusion etching his features. "You need sunscreen too." She said, squeezing the lotion into her palm.

"Nah, I'll be fine." Jake replied shortly.

"But Jake, I already have it on my hands." She gestured with her other hand.

Jake just stared at her, vaguely registering that she was using his given name.

Her argument was logical, but he wanted just about anything else in this world right now other than Lexi putting her hands all over his back. But he was afraid if he put up too much of a fight and made a big deal of it, it would be worse, so he turned his back to her wordlessly and waited.

Lexi gasped inaudibly when she saw the reason he had hesitated. There were silvery scars lining his back in crisscross patterns. Lexi had seen marks like these before; she had seen more than her fair share of child abuse survivors. She rubbed her hands together and didn't say anything to him. He was obviously embarrassed about them and she didn't want to pry, but the way he'd reacted when he removed his shirt before now made perfect sense.

She smoothed the sunscreen over his back, taking care to not disrupt his stitches, and marveled at the stark difference that was Jake Jackson from nearly every other guy she knew. Her fingers slipped over his skin as she gently rubbed in the lotion in over his shoulders, moving lower. She knew they probably didn't hurt at this point, but still she tread with a lighter touch over the silvery lines that marred the expanse of his back.

Jake held his breath as she began applying the lotion. Her hands were soft, but she had a surprisingly firm but gentle touch. Something twisted deep in his gut as she worked the lotion over his flesh, slowly and methodically. He didn't think he had ever felt anything better in his life than Lexi's hands on him and whatever that something was in his gut; it twisted even harder.

"All done," she announced as she pulled her hands away all too soon. He turned to face her, expecting the requisite pity, but her face was just lit up in that smile he'd come to expect. Soft and sweet.

"Let's go get our feet wet." She began walking down toward the water and Jake just dumbly watched her go, following behind her by several seconds.

She hadn't said anything about his scars and he wasn't sure what to think about that. Anyone who had ever seen them had either had a million questions or he had gotten that look of pity that he came to hate the most. Jake never relished the idea of talking about it, but he'd rather answer questions than see that look on someone's face.

Lexi was putting her toes in the water, letting her feet sink into the sand as the waves washed up. There was hardly anyone else out on the beach. Of course they did have the advantage of being the last house on the strip before the island made a hard turn and much of the geography was uninhabited on that stretch of beach for several miles southward.

Jake joined her at the edge of the water, trying very hard not to look at how good she looked in her swimsuit, one he'd held in his hands as he'd helped Chloe pick them out. Looking out over the waves cresting higher and higher with the tide, he wished he had brought his board out. Maybe the surf would still be good in the morning, he thought. It had been a long time since he had been able to surf or kite-board.

"You ever been kite-boarding?" He asked Lexi on impulse, attempting to steer them into neutral waters, pun completely intended.

She turned to look at him. "What's that?" She was fighting a losing battle to keep the hair out of her face, the wind whipping it about every few seconds.

"It's like a surf board with a big kite attached to it. It's powered by the wind and waves. I could teach you, if you want." He looked at her sideways, the words having spilled out before he could think about what he was offering.

"That sounds like fun. When can we do it?" She asked eagerly looking out at the waves building off the shore a ways.

"Oh no, not out there. We'll start in the sound." Jake gestured behind him over his head in the general direction of the Pamlico Sound, the body of water between Hatteras and the mainland. "Water's much calmer, but the wind is still good."

"Oh," was Lexi's only reply, feeling excited that he wanted to show her something new and different. Almost like they were on a long weekend trip to the beach. Almost.

She kicked at the water a bit, wading in deeper. It was cold, but refreshingly so. The water inadvertently hit Jake at the waist and he jumped back slightly.

"Hey!" He protested.

It had been a total accident, but his reaction was so funny she did it again, this time on purpose.

"Oh woman, you do not want to start this with me," he warned her, his eyes drawn down in a mock scowl.

Lexi either saw straight through him or didn't care, because she splashed him again, this time soaking the entire front of him, her eyes dancing with laughter.

"Okay, but I warned you," he said, but his words held no bite. His hands cut a wide swath into the sea, creating a wall of water heading her way, the force of it getting her completely drenched from head to toe. She looked up at him in surprise, her jaw dropping open.

"I tried to tell ya," he informed her, but he couldn't help but grin. She was soaking wet, her hair dripping around her face and into her mouth that was still hanging open in surprise. He decided she looked pretty. *Real pretty.*

Lexi sputtered at the briny water washing down over her nose and mouth. She knew she looked ridiculous with her hair plastered to her face. "You are so going to pay for that, Jackson." She told him, her eyes narrowing as she planned her attack. She bent down and scooped up as much water as she could and aimed it for his head, grunting in frustration when he ducked and she missed.

He laughed and splashed her again, the water again pummeling her everywhere at once.

Lexi moved to splash him again and with the oncoming wave, lost her footing. She grabbed at the air, knowing that she was going to land in a big heap and the waves were going to bury her. She hadn't expected Jake to reach out and catch her. She landed easily in his arms as he steadied her and kept her from falling face first into the water.

His arms gripped her at her elbows and she reached out to grasp his forearms until she got her balance. Unfortunately, another wave came crashing at that moment and they both toppled over onto the sand at the edge of the beach, Lexi landing on top of Jake with both hands braced on either side of his head.

It was a hell of a situation to end up in, she thought. She could feel herself pressed up against him in every way and she blushed furiously and hoped he would mistake the fire in her cheeks for the warmth of the sun.

Jake had tried to steady Lexi but the waves were getting rougher and before he knew it, he was lying back on the sand and Lexi was on top of him. All the teasing was gone from her and it almost looked like, well it looked like she wanted him to kiss her.

He shook his head, trying to clear the mental image and glanced down. Jake could see that her bikini top had skewed to the side, exposing a generous amount of breast. He cleared his throat and looked away. Finally her gaze was pulled from his as she realized her predicament, hurriedly attempting to adjust her top as she moved to sit beside him on the sand.

"Told you not to start it," he told her, looking at her from the side, brushing the sand from his hands. He smiled at her, rather enjoying watching her try to wring the water out of her hair.

"A gentleman never tells a lady *I told you so*," she informed him primly.

"I ain't no gentleman." And it was true too. Nobody had ever accused Jake of being anything of the sort.

"Sure you are." She said matter of fact, her smile bright as she looked out upon the ocean, finally giving up on getting the water from her hair.

The thing of it was it didn't matter that she looked like a drowned rat with her hair dripping around her and plastered to her head. She was still beautiful. Too damn beautiful. And he could even in the short time that he'd known her that she was genuinely a good person. Too damn good for him.

"How you figure that?" He asked her, tracing lazy patterns in the sand between the two of them.

"Well you went back to get the sunscreen," she offered. "So I wouldn't burn."

He raised an eyebrow at her and she laughed, knowing that her argument was pretty weak. "Okay, what else you got?" He replied.

"Well you're saving my life right now. That's pretty gentlemanly." She looked at him seriously. "Thank you, Jake". Her face was sincere and bright and reminded him for some reason of his first grade teacher, Mrs. Moss. He hadn't thought of her in years but she had been the nicest teacher he ever had. She had taken a liking to him and had always brought him cookies and snuck them to him at lunch time.

"Yeah, thank me when that bastard is behind bars," he told her. And it was true. He couldn't rest until Thomas Garner was either in jail or six feet under. To keep everyone safe, it really didn't matter much to him which one it was.

Chapter 9

Lexi stepped out of the shower, glad to have rinsed off the saltwater from her skin. She had been hoping the shower would also quench some of the burn. Despite all her precautions, she had still ended up getting a tad scorched from the afternoon rays. Not badly, but enough that it was going to be uncomfortable later tonight.

Her thoughts turned naturally to Jake and how she burned in a different way. She felt lit afire from all the looks she had received from him on their afternoon at the beach.

Then when she had fallen onto him in the sand; well her skin was still tingling in all the places their bodies had touched. She could only imagine what it would be like if they ever-.

Lexi wouldn't even let herself finish that thought as just the thought of him pressed up against her on the beach had her breathing funny. She found herself wondering idly what Jake had thought about it. He probably thought she was a total klutz falling all over him like she did. But she knew she hadn't imagined his smoldering glances after applying the sunscreen.

She wasn't stupid. She knew she was turned on by Jake. She just didn't know what to do about it or if he would even reciprocate. Not to mention that it would be an extremely dangerous move considering their current predicament.

She wished she could talk to Laurel right now. Or even Vivian, Matt's wife. She had been best friends with Vivian practically since she started working with Matt. Vivian would definitely know what to tell her about Jake. She knew she would be able to decipher the signals it seemed like Jake was sending her.

Vivian and Matt had been together forever and while things hadn't always been happily ever after for them, they had made it all work. Lexi hoped to one day have a relationship with someone like what Vivian and Matt had. They really loved each other, she thought as she pulled on a pair of white capris that fit her perfectly. She threw on a navy and white tank and a white sweater over that. Jake had said it might get cool out on the open water and to bring a jacket.

Jake had run out and gotten her a pair of flip flops earlier and she donned them now before running a hand through her hair one last time and securing it into a messy ponytail. She wondered about Ocracoke and specifically at the fact that they were getting paperwork from someone that lived there.

It seemed a very unlikely place for any sort of criminal activity much less ones that required false identification. Then again, that was precisely why they were going there that day so she guessed it made sense. She made her way down the hall seeing that Jake's door was opened. It likely meant that he was waiting for her in the living room.

She walked into the living area and drew in a shaky breath when she saw him standing there. He was standing in the doorway, the door propped open with one foot and leaning against the door jamb, smoking a cigarette.

She hated cigarette smoke and usually despised it when someone smoked around her but for whatever reason Jake Jackson looked sexy as hell standing in the doorway, the smoke gathering around his head as he exhaled and swirling up into the beach air. She smoothed her hands down over her pants, rubbing away any make-believe wrinkles or imagined fuzz.

He was wearing a pair of khaki cargo pants and a button up chambray shirt, tucked in at the waist. She took a deep breath as she approached him.

"Well you clean up nice." She said lightly, hoping he hadn't noticed her ogling from the doorway. That would be embarrassing.

Jake stubbed out his cigarette and pocketed the butt to throw away in the trash can. "Thanks." He muttered. He never knew what to say when women said stuff like that to him. He had never considered himself to be a Casanova or whatever. But women liked him and often told him he was handsome or some shit and he just looked at them dumbfounded.

Jeb on the other hand; he had always been a looker and knew it; bragged about it even. Where Jake lacked confidence in women, Jeb more than made up for it. Suave and debonair were his middle names and it was true that Jeb always had a steady stream of different women that he paraded around town on his arm. It was also why Jeb often had the clap, Jake smirked to himself. Really, it had only been the one time, but Jake wouldn't let him forget it.

He shut the door and motioned for Lexi to follow him out to the car. The plan was to drive down to the marina and board his boat. He had already checked the weather and it looked to be a good night for a trip across the water to Ocracoke Island, which was about five miles off the southernmost tip of Hatteras Island.

Ocracoke had long been one of his most favorite places to visit but he didn't get to go too often anymore. He had always wanted to live there but had just never found the time to find the perfect place. Beachfront property that was up to perking standards was hard to come by on Ocracoke. The families that owned the land tended to hold onto their property generation after generation, so it wasn't like real estate was plentiful on the small barrier island.

Jake had a scout on it but so far, there had been nothing too exciting to go and see. So he waited.

He made good enough money in his line of work and knew that most people wondered about that. He was grateful that Lexi hadn't asked him about how he afforded the things he had, but he suspected she knew most of his history anyway.

His SUV was a top of the line Cadillac Escalade. He had the beach house there in Hatteras Village and she hadn't even seen the boat they were getting ready to board or his condo he kept in Atlanta. He wasn't filthy rich by millionaire standards, but he was quite comfortable.

He had worked hard and had been smart in his investments. He tried not to think of all the blood that had been spilled over those hard earned dollars. In the end, it really hadn't mattered.

Whether he was the one killing Mexican drug lords or it was someone else, they were going to end up dead anyway. Might as well be him who did it. It was always quick and painless. He wasn't a sadist; he never wanted another living thing to suffer. Maybe that was part of his upbringing. He had seen firsthand what pain inflicted on a human being could do. He never wanted to be the cause of that to someone else.

He knew it was a screwed up values system, but it had worked for him. He was glad that he was comfortable enough now that he didn't have to be a full time mercenary any longer, but it was a part of him and it always would be. Some might call it a life on the run and maybe it was. He would always be running from the ghosts of yesterday that seemed to find him wherever he went.

Jake shook his head as they entered the marina parking lot and pulled into his allotted space. He didn't know what had set him on this morbid train of thought and decided that it had to be the small blonde beside him. She stepped out of the vehicle and looked around with interest.

He walked down to the dock and turned left to get to his slip, where his boat "Zen Goddess" awaited. It was a 24-foot Cabin Cruiser with ample deck and a cabin underneath that could sleep four people. He had gotten it used and refinished it himself over the course of two years. His blood, sweat and tears had been poured into her and she was a labor of love. He ran his hand over the smooth finish as he stepped aboard and then reached down to help Lexi climb up after him.

She stood at the bow of the boat while Jake checked over the instrument panel and readied it for sailing the across the channel of waters that would take them to the marina on the other side of Ocracoke.

She had to wonder at what Jake did for a living besides helping battered women escape their husbands or save their sister from certain ruin. It helped that she had read the file her friend had given her on him before hiring him for Laurel.

She guessed she just never knew that mercenaries could clean up like this. The house he had on the beach had to cost at least 5 million dollars on beachfront property such as that. When Jake had said they were taking a boat to Ocracoke, she had imagined a small skiff or maybe something akin to a row boat with an attached outboard motor, not this luxury boat.

Jake started the engine of the boat and pulled out of the slip, careful to stay below speed during the no wake zone until they pulled out into the channel that led to the open water. The waters off the coast of the Carolinas were no joke, especially in and around

Hatteras. They didn't call it the Graveyard of the Atlantic for nothing.

He guessed the real reason the place had always appealed to him was because of all the great pirate stories that originated there. As a young boy, books were his escape and he would read everything he could get his hands on about pirates and knights and dragons. He didn't know why that spoke to him so much but he just loved hearing about Blackbeard and the general badass he was.

According to the history books, Blackbeard had been killed by the British right off the coast of Hatteras. Urban legends boasted that his ghost still roamed the shores. He didn't know if he believed all that, but he had told himself when he was younger that he would go to Hatteras someday.

The day he had first come here had been after his first really big job as a mercenary. It had been a big pay day, his biggest ever and he had bought his first place in Atlanta then and taken a long vacation, renting a house right there on Hatteras. After that the rest was history, as they say. He knew someday he would retire there if he didn't get himself killed before then, he thought wryly.

Lexi looked at Jake who was driving the boat and staring straight out at the horizon. It was late afternoon and still the sun was beating down on the open water. Lexi was grateful for the canopy that covered the helm and adjacent seat where they were currently sitting, otherwise she would be getting further burned.

It struck her suddenly that Jake hadn't spoken a word to her since they had left for the marina and he didn't look any closer to talking to her now than he had before. In fact he hadn't said more than two words to her since that awkward fall on the beach in the water, when she thought about it.

That was it. He had to think she was the biggest idiot in the world and he didn't want to spend any time with her. He was really just doing his job right now. She couldn't believe how incredibly stupid she was. She knew she was behaving irrationally, but she couldn't help it. This was why he kept calling her kid and half-pint; she was nothing more than an annoyance to him.

Jake was trying very hard to train his concentration on getting the boat safely through the channel following the channel markers carefully. The water was a bit choppy this evening, he noted as he looked out over the choppy waters, the white caps glinting in the late afternoon sun. He was refraining from looking in Lexi's direction.

She kept looking at him; he didn't miss that. But she was looking at him like she expected him to say something or do something. He wasn't sure what that meant. He had never had somebody that had any sort of expectations of him before so it was a strange concept to him. He just did as he was told when he was working and did whatever the hell he wanted to do when he wasn't.

He finally figured out why she made him so nervous. He had never had to spend this much time alone in someone else's presence, least of all one of the female persuasion. As Lexi turned to look out over the water, Jake glanced at her. He was no stranger to beauty; had seen his fair share of beautiful women in his time.

But there was something about Lexi's beauty that made you stop and take notice. Maybe it was the innocence that accompanied her smile.

Jake thought about a time when he had been on a rescue mission deep in the jungles of South America, he had gotten his assigned target who had held an American man as his hostage, a soldier. The man had been kept in a thatch covered hole in the ground for several months with very little exposure to sunlight. The man had squinted for at least half the day when Jake had rescued him.

Jake decided that being with Lexi was much like that. After a lifetime of darkness, being around her was such a bright and shining light. He had to take it in small increments or he might go blind.

Thirty minutes later and more tumultuous thoughts later, they were pulling into the marina at the southern tip of the island.

They still had a full ten minutes before they had to be at Jerry's office. He had worked with Jerry back in his early mercenary days. Had even done a couple of missions with him and there was nobody he would rather have his back than Jerry Helms. The guy sometimes was annoying and he often spoke before he thought, a trait that often drove Jake crazy, but he trusted the guy and trust was something you had to earn with him.

Jake tied off the boat and helped Lexi onto the dock, her hand firmly in his grasp as the transfer was made. But as soon as her feet were firmly on the ground, he released her as if he couldn't wait to get away from her. Lexi cursed herself silently. It was obvious now; he couldn't even stand to be around her. She should have known that she had imagined whatever she had thought she sensed from him.

Jake knew he was acting like a jackass but he just couldn't help himself. If he didn't have to touch her, he would be fine. But he swore every time he touched her, in one way or another, it felt like his skin was on fire. When he reached for her hand, all he really wanted to do was pull her to him so he could kiss her.

He knew was ridiculous for him to be so worked up about something as practically innocent as a kiss. But Jake knew he was kidding himself. Kissing Lexi would be anything but innocent and he damn well knew it.

The whole thing just pissed him off. He was a professional dammit, he thought to himself. Surely he could control himself better than this.

They walked the short distance to Jerry's office and entered it, a bell ringing when they closed the door. Jerry came out from the back of the house-turned-office and greeted them.

"Jake, hey man," Jerry said enthusiastically. At first glance, with Jerry's long hair that fell over one eye and broad shoulders and California accent, he looked like an old school surfer. You would never suspect he could take down two goons in one shot, but he was a force to be reckoned with.

Jake shook his hand firmly and introduced Lexi to him. "Lexi, this is Jerry."

Lexi smiled and extended her hand. "Nice to meet you." She spoke with her slight southern lilt.

"Ahh, Jake man. You sly dog you." He motioned to Lexi and handed Jake a thick manila envelope.

Jake swore under his breath as he took the papers from him and closed his eyes. There he went again, speaking without thinking, he thought.

Lexi flushed as the implications of what Jerry had said sunk in. She glanced at Jake who was clearly pissed. It bristled that he thought so little of her.

She knew it was silly to feel this personally affronted, but she quickly excused herself and went back out the way they had come. She wasn't going to go far, but she could not be in that room with Jake one minute longer. It was just too humiliating that he thought of her as little more than a nuisance or a job to be done. She didn't even know why she was reacting this way, but she decided that being angry was better than feeling humiliated, so she just went with it.

She headed down the street a little ways and stopped at the edge of the sidewalk in front of a building marked "Post Office" but it was clearly long-abandoned. This whole street was abandoned actually.

It gave her a start suddenly, being this isolated in a place she didn't know. Maybe she shouldn't have left Jake. If he couldn't find her and someone came after her, she would only have herself to blame. She had barely had time to finish that thought before she felt someone's hand on her arm, spinning her around.

Jake had cursed loudly as Lexi stormed out of the office, letting the door slam on the way out. Jerry had muttered an apology, which he had ignored.

"What do you think you're doin' runnin' off like that? You want to get yourself killed fine, but not on my watch. Got it?" He was angrier than he had been in a long time.

She spit his words right back at him. "No I don't *got it*." She emphasized. "I am a grown woman. Not a kid. Not half-pint. Not a *girl*." She fumed and raised her chin a few inches, seething as she forced herself to take a deep breath. "I can take care of myself."

He had her backed against the wall of the building. Jake breathed in and out and tried to keep himself from punching the wall behind Lexi's head. He didn't know what the hell he had done to deserve this woman constantly making him have to figure out her whereabouts but he sure would like to thank that bitch called fate that had caused them to cross paths in the first place. He wasn't being rational; he knew this. But he couldn't seem to stop himself or this well of feelings that kept coming whenever he was around her.

He stared down at her and she was leaning against the wall, hands on both hips, her bright blue eyes somehow managing to blaze heat when their very color belied any warmth. Her cheeks were flushed and her lips were set in a thin, hard line. She was about five feet nothing, but at that moment she looked much taller, her anger and passion lending height to her small frame.

As he looked at her lips, her eyes dropped so he couldn't read her expression and she ran her tongue lightly over her bottom lip and then bit down on it. She moved her eyes back up to him, all that white heat suddenly gone and replaced suddenly by something else. Something much fiercer. He swore he could hear a breathless sigh escape her lips as they parted ever so slightly.

His fists clenched at his sides as his body responded to her. His breath was coming faster and he knew what it meant. Jake was no stranger to desire. Had felt it many times in his life. The only thing that was foreign about it was the fact that he didn't feel in control at all. He felt like a snake about to come uncoiled. He could feel it swirling into the pit of his stomach. His hand moved of its own volition, as if it was not a part of his body, up to smooth her hair

99

back from her neck as he dipped his head down, letting his eyes slide closed and knowing as their lips met that he would ignite from in the inside out and incinerate on the spot.

Jake imagined tasting Lexi would be like warm sugar and vanilla, all sweetness and velvety softness. He imagined being with her in any way would be like sewing himself inside of a cocoon. Safe and suffocating all at the same time. He knew this, because right now it was getting harder and harder to breathe. Her lips parted beneath his and he swallowed her answering moan.

Lexi fisted her hand into Jake's shirt as his lips claimed hers, feeling a sigh escape her, like a soft slow breath of relief. She parted her lips and accepted his tongue. His hands were cupped on either side of her face now and he was leaning into her lightly as he kissed her like she'd never been kissed before.

She instinctively widened her stance a bit as he moved his leg between her thighs, trapping her against the wall and against the length of him, hard in all the places she was soft. Lexi pulled her lips away from him and tilted her head to the side, exposing her neck, not knowing what she wanted exactly, but instinct was telling her to make every inch of herself accessible to his mouth.

Jake accepted the invitation she had given him and spread kisses along her neck, spending extra time at the hollow of her neck, savoring the softness and the scent of vanilla and flowers filling his nostrils again.

He moved his lips back up along her jawline and kissed his way back to her mouth, claiming her lips again and angling his head so he could better access her, not thinking too much and letting himself just feel everything that he had wanted since the day he met her in the bar. He knew that they had only known each other a span of less than 48 hours but it seemed like there had never been a time that he hadn't wanted to kiss Lexi Green.

When she moved her legs, he moved his knee up to her and could feel where her thighs met, all warm and pliant and suddenly his jeans fit just a little too well. He could feel his hardness pressing against the zipper and that was his wake up call. He pulled away from her suddenly, rubbing his hand down over his face. "We gotta go. Got dinner reservations." With that, he turned around and started to walk off, readjusting his pants and hoping like hell she hadn't noticed just how aroused he was.

Lexi felt him pull away and watched as he tried to regain his composure. She should have said something. She should have yelled at him for manhandling her. She should call him out on breaking their kiss because it had gotten too hot to handle. But she didn't and maybe it was because her lips were still tingling from where he had kissed her. Maybe it was because her skin burned from where he had touched her. And maybe she should be angry, but instead she was just happy. She followed after him, feeling very pleased with herself.

Because at least now she knew she had not imagined all of it. And he didn't think she was a klutz after all. Well he might, but when he had kissed her, she had felt his hunger and it was as palpable as her own and she was not thinking at all about that awkward exchange on the beach.

What was more; she could see how bothered by the whole thing he was. He could barely even look at her after kissing her like that. She had made him nervous and he didn't know what to do with her. Lexi smiled to herself as she walked beside him. He did like her; maybe a little too much and it was killing him, she decided.

Lexi had kissed guys before, sure. But kissing Jake far out-did anything she had ever experienced with her past boyfriends. Kissing them had never made her feel like this. Like she was going to burn up from the inside out. It was exciting, it was heady, it was scary; but she didn't care. She had never felt more alive in her whole life.

Chapter 10

Dinner was an extremely awkward affair. They ate at a tiny establishment called "Pelican's Watch", a very upscale place right on the marina. Jake had been here many times before and the wait-staff knew him but were discreet about it. Jake was really in no mood to eat anything after the tense walk to get here, but they had the reservations so he figured they may as well make the best of it. When the food got there though Jake dug in with gusto, realizing that he had skipped lunch that afternoon while at the beach with Lexi. He figured there was no sense in punishing his stomach for something his mind (and the rest of his body) had done.

He glanced over at the source of all his thoughts to see that she was picking at her shrimp salad, moving items around on the plate rather than actually eating anything. "You should eat," he muttered between mouthfuls.

"I'm not hungry." She looked up at him, her eyes sparking in those bright blue crystals that he had gotten used to, or at least should be used to by now anyway. But whenever she looked at him, she had a way of seeing him like she knew his innermost thoughts and secrets, right down to his very soul. He wasn't sure how he felt about it. He had never let anyone get as close as he did Lexi Green. He'd sure as hell never let anyone see the scars on his back, the scars that ran much deeper than the surface of his skin.

He brought his glass to his lips, taking a tentative sip of the water. His lips were still swollen from kissing her, he realized. He might have been a bit overzealous when he claimed her lips with his own. He suddenly found himself wondering if hers were aching like his were.

She was studying the food on her plate like it might get up and walk away any minute and this amused him. He smirked at her as he swirled his iced tea in his glass. "It's dead already, you know."

He couldn't help but notice the small smile that crept into her features and he liked knowing that he put it there. It made him feel special for whatever reason and he found himself looking for something else to say that would elicit a bigger and brighter smile from her.

He wiped his mouth with his napkin and placed it in his plate. The waiter moved to bring him the check right on cue, but he held one hand out. He could see the waiter retreating out of the corner of his eye. He wanted to give Lexi a chance to finish her dinner, although it pretty much appeared to be a lost cause right now.

"Want me to get you something else?" He offered, but Lexi shook her head. He didn't know why he was being so nice to her. It really wasn't in his nature to coddle someone, but he felt genuinely bad, guilty almost, about kissing her like he did and then just leaving her standing there. He just didn't know how to deal with everything that kept popping into his head.

Besides that, he reasoned, right now it was his job to protect her. She may have hired him to pilot her sister to safety but now he was off her clock so to speak. He was no longer operating as her employee, he was acting as her sworn protector. He had his orders. He was to guard her at all costs. He didn't know how in the hell he was supposed to protect her, if he had to keep her at arm's length, but it was something that he was just going to have to sort out.

The constant circle that his thoughts kept traveling in was about to drive him crazy. But Jake did the only thing he had ever done when he was faced with a hard situation. He ran from it. Since he couldn't very well run away from her, this would have to do.

Lexi sat back from her plate. "We might as well go. I'm just not hungry. Sorry." She looked up at him and the effects of the past few days looked to be wearing on her. Jake nodded and motioned for the waiter to bring their check.

When they were on their way back to the marina, it had grown dark out. A light breeze was blowing and Lexi inhaled deeply, breathing in the thick briny air. People could say what they wanted, the beach had a definite calming effect for her. She was going through a pretty tough time in her life right now and just being near the ocean had minimized the effects greatly. She only hoped that Laurel was faring half as well.

Jake watched as Lexi kept falling asleep beside him. He slowed the boat as he came out of the channel and entered the marina at Hatteras Village. After about a minute, she had given up the fight and her head came to rest against his left arm. He took to steering the boat with his right hand, directing it towards the slip, the headlight of the boat cutting a yellow path across the brackish water of the marina. She felt oddly heavy lying against him, but it was a good kind of weight. Her hair was falling out of her messy ponytail and the strands were fanning out over his arm, tickling the skin everywhere it touched him.

Jake took a deep breath in and knew suddenly that he hadn't breathed this deeply in a while. This girl beside him had a palpable calming effect on him and while it puzzled him, he was thankful for it. He started to imagine what it might be like to kiss her again; if it would be half as explosive as the first time. He found that he was trying to convince himself that the passion behind their kiss, their argument was what fueled it and that was why he had felt like he might burn up from the want of it.

He pulled the boat into the slip and gently nudged her awake, wanting all at once to watch her sleep and wake her up so he could kiss her again to see if he could prove his theory; right or wrong, he couldn't remember which and he wasn't sure it mattered.

He got up and motioned for her to follow him as he tied off the boat and stepped out onto the dock. She extended her hand to him and he helped her down, enjoying the feel of his hands just above the crest of each hip as he lowered her down to the dock in front of him. As she slid down to the dock, her sleepiness had made her just the least bit limp and she slid against him pleasantly and he could swear he heard her sigh.

Lexi felt at peace suddenly waking up beside Jake. She knew she hadn't been asleep more than a few minutes but it had felt like hours and when she awoke, she could sense the change in Jake and she wondered what had happened to change him from the surly person earlier to the almost tender one in front of her now.

"Want to take a walk on the beach?" He asked her, extending his hand. The moonlight was great and the crabs that usually roamed the beach at night shouldn't be too much of a problem.

She nodded her head at him as she took his hand and their fingers naturally entwined like they held hands like this every day. He led the way down the path across from the marina parking lot. The beach was several hundred yards away but in the cool evening air, they crossed it in no time and drew close to the water lapping at the shore in the silvery moonlight. It didn't escape her that once they had reached the beach, he didn't release her hand. Instead he seemed to grip her fingers tighter within his, walking slowly so she could keep up with his longer strides.

Jake snuck a glance at her. She didn't seem to mind him holding her hand and for that he was glad. He figured if she let him hold her hand, maybe he really could kiss her again. At first he had considered going back to the house and kissing her goodnight outside her door. But then his imagination had gotten the best of him and he thought better of it.

He knew if their second kiss was anything like their first, it would be all too easy to open the door to her room and carry her to the bed, consequences be damned. No, he thought, it was better this way.

When they reached the curve in the island where it started to cut back into the marina, they circled back around and followed their fading footsteps back across the sand. Quickly before he could lose his nerve, he spun her around to face him.

Lexi was surprised by the sudden change in posture and she looked up at him and barely had time to register the emotion on his face before his lips met hers. He brought his free hand up to cup the back of her hand, his fingers threaded through her hair and pulling her to him.

For the second time this evening, she found herself in this man's tight embrace and she didn't mind it one bit. She brought one hand up to his biceps and then to the back of his head, pulling him closer as their kiss grew more urgent. Lexi opened her mouth and accepted his tongue as it licked the inside of her mouth, sampling, tasting and Lexi pressed herself against him instinctively, needing to feel him ever closer.

He let her fingers go and she whimpered until she realized this freed her hand up as well. He moved his hand up under her sweater,

106

under her tank as he ghosted fingers lightly up over her bra and back down again and she involuntarily shivered as she felt her nipples harden beneath the fabric. She skimmed her hand at his abdomen and reached up under his shirt, splaying her fingers over his rock hard abdomen. Her fingers at long last explored the hard planes of his stomach and reached up higher, inching her way up to his chest and she felt his breath hitch.

Jake moved his hand up to her ponytail and removed the elastic that held it all together, running his hands through the long locks of golden silk, loving the feel of it between his fingers. If it were up to him, she would never wear her hair in a ponytail again, he thought.

He angled his mouth to possess hers better and found that he couldn't get close enough to her. Somewhere in the back of his mind some part of him was recognizing the fact that he had proved his point. It hadn't all been in his mind. This kiss was every bit as passionate as the first and then some. He dragged his mouth from hers and leaned his forehead against hers, taking a deep stilling breath, meant to calm him but he found instead that he was thinking how he could get his lips back to hers again.

Lexi had a million thoughts running through her head as Jake kissed her again, leaving her breathless and just wanting more. She just couldn't use those thoughts together to form one single coherent one. When he took her hair out of the ponytail she actually felt sexier. And the way he kept one hand on her at all times, like he didn't want to let her go, made her feel special. Wanted. *Safe.*

Then all too soon he had pulled his lips away and was resting his forehead against hers. Lexi was afraid to say anything; afraid to spoil the moment but the silence was louder somehow than the beating of her heart.

"Jake." She said his name anyway, needing to feel it coming off her lips, the whisper behind it implying the passion she felt.

"Lexi." His voice was rough like wheels on a gravel path and he seemed just at a loss for words as she was.

"What are we doing?" She asked him finally and it was a valid question. But that one question spurned a thousand others and Jake didn't know how to answer it. He wasn't sure what to say. Hell if he knew what they were doing. Instead of answering her, he dipped his head back down to claim her lips again. And as he stood there kissing Lexi on the beach, he wasn't sure he would ever be ready to answer that question.

Chapter 11

Lexi hung up the phone and let out the sob that she had been holding in once she heard her sister's voice. Laurel sounded good; so much better than the last time she had talked to her. It had been three days since Jake had first kissed her and he hadn't done it since. In fact, he hadn't mentioned it at all. He had never answered her question of what they were doing either.

She cracked the cell phone into two pieces just like Jake had shown her and threw it into the waste basket in the bathroom. She then turned on her heel and headed out to the deck outside her bedroom. It would be easier to have her cry outside where Jake couldn't hear her. She leaned over the railing and breathed in the warm sea air. The sun had just set and the water was very calm. It had been a very hot day and the heat of the day still lingered in the evening air, sticky and cloying.

Lexi was dressed in a pair of pajama shorts and a tank top and the slight breeze blowing raised the flesh on her arms despite the warmth. She let the tears fall without even bothering to wipe them away. She was glad that Laurel was doing well, but it was killing her being separated from her. From Vivian. She even missed Matt right now. She realized with a start that she was homesick.

It really didn't help that Jake had been in such a surly mood the past few days. He had kissed her outside her bedroom door that night and she had lain awake most of the night tracing her fingers over the places his lips had touched, her skin feeling scorched by the contact. He was a really good kisser.

She had shared many stolen kisses with prior boyfriends, but they hadn't been anything remotely as hot as kissing Jake Jackson. Though she still didn't have resolution in her mind about what they were doing exactly, it had allowed her thoughts to stray beyond more pressing matters. Thinking about Jake and kissing him, she was able to stop crying finally. At least, that was something.

The sliding doors adjacent to hers opened and Jake stepped out onto the deck, lighting a cigarette before shutting the door to his room. He evidently didn't see her in the corner of the deck. She hurried to wipe her tears away and wondered briefly if she had summoned him out here with her thoughts about him.

"Oh hey, I didn't know you were out here," he said to her almost apologetically and she wondered if he had a guilty conscience. He should, after practically avoiding her for the past three days, she smirked.

Jake wondered at how just watching Lexi leaning over the railing in the corner of the deck had his thoughts right back where they shouldn't be; thinking about his hands and lips all over her. He had been doing pretty good avoiding her out here most nights.

She usually was in by now, watching something on the television in her room or reading a book. He walked over to where she stood and saw the telltale tear tracks on her cheeks and met her eyes, bloodshot and still watery.

The hell of it was she was trying to hide it from him and he immediately felt like shit for acting the way he had the past few days. It wasn't her fault he was so screwed up. Then he thought he'd heard her talking to her sister and maybe something had happened. "What's wrong?" He asked, immediately concerned and he turned her shoulders gently to face him.

But Lexi was having none of it. She jerked her shoulder from his grasp, a flash of sudden irritation. It was annoying the way he seemed to turn his feelings on and off. She wished she could be that lucky.

She faced him with barely disguised anger and shrugged. "Why do you care? You've been ignoring me for days." She said softly and turned back around to face the Atlantic. Right now, the waves out beyond the dunes were less tumultuous than what was going on inside her mind; inside her heart.

Jake reeled back as if she struck him. He guessed he deserved that. He had been very distant, but it had been necessary. What he was feeling for Lexi scared the ever living shit out of him. He couldn't tell her that, but it was just as true. He figured the further he stayed away from her, the less likely he would be to hurt her. Because he wasn't nearly good enough for her and he never would be.

But now he felt like the worst kind of prick for making her feel like he didn't care. That was the thing; *he did*. Too much. Against his better judgment he ground his cigarette out and put both hands gently on her shoulders, leaning close to her ear. "'M sorry, okay. I ain't good at this." He turned her to face him, a dagger of sorrow piercing his chest when he saw the tears tracing their way down her cheeks and knowing he was the one to put them there. "Damn, I didn't mean to make you cry."

"You didn't." She replied. "I just got off the phone with Laurel. She's okay. I just miss her." The last part came out in a sob, to Lexi's horror. So much for not letting him see her cry. She just stood there helplessly, letting the tears fall.

He took her into his arms wordlessly and it was like they melted into one another, falling into that position where her head fit under his chin so perfectly. She pulled away to look up at him. "I'm sorry to be a cry baby."

Jake could not believe she was apologizing for crying. He had never met anyone like her. She was so good and so sweet, it made him ache. Made him want her even more than he already did and damn it to hell, he was tired of keeping himself away from her. Because if something was that good, that pure and it felt that natural to him, then it couldn't end badly. It couldn't. He just wouldn't let it.

He felt all his solid resolve melt away and with that, all reasonable thought went out the door as he bent his head to hers and took possession of her lips. A tiny gasp of surprise sprung from her lips just before he silenced it with his kiss. She parted her lips willingly under his and wound her arms up around his neck. He ran his hands down her back, fingers splayed over her lower back as she arched herself into him, pressing against him in all the right ways.

She was soft and pliant in the way a woman gets when she is ready. The fact that this girl was ready in that way for him made his pants tight instantly. He deepened their kiss and she moaned into his mouth as he lightly bit her lower lip. Her shirt had rucked up in the back and allowed him a touch of bare skin, so soft, so warm. He gently pulled her flush against him, no longer giving a damn if she could tell he was aroused or not. He wanted her to know how much she turned him on.

Jake was kissing her again like the past three days hadn't mattered and Lexi just didn't have the sense or the willpower right now to question what was going on. She wanted him desperately; in all the ways she had read about in all those romance novels Laurel hid from their Mama.

At that time, she had never imagined she would be kissing someone like this. Even a week ago she would have never believed someone if they told her she would be acting so wantonly. But his mouth on hers was like being branded by fire and she didn't care about propriety.

Her head dropped to the side as if on a string and he didn't waste time in ghosting his lips over her jaw and down her neck, his mouth tracing a fiery path that he created, threatening to consume them both. He pulled her against him and she could feel his erection in his jeans, pressing up against her. She splayed her fingers over his back, enjoying the feeling of the hard planes of his body, so different from her own.

Jake reached down to cup her ass and hoisted her up to straddle him, his lips meeting hers in a frenzied mix of teeth and tongue and he walked them to his door and kicked the door open with his foot and stepped into his room, the coolness of the house hitting them as soon as they hit the carpet. He never broke contact with her lips as he walked her over to his bed and gently laid her down, her hair fanning out over his pillow, the bright blond a sharp contrast against the black microfiber sheets. She looked up at him expectantly, her eyes half lidded with desire.

Lexi pulled Jake down beside her as he laid her on the bed, scarcely daring to believe that this was happening. She instinctively raked her nails lightly over his back, hiking her hip up over his leg, needing to make contact between where she knew their two bodies would join perfectly.

Jake was so hard, his erection straining against his pants and he wished he had thought to remove them before he laid down beside her. But now that she was laid out beside of him in all her perfection, he didn't have the strength or the fortitude to tear himself from her for any length of time. She was pressing herself into him. He reached up between them and skimmed his fingers up under her tank top and was pleased to discover she was not wearing a bra. He moved his hand up over her breast, kneading his hands and bringing his thumb up over her nipple, feeling it pebble beneath his touch. Lexi arched her back against his hand. Jake ghosted his fingers back down her body, down her stomach and slipped his hand down over her shorts and cupped her with his hand, feeling the warmth seeping through the fabric. He traced her slit over top of her shorts and he could practically taste how sweet she would be.

Lexi clenched her thighs shut as if to trap Jake's hands over the apex of her thighs, wanting, no, *needing*, friction and her hips writhed back and forth, her body sensing what she needed. She wanted his hands *there*. His fingers *there*. His mouth *there*. There where she ached for him, throbbing pulsing desire just erupting beneath the service.

Lexi was no stranger to pleasure. She was a grown woman after all and she knew which buttons to push to bring on her orgasm. But she had never had a man bring her to that point. Brandon had tried, but it just hadn't ever happened for her with him.

She was curious to know if Jake would know her body as well as she did. With the way she was feeling right now, she didn't think he would have any trouble figuring out what she liked and she smiled against his mouth at the thought.

As Jake continued to caress her at the apex of her thighs, he could feel her wetness through the fabric and it was nearly his undoing. He wanted nothing more than to remove every stitch of her clothing and have his way with her, but there was no way he could do that to her. Lexi was not someone you simply screwed. She could never be a one night stand. He tried not to think on this too much. He just knew that he wanted her more than he had ever wanted any woman in his life.

He dragged his mouth back to hers once again, his mouth punishing hers with an intensity that was leaving them both breathless.

Just then, he heard the front door slam. "Hey Jakey boy, where ya at?" That unmistakable voice called out down the hall.

"Dammit." Jake swore softly. "*Jeb.*" His brother had always had the worst timing. He sat up quickly, hoping to get to the door, but it was too late. Jeb came sauntering in, a beer already in his hand.

114

"Woooo-weee, son, didn't know ya had company back here. Yeah, I'd hit that too." He laughed that very Jeb laugh and walked back out the door, leaving Jake staring after him and looking to Lexi whose face was flushed and confused. Dammit to hell, the only thing worse than Jerry the other day would be Jeb showing up and wrecking everything. He ran a hand through his hair.

"Who's Jeb?" She asked him, moving to get up.

"My brother." He muttered as he got up to go face the music. "I'm sorry. He's a pain in the ass; I'll try to get rid of him."

Lexi just nodded and stared after him as she watched him leave, unsure of what to do. She was pretty sure there wasn't a handbook out there for what to do if your boyfriend's brother interrupted you making out like two teens. Then she stopped herself at the word boyfriend. How had that thought even crept into her mind? Jake was nothing of the sort.

She decided her best course of action was to go to her room and change to something a little less revealing and go out to meet Jake's brother.

Chapter 12

Jake walked out to the living area where Jeb was already propping his feet up on the coffee table and had switched the television on to some stupid reality show.

"Jeb." It was a statement. He never knew what to say to his brother after his long disappearances. He never said where he was or what he was doing during his absences, but if Jake could hazard a guess, it was probably nothing good.

"Who's the piece, little brother?" Jeb drawled and Jake clenched his jaw. The thing with Jeb was you didn't let him know he got under your skin. It was better that way. If he got any whiff of weakness he would pounce on it like a cat on its prey.

"It's complicated." Hell would freeze over before he would tell Jeb anything about Lexi Green. He didn't even want him to look at her.

"Why don't you bring her on out here? Let old Jeb decide if it's complicated or not." He chugged down the rest of his beer and sat the bottle down on the table loudly.

"Hey, careful." Jake didn't know why Jeb had to be so hard about everything. Sometimes he wondered how they could even be related. But, he was blood and that counted for something in Jake's book.

Lexi walked into the room, having changed into yoga pants and an oversized sweatshirt with the OBX logo. She had found it buried in the back of the closet in her room. She had brushed her hair back into some semblance of a ponytail and she sat down on the sofa beside Jake. Jeb was seated across from them on the overstuffed arm chair.

"Hey there sugar, I'm Jeb." Jeb drawled out his name. "Jakey here hasn't told me how you know each other yet."

Jake hadn't been planning on telling him to be honest. It wasn't any of his business for one thing.

Lexi looked to Jake expectantly out of the corner of her eye. Lexi was starting to think she should have stayed in the bedroom after all. But she put on a brave face. "I'm Lexi Green, U.S. Marshal." Lexi decided to go with her professional title. Sometimes it was disarming to people and Jeb seemed like he might be one of those people.

She seemed to remember in reading Jake's file, a mention of his brother who was somewhat of a wild card. He had been in trouble with the law in the past and had appeared to clean up his act but often disappeared for months at a time and no one ever seemed to know where he went.

Jeb seemed overall unaffected though by her announcement. "Is that right?" He feigned complete interest and Jake watched him warily. He looked to Jake. "What's the story, little bro?"

"She's my assignment for now. Her sister is married to Thomas Garner." He explained. Jeb was well versed in the crime rings of the Southeast United States. Hell, he'd been part of them at one time or another.

Jeb let out a low whistle and addressed Jake. "Not like you to mix business with pleasure, little brother." Jake clenched his jaw and fisted his hands at his sides. Just like Jeb to jump right to the point of the conversation. Big fuckin' mouth and no tact to go with it.

"Come on, Jeb. Let's have a drink." He had to get the topic of conversation steered away from Lexi before he killed him. Because he swore if he said one more derogatory thing about her, he was going to have to punch his own brother in the face. And a fist fight between him and Jeb was never a good thing.

He walked over to the mini-bar in the corner of the living room and grabbed a bottle of Jim Beam, intending to get Jeb drunk. He grabbed two shot glasses, then a third just in case. He didn't know if Lexi was a drinker, but he got her a glass anyway.

He sat out the three glasses on the coffee table and looked to Lexi before he filled the last one with the amber liquid. To his surprise, she nodded at him.

Lexi had never really developed a taste for alcohol. Her Daddy had been a recovering alcoholic, but this past week had been so unnerving that she wished she had known the mini-bar was well stocked earlier. So when Jake offered to pour her some, she nodded her consent.

Jeb and Jake both took their shot glasses and raised them and she did the same. She sniffed it delicately and tossed it back, feeling the liquid burn all the way down. It wasn't awful, but she wasn't sure if she wanted another glass.

Jeb and Jake had another immediately and soon Jeb was laughing more riotously than before he had started drinking.

"Were you followed here?" Jake asked him. He couldn't have Jeb fucking up his operation here. No one knew where his house was except for his brother and he intended to keep it that way.

But Jeb just shook his head. "Relax. You know old Jeb is lookin' out for you. I gotta tell you though, you sure stirred up the shit pot back home." So it seemed like Garner had spread the word about things. Word traveled fast in those networks, he supposed.

Jeb poured another drink for himself. "Want another, blondie?" He asked Lexi and she just shook her head. She was still feeling dizzy from the first shot. She figured she better quit while she was ahead.

"Whadya mean?" Jake thought he better slow down. He didn't mean to match Jeb shot for shot but that was what was happening. He found he was starting to slur his words. He was feeling almost pleasant. He reached over and squeezed Lexi's knee, letting his palm rest on her leg when she didn't move his hand.

Lexi looked up in surprise at Jake and realized with a start that he was drunk. And drunk Jake was funny. He was completely relaxed, the opposite of what he normally was. He stayed wound so tight it was a wonder he could even function. She placed her hand over his, for the moment going with whatever this was.

"Garner has his weasels looking for her sister all over the place. Word is he's tracking her down to Florida." Jake nodded thoughtfully, pleased that the plan had worked so well.

Lexi watched the interaction between the two brothers and it was the strangest dynamic she had ever witnessed. They seemed to love each other and hate each other equally. As abrasive and boisterous as Jeb was, Lexi couldn't help but wonder how two brothers could turn out so differently.

Jeb was laughing again at some story Jake was telling. "And then he just sat there holding the toilet seat in his hand." Lexi smiled as both men laughed riotously. She almost felt like she was intruding on some private moment.

She got up and excused herself. "I'm going to head to bed boys. Don't stay up too late now." She told them and winked at Jake daringly.

He pulled her down to him for a quick kiss on the lips, which also startled her. What was up with him tonight and all the public displays? It had to be the alcohol, she thought and she was amused as she headed back to her room. She really was tired.

Crying as hard as she had earlier had her eyes feeling raw. Plus all the things that had happened, making out with Jake, to the point that they had almost had sex, then his brother showing up and the whiskey shots she had just downed. All of it had her feeling pleasantly sleepy.

She changed back into her shorts and tank top and crawled beneath the covers, relishing the feel of the cool sheets on her flushed skin, knowing it was a side effect of the alcohol.

It seemed like she had just closed her eyes when she heard Jake open and close her door loudly and stop by her bed. "You awake?" He whispered loudly.

She smiled at him sleepily. "I am now".

"Lexi. Lexi. Can I lay down here, Lexi?" He asked her. It was like he couldn't seem to say her name enough. His hair was disheveled in the most disarming way and the effects of the alcohol had relaxed his usually stern facial features. He looked happy. It looked good on him, she decided.

She moved over to allow him to climb in beside her. She didn't know what to expect but him passing out as soon as his head hit the pillows wasn't it. She laughed as she pulled the covers up over both of them.

"I love you." The whisper that fell from his lips was so soft she almost didn't hear it. Lexi nearly fell out of the other side of the bed, not sure if she had heard him right. Because there was no way she had heard him say those three words.

"What did you say Jake?" She shook his shoulders lightly and got no response. By the time she fell asleep two hours later, she had almost convinced herself that it had been a trick of her mind. Almost.

Chapter 13

He was back in the fields again. He breathed her name; Maria. He glanced behind him and he was pulling her along, trying to push her ahead of him. But still, no matter how fast he ran, or how much he tried to propel her forward, he still felt the pull of his hand as she fell to the ground, the guerillas having taken her out. He yelled her name and screamed "No" over and over again. He killed the men who had just murdered Maria in cold blood and went to pick her up off the floor of the field of orchids. Orchids. That was the smell. Suddenly when he looked down, it wasn't Maria in his arms bleeding out her last drop of blood. It was Lexi.

Then suddenly, someone jerked his shoulders, shaking him.

"Wake up Jake." Jake opened his eyes to find Lexi hovering over him. His head ached something awful. He glanced at his surroundings and vaguely remembered thinking it was a good idea to come visit her after his late night with Jeb. She smoothed his hair back from his forehead. "You were having a dream".

Jake sat up, still fully clothed and ran a hand down the scruff on his face. He had the dream again, but it had changed this time. Instead of Maria, it had been Lexi that had died in his arms. He glanced over at her and she was watching him carefully in the pale moonlight streaming through the window.

Lexi didn't quite know how to handle Jake, all vulnerable from sleep and the nightmare that he had clearly just had. Not knowing what his reaction would be, but hoping that he would open up to her, she asked him. "Who is Maria?"

Jake looked up at her in surprise. He must have said her name in his sleep. Thank God he hadn't said Lexi's name. That might have been a bit embarrassing and hard to explain since he didn't understand it even himself. He brought his hand back to his head and massaged his temples there, trying not to notice the way his fingers shook.

Even he didn't want to admit how much the dream disturbed him. It always did. Lexi was still waiting on his answer and blame his state of mind or blame the after-effects of the whiskey but he told her. All of it.

She just listened quietly, nodding here and there and asking intelligent questions. He had never told anyone about Maria, ever, not even Matt. He didn't even want to think what it meant that he was telling Lexi. Someone he had just met, no less. But he felt comfortable with her in a way he had never experienced before with another person.

Lexi looked at Jake and watched his pained expression as he told the story of how he met Maria and the horrible way she had died. It was obvious from his words and how deeply affected he was by the dream that he had loved her. "I'm sorry," Lexi said simply. The occasion really didn't call for much more than that. She reached over and squeezed his hand and he let her.

There was something familiar about Lexi Green. Something that felt like home and it scared the shit out of him, to be honest. He pulled his hand away where she had just grasped it. He knew she was trying to be nice and that he was an asshole but he suddenly felt the need to put as much distance between him and Lexi as he could.

Again. He got up and scooted off the bed, standing to leave. "I'm sorry I woke you up." And he walked out of the room, closing the door softly behind him.

🍎 🍎 🍎 🍎 🍎 🍎 🍎 🍎 🍎 🍎

Lexi watched him go, feeling strangely bereft. Some part of her knew that it had to have been hard for him to tell her about Maria. But after what had happened between them yesterday, the kisses they had shared, him whispering I love you as he fell asleep; she knew that she hadn't imagined it.

But then he went and dreamed of some other girl from what sounded like a lifetime ago. She wasn't mean-spirited and never had been, but she realized with a pain that she was jealous and that seemed ridiculous to Lexi. She was envious of a ghost of a woman that still haunted his dreams. And it didn't feel good, not at all. She laid back down and tossed and turned before finally falling asleep in the early grey light just before dawn.

🍎 🍎 🍎 🍎 🍎 🍎 🍎 🍎 🍎 🍎

Jake went back to his room when what he really wanted to do was go grab that bottle of whiskey and down the whole damn thing. But he knew that wasn't the answer; it never had been for him. He guessed his old man had done enough drinking for all of them in his opinion. So he trudged back to his room and pulled back the covers to sleep, but just sat on the end of the bed instead.

In the dream it had been Maria at first, but then it had switched to Lexi. Seeing her, even in his dream state, covered in blood was deeply disturbing and left him with a lead ball in the pit of his stomach. He couldn't bear to lose anyone that way again. He couldn't bear to lose her. Period. And that scared him because he didn't know when the hell it had happened; when had Lexi Green, his assignment become an important part of his life?

Jake had never been the kind of man who looked to the future and wanted true and lasting love with someone. He never thought he deserved it. Hell, he probably still didn't deserve it. But this girl made him want those things. With her. And it was absurd.

Jake clenched his fists at his sides. He had no right to feel that way about her. She was so good and represented everything that Jake didn't possess. Even if he was a better man, *and he wasn't*, he would only get her hurt or killed. Like Maria. And he was not about to let that happen.

The next morning at breakfast was nearly stone silent, save for the clattering of plates and forks. Lexi had gotten up and made breakfast for everyone and Jeb and Jake were digging in with gusto. The otherwise quiet room was nearly deafening.

Jeb glanced back and forth between Jake and Lexi and it was clear he was trying to fit pieces of the puzzle together. She almost had to laugh, because so was she.

"What's the matter Jakey boy? Trouble in paradise?" Jeb laughed at his own joke and looked to Lexi who just smiled tightly.

"Keep your trap shut, Jeb," Jake warned him, sending a glare across the table to his brother. He wished to hell he had never shown up here. "How long you stayin' this time anyway?" Jake asked.

"Aww, now you done gone and hurt old Jeb's feelings, but since you asked, I'm probably leaving tomorrow," Jeb drawled but there was a chuckle behind it, negating the words he spoke.

Jake rolled his eyes and cleaned his plate off the table, fully intending to do the dishes.

Lexi stopped him. "I'll get them." She said softly, meeting his eyes across the room. He hadn't spoken two words to her all morning. She wished they could just go back to when they were making out the day before.

Jake shook his head. "Fair is fair. You cooked. I'll clean." Like this rift between them was some domestic squabble over forgotten chores. His words were logical, but the look on his face was breaking Lexi's heart. He looked a little like a kicked puppy, she realized. She hoped she hadn't put that look there. She couldn't think of anything that she had said that might have offended him.

"I can do them. I don't mind." She placed her hand on his at the counter. He didn't move his hand. He just looked at her as if he wanted to say a million things, but he didn't utter one word. Not even an argument for the dishes.

Jeb excused himself from the room and Jake almost wanted to congratulate his brother for realizing something was going on bigger than himself for once.

"Lexi what's happening with us…I don't know what it is. *But it can't happen*." He looked at her, his bright blue eyes conveying so much pain, she didn't know if she could do what she thought he was asking.

He turned on his heel and walked out to the deck. Lexi didn't want to fight with him, but he wasn't going to get off that easy. She followed him out the door and shut it behind her. At least out on the deck they had a bit of privacy. On the one hand, she was heartbroken at his words and on the other hand, she felt like it wasn't just his decision to make on where they went with whatever the hell this was.

"You don't get to do that, ya know." Lexi informed him primly, both hands on her hips as she faced him.

126

He stared at her disbelievingly. "Do what?" He asked.

"You don't get to just come in and make me feel things and then just announce that it's not going to happen." She gestured wildly with her hands, words strangely inadequate to her all the sudden. "It's already happening if you haven't noticed."

Jake looked at her in surprise. By what she was saying, it meant she was feeling something too. Sometimes it was hard to remember if what he thought and what was actually happening were the same thing. His mind was in such turmoil, he couldn't think straight anymore. It made him angry.

"You don't know how dangerous this is. This thing? With us? It just can't happen." He ran his hand over his head, frustrated with his lack of eloquence. "You'll get hurt, Lexi. Or worse. And I can't have that." Jake bit out the words. "It ain't happening." He stressed the rest of it, mere inches from her face now.

She felt the stinging of tears at the back of her eyes and she willed them away. She would not have him see her cry. Not again. "It's bullshit". She said to him. He wanted a fight. He was going to get a fight.

"Bullshit, huh?" He said and then laughed mirthlessly.

"Yeah, bullshit", she repeated. "You look at me and you see another dead girl's face. You think just because you lost someone that somehow makes you special. Well guess what, it doesn't! I've lost people too and I don't walk around acting like the world owes me something. Just because you're scared." She shouted the last word at him.

"I ain't scared of anything." He was fuming now. How dare she come in here and insinuate that she knew how he felt? That she had walked one mile in his shoes? She had no idea what he was up against; what they were up against and how very dangerous it all was. Except that she did and deep down he knew that. Just like he knew he was losing this argument.

She sent him a calculated look. "You were scared last night. And you're scared right now. You feel something for me and you can't handle it. You are afraid of us, Jake."

He stood back a minute and studied her, calling him out on his bullshit and he couldn't recall a time in his life when anyone had ever stood up to him before. Not like this girl. He didn't know how to take that. He didn't know how to handle someone like her. Who saw straight through him to his very soul, as black as it was.

She thought he was afraid of what was happening between them?

She was right.

But instead of telling her she was, he just walked away, heading quickly down the steps, knowing that he was running away from her for the second time in the past several hours. It didn't set well with him, but he didn't know how in the hell to process any of this shit with her standing right in front of him demanding answers to her questions and he just didn't have any right now.

The sea air would maybe clear his head. He caught a scent on the wind, it was her hair. Suddenly he was thinking of his dream again and he remembered the field of orchids where Maria had died. He remembered that they were special orchids; vanilla orchids. He would never forget the smell as long as he lived. The air that day had been pungent with their distinctive fragrance.

When he had come back, he had wanted to get some of the same orchids for his garden but they didn't smell the same. It wasn't until after he consulted a horticulturist that he found out the truth of it. Vanilla orchids were what made vanilla and the reason they were so distinctive was because they were pollinated by a special species of bees. The pollination process of the orchids was almost solely responsible for giving vanilla its heady scent. Lexi's hair smelled exactly like those fields.

Jake paused at the dunes and looked out over the expanse of the Atlantic. Why his subconscious brain had picked up on all that he couldn't figure. Jake hadn't cried in years, but as he stood there he felt like he was finally mourning the passing of Maria. He finally felt ready to let go of her memory and he cried.

Chapter 14

Jake was still standing there an hour later, watching the waves come and go, trying to decide how he was going to swallow his huge amount of pride and apologize to Lexi. It went against his very nature to say he was sorry, but when he was wrong, he admitted it. He was loathe to do it, but he would.

He walked back up the steps, trudging slowly. It felt very much to him as if he was going to the guillotine. He slid open the doors to the deck and found a note on the table. If she had gone and run off, he was going to wring her neck himself, he thought. She wouldn't have to worry about Thomas or his goons being after her.

But the note wasn't from her. Instead he recognized the scrawl upon closer inspection as that of his brother.

"Back in a few days, J."

It was strange for his brother to make that trip all the way down here to leave so soon. It was a far way down to the tip of this island where Jake's house was located and wasn't an easy trip to make but he wasn't his brother's keeper. He figured he never had been. It just wasn't much the Jackson way to keep tabs on the whereabouts of the only family he had left.

He tried not to feel guilty for feeling relieved that Jeb had taken his leave. This visit was just not happening at a convenient time. He wasn't really sure there ever would be a convenient time for his brother to make an appearance but with Lexi there, it was too much for him to handle.

He looked in the kitchen and living area and didn't find Lexi in either place. He knew she wasn't on the deck because he would have seen her as he walked up from the beach. He walked down the hall to her room and found the door standing wide open.

He retraced his steps. Maybe she had found her way up to the library. The room was a loft area just above the living area in the main part of the house. It served as an observatory as from that high elevation, you could look out one set of windows to the ocean and the ones on the opposite side of the room gave a beautiful view of the sound.

He hardly ever went up there anymore and often forgot it was a good place to hide out from the world. He guessed if anyone deserved to be avoided, it was him.

He sighed as he started up the steps. He could already smell the sweet scent of vanilla and flowers that he had come to love. As he came to the top, he saw her curled up on the sofa, ponytail all askance, a book laid across her chest. His heart caught in his chest at the sight of her. She was so damn beautiful, it almost hurt to look at her, and in slumber she was even more so.

He went to turn to go back down the steps. He didn't feel like he had the right to wake her up. Seems like he had already done that last night and that was the main reason he was in the most distasteful position of having to say he was sorry in the first place.

For what, he didn't know. He still thought it was damn dangerous. Not to mention the ethical dilemma he faced from her being a business associate. Jeb hadn't missed his mark on that one.

He never mixed business with pleasure. But Lexi just didn't seem to fit into the pleasure category, at least not in the conventional sense. He had already kissed her several times and he knew that sex with this woman would be pleasurable. Hell, he figured they might burn up on contact once they got around to it. But he was getting way ahead of himself. Besides the fact that casual sex didn't even seem to be the right term to describe anything of the sort with Lexi.

"Hey." The subject of all his thoughts called from the couch with a wary look.

Lexi sat up and moved the book beside her. She didn't know at what point she had fallen asleep. She had been so angry when Jake had left her standing there after their argument that she had gone in search of any kind of distraction.

She had found this room and the peace she had sought and curled up with a book. She hadn't intended to fall asleep, but it seemed the nap had done her good. She felt considerably better about things, even if she wasn't quite sure why he'd come to find her after the horrible things she had said to him. She couldn't force this with them. He had to want it too. And maybe he wasn't ready for anything like this; whatever this was.

"Hey," said Jake softly as he walked back up the three steps it took to get to the top landing. He walked over to where she was sitting, feeling ridiculous to ask her if he could sit down in his own damn house, but that was exactly what he did. "Can I sit?" He gestured to the sofa beside her.

"Sure," she answered, sitting up more fully and running her hand down over her hair, adjusting her ponytail, as he sat down next to her.

"I'm-." She began.

"I wanted-." They both started to speak at the same time and then laughed nervously. He motioned for her to go first.

"I'm sorry, Jake. I had no right to say what I said to you. What happened with you and Maria was awful and I didn't have any right to bring that up. I'm pretty ashamed of myself." The look on her face was a cross between embarrassed and guilty and, for a minute, he forgot what he had been going to say.

She was apologizing to *him*. He was thoroughly confused. He had never met anyone like her. He had only ever had one-sided relationships. This give-and-take thing they had going on was foreign to him. He wasn't sure how to take it, so he just forged ahead.

"No, *I'm* sorry. You were right." Damn, if those weren't the bitterest words he had ever had to utter. They actually didn't taste quite as bad as he thought they would, though.

She raised her eyebrow at him. "I was?" Her voice was at least an octave higher, then she added quickly. "Go on," she said, her expression now one of open curiosity. This was definitely not how she expected this would go.

"I don't get to make the decision by myself. I don't know what's going to happen. I still think it's dangerous. But if you want to try whatever this is between us." He ran his hand through his shaggy hair, not really sure what else to say and he held his hands out to convey this to her. "I *am* afraid. I haven't never been afraid of anything in my entire life. But this? With us? Yeah, it scares me." He took her hand and moved it to his chest, right over his heart. "*Feel*".

Lexi could feel his heartbeat thrumming beneath her fingers and she gripped his shirt, even as he moved his hand down to take her other hand in his. She looked at him and realized that his guard was completely down for the first time, maybe in his whole life and she was so moved by his speech that she moved her hands up on either side of his face and searched his eyes, finding that cold steely glint behind his bright crystal blue eyes was gone. In its place was one of the most searchingly tender gazes that had ever shone upon her. She let her eyes flutter closed to signal her intention and leaned closer to him to move her lips over his.

As her lips met his, Jake groaned and moved his hands to her waist, his fingers skimming the soft flesh of her hips as his mouth slanted over hers and he felt her own lips part willingly under his. He teased the seam of her lips with his tongue and moved to draw her in even further, knowing that there was no turning back now.

Lexi pulled away breathlessly to look at him for a minute, bracing one hand on his chest to steady herself. He had kissed her to near breathless and she thought her own heartbeat echoed that of his. Rapid and steady but like that of a frightened rabbit. She felt very much the same way and he deserved to know that he wasn't alone. "It scares me too, Jake. We can figure it out together if you want," she offered.

Jake knew that he had never heard anything so wonderful in his life. This beautiful person sitting here before him, telling him, Jake Jackson, that they could just wing it together. He brought his lips to hers again, wanting to consume her, cherish her, *love* her. No one had ever said anything like that to him before. Like it was him and her against the world.

The world was a scary place and always had been for him. It sounded like she was much the same way. But with the two of them facing off against whatever obstacles were in front of them, he felt like they just might come out on top. As he leaned in to kiss her, the light from the moon spilling over them in this place high above the rest of the world, he felt like they might even conquer it.

Chapter 15

Lexi marveled at the man before her. He had gotten up from the sofa and pulled her up beside him, taking her hand in his and led the way down the stairs. She followed him down the steps, feeling very much like the princess that had been rescued from a tower and was following her dark prince to his chambers. It was that surreal to her that this was all happening and following him, holding his hand tightly within hers, it was hard not to draw those parallels.

She smiled to herself as he kept walking past her room in favor of his, like they had last night before they got interrupted. It seemed like it was much longer than yesterday, but it was funny that way; time with Jake.

It was as if it sped up and slowed down all at once and it made her dizzy. Or maybe it was because Jake swept her up in his arms just before they crossed the threshold to his room. She squealed in delight and nuzzled her head to his chest as he carried her across the room, lowering her gently, but with purpose in his gaze, just beside his bed.

She couldn't help the little gasp that sprung for her lips as she felt his hardness melded to her softness, letting her body slide all the way down his, the friction building between them and igniting a fire deep in her core.

Suddenly, everything slowed to a crawl and she felt butterflies in her stomach at the look that he was sending her, his eyes smoldering into hers as if he was undressing her down to her very soul.

Lexi shivered involuntarily and unconsciously dropped her head back, exposing her neck and Jake took the invitation as he was meant to, dipping his head slowly to nip gently at the tender flesh there, spreading soft slow kisses all the way up her jaw line until finally resting on her lips.

Jake moved his hands to Lexi's hips and looped one finger in each belt loop on her shorts, pulling her against him, her body molding to his; soft in all the places that he was so very hard.

He had a sense as he was kissing her that it was some sort of forbidden pleasure but at the same time, he knew that his lips were meant for hers. His hands were meant for her hands. His soul was meant for her soul and he knew it sounded corny, but he figured he had never asked for a damn thing in his whole entire life.

Just maybe it was his turn for something good to happen. Lexi was so achingly good to him that the more he was around her, the more he craved her presence. The more he touched her, the deeper his need grew to draw her ever closer. It was maddening but at the same time, it kept him grounded.

Lexi sighed against his lips as he deepened the kiss, his tongue probing her mouth, exploring, tasting; teeth nipping lightly on her bottom lip as he grazed back over them again. Her heart was hammering in her chest so much that she was convinced it was louder than the ocean outside their door.

She felt like she had that summer they had gone to Six Flags. She had ridden the roller coaster and it had dipped down suddenly in a drop that had made her feel as if her stomach had dropped out beneath her as it seemed they fell into nothingness. She had a fleeting thought that maybe that's what love was; a wild dip on a roller coaster ride where your heart raced and you felt like laughing and screaming at the top of your lungs at the same time. Because that's sort of how she felt now as Jake's lips moved with a frenzy over the surface of her skin; like she was falling in love.

She was convinced that was what was happening here. Before last week she hadn't known of his existence and now she loved him? No it wasn't a question. It was fact. *She loved him.* Beyond reason, beyond anything that she had ever experienced. Jake was everything that she had been missing in life.

"We don't gotta do this, Lex," he was saying and she just shook her head.

"I want this, Jake. I want *you.*" She said to him softly and ran her hands up his chest, playing with the buttons on his shirt, unfastening the top one and waited for his reaction.

Jake sucked in his breath at the implied direction things were moving and she bravely undid the next few, sliding the fabric from his shoulders. She glanced to him for an answer to the question her hands were asking and he nodded because he was incapable of words. She wanted him and yes, he was physically desirable, the way she said it, the way her want reached her eyes; he didn't think anyone had ever truly wanted him in that way before.

He moved his hands to her pullover and skimmed his fingers up over her ribs, feeling her sharp intake of breath and feeling a thrill that he could make her react that way. He had thought they would incinerate on contact but he had been wrong. What he was experiencing right now was a low heat; a slow type of burning, a smoldering so they didn't catch fire.

He pulled himself back and stilled his hands just beneath her breasts, looking into her eyes but the answer was there loud and clear, her pupils dilated into deep pools of desire. She wanted this just as badly as he did. Jake moved his hands up to cover both of her breasts, palming them softly and groaned as he felt her nipples harden beneath his exploring touch.

Lexi reached between them and leaned back to pull her shirt off in one movement, leaving her well and truly bare to his sight and it felt positively delicious watching him appraise her with his eyes as his hands explored the newly exposed skin and then he dipped his head to take one nipple into his mouth while the other massaged her other breast. A burst of star-bright pleasure pulsed behind her eyes, his mouth so warm, so wet on such sensitive flesh.

Jake sucked on the pert bud, drawing it into his mouth, laving his tongue over the surface, feeling Lexi arch her back more firmly into his face. He moved his fingers down to the button on her jeans and pulling back, watching carefully for any sign of doubt.

Finding none, he opened the button and slid the zipper down as she moved her hips, helping him along in the process. Jake hooked his fingers in her shorts and pulled them down, feeling her shimmy a little until they fell in a heap and she stepped neatly away from them and back into his arms.

Lexi groaned against his mouth and she reached between them to the button of his pants and nearly wept in frustration at finding that he had on button-fly jeans. She painstakingly unbuttoned each one as she kissed him, slowly, feeling him smiling against her mouth.

Before unbuttoning the last button she reached up and pulled his hips to hers roughly and she could feel the evidence of his desire pushing against her.

She pulled away to smile at him, a wicked glint in her eye, feeling satisfied when she heard his gasp of pleasure. She liked the feeling of power she had in pushing all of Jake Jackson's buttons. She may not be all that experienced but learning what Jake liked was as easy as reading a book, for his face was an open map of desire.

Lexi finally managed to undo the last button and pushed his jeans and boxers down at once, taking in his length and girth as his erection was freed from the confines of his pants.

Never taking her eyes from his she stepped away from Jake as he stood naked before her and looped one finger in each side of her string bikini panties, letting them drop to the floor at her feet. She never looked to see where they landed, just looked into his eyes the entire time she removed the final piece of clothing that stood between the two of them. His eyes seemed to rake over her all at once before he pushed her gently back on the bed and for a moment he just stood there and looked his fill.

"Lexi, you are so goddamned beautiful." Jake said finally, like he'd been waiting a lifetime for that admission, as he laid down beside her. He moved his hand over her breast as he brought his lips to hers, kissing her slowly, wanting to savor each moment. He continued kissing her even as his fingers traveled south, skimming over her flat stomach, over that slight curve of her hip and ghosted even lower until he reached the apex of her thighs.

Lexi delighted in all the sensations that were washing over her. His lips coursed over her skin, like he was tracing a path only he knew and she was just along for the ride, tiptoeing along in ecstasy. She felt her pulse throbbing between her thighs and could feel dampness gathering there.

He parted her gently with one finger, tracing over her sex lightly and she swore she lost her breath. She shivered against him, molding herself to him and doing his bidding, letting her legs fall open as he delved one finger into her heat.

Lexi was every bit as soft and wet as he expected her to be and he groaned aloud as he felt how ready her body was for him. She was so damned tight it made him throb even harder and he could feel his length twitch against the side of her leg. He loved the soft little gasps he was eliciting from her pretty pink lips, cheeks flushed with pleasure, as he moved his finger up to that tight bud at the top of her sex and began to move it in rapid tight circles.

He may not have much experience with pleasuring women, preferring to keep things to just the most basic needs, but she was making it easy for him to figure out her ways. She practically purred with the tiny little moans that were erupting from her throat with each pass of his thumb over her clit and it was only minutes later that he could feel her come undone beneath his hand.

Lexi could feel it building deep in her core and it was like hitting a great wall of white every time he hit her in just the right way until finally she was punching through the surface, like she'd catapulted off into the stars. The deliciously aching throb in her core completely spiraled out in waves, making every muscle quiver as they tensed and released continuously until her climax ebbed off.

It may have been minutes or hours as she came down, her lover stroking her thighs lovingly as she rejoined him on this plane. Then he moved his lips back up to her neck and whispered, "You ready for me?"

She smiled into his shoulder before he finally pulled back and she was able to meet his eyes as he positioned himself over her. She had never moved to cover herself and this surprised her a bit. She had always been shy around Brandon, but with Jake it felt completely natural and she wasn't the least bit self-conscious.

Something about being with him like this made her feel incredibly sexy and every bit a woman, like her body was made for what he was doing to it.

"Please." Was her one word reply and she didn't think she recognized the wanton timbre of her voice for what it was. But he must have. For he settled into the cradle of her hips with purpose, an arm coming to rest on either side of her head, placing himself against her wet opening, teasing the tender flesh there with the head. Then finally, slowly, he was easing himself into her as her hips arched upward to meet that first thrust and they both groaned in pleasure.

Jake breathed her name as he felt her wiggle her hips, making the friction almost unbearable. "Lexi." he whispered. "I ain't gonna last long, baby." He barely had time to finish that sentence as she moved yet again whispering for him to hush. So he did.

Lexi got lost in their love-making, her body taking over and her mind going somewhere else completely, far above this plane where the only sound that could be heard was their two bodies, moving in rhythm, peppered with gasps and moans and the slide of skin against skin.

She felt like she was floating high above them while her body was tethered to this undulating feeling, pulsating waves, building and building until it crashed over her and she was caught in the undercurrent of her release.

For Jake, making love to Lexi was like nothing else he'd ever experienced. Her breathing was coming in gasps and he could tell she was edging towards release again. As such, her movements had become a bit frenetic beneath him. It was too much and he fought with himself to reach down and grip her hips in his hands, and pace their movements, but he found he couldn't do it. It felt that good. Besides, he was fine with her setting the rhythm for their lovemaking as long as she didn't mind a do-over when he couldn't hold on anymore.

After her orgasm eased off slightly, he began to pulse himself into her heat, with longer, slower drags, his pace matching the one that she set. He pulled back to look at her, watching her eyes as they dilated further and her mouth dropped open. He longed to kiss her, but he didn't want to miss even one moment of the rapture on her face. Instead, he made himself content with weaving his fingers through her hair and undoing that damned ponytail, the soft tresses spilling over her shoulders to cover the creamy tops of her breasts.

God, she was pretty.

She met his thrusts with each movement of her own and the pace was becoming so regular now that his body knew the rhythm and was acting accordingly. He could feel the pressure building in the base of his spine as he got even harder inside her the moment before he felt the tight cords of tension release all at once, uncoiling deep in his belly as his muscles clenched and relaxed, sending waves of pleasure to wash over him again and again until he was spent, spilling his seed deep inside her.

For the first time in his entire life, Jake Jackson had not worried about any form of reasonable precautionary measures or if the whole damn world came crashing down on top of them. He got lost in the moment and he couldn't even find that he was sorry for it.

In looking down at Lexi, she smiled up at him and he rolled off of her, grabbing a towel off the nightstand and handing it to her. She wiped herself off quickly before curling against him and he brought his arm around her as she rested her head on his chest. "We didn't use anything," she said softly as she smiled up at him sheepishly.

"I know. I'm sorry about that." He told her. And he guessed his original thought had been a lie. He guessed he was a little sorry.

"I don't care. That was amazing," Lexi exclaimed with a half giggle in the back of her throat. She grinned up at him, that bright smile that he had come to love and he chuckled.

"Is that so?" He murmured against the top of her head.

"Umm, yes!" she said, emphasizing the last word and then looked at him shyly. "It's never been that way for me before. Just with you." Her last words trailed off in a solemn whisper and his heart lurched into his throat because he felt the same way.

"Me too." He whispered. He hauled her tiny form up his body to rest firmly in his arms, bringing his lips to hers as he kissed her thoroughly. It was a different kind of kiss he realized. It was the kind of kiss shared between two spent lovers. As he pulled away, the words fell from his lips before he could stop them.

"I love you, Lexi." Her eyes met his in wide surprise and for a moment, he regretted his admission. What if she didn't feel the same way? He opened his mouth to temper his words with something, but he didn't even know what he could say. As it turned out, his fears were completely unfounded. The answer was clear in her eyes.

"I love you too, Jake, so much," she whispered as she brought her lips back to his and kissed him.

Suddenly his whole life had shifted focus and as off kilter as it was, he didn't give a damn. He was with Lexi. She made him happy. And for once, he let himself think that he deserved it. That he deserved her.

He breathed in the intoxicating musk of vanilla and orchids and found that the only thing he saw dancing behind his eyelids was a beautiful blonde girl with bright blue eyes. His past was fading away and his future looked brighter every moment. All because of her. *His Lexi.*

Chapter 16

When Lexi opened her eyes the next morning the first thing she was aware of, actually hyperaware of, was the ache between her thighs. It was slightly unfamiliar, as she'd never made love that many times in the space of so few hours, but it wasn't altogether unpleasant. Thinking of why she ached changed the overall sensation to a pulsing desire and she was shocked at her body and to what limits it was willing to take itself.

She stretched slowly, feeling Jake stir beside her and she turned to face him, hoping to God that she didn't have morning breath and daringly reached her hand over to creep over his chest, her fingers ghosting over the surface as he opened his eyes and looked at her and smiled.

"Good morning", she whispered, pressing a chaste kiss to his lips. She let her fingers drift downwards, stopping just as she reached the triangle of coarse curls just below his abdomen. She felt him suck in his breath. They had made love twice more in the night and she couldn't believe that she was ready for more already but she just wanted to explore every single inch of him.

Jake placed his hand on top of hers underneath the covers and stilled her fingers for a moment. "You tryin' to kill me, girl?" he groaned. "I'm an old dude." He protested gently. They had gone and taken a shower together after the third time, their energy finally having been spent and they had gone to sleep sometime in the hour just before dawn, the last bit grey light slipping from the sky and the first tendrils of sunshine breaking the horizon.

Now, it was full on daylight, she was wanting him again and he couldn't deny that he was wanting her too. If she skimmed her fingers a bit lower, she would be met with his hardened length as it twitched against her palm. He found that he was willing her to do it before he realized that he still had her hand imprisoned in his light grip.

"You didn't act all that old last night". She said suggestively, her eyes dancing with mischief. He sighed as he released her fingers and he saw a smile play across her features before she kissed him.

"Is that so?" He was teasing her and she loved it. She giggled and nodded her head.

"Why don't you show me again," she suggested with that little grin on her face; a decidedly dirty grin.

Well, he could be dirty too. "Thought you'd never ask." He planted a quick kiss on her lips, then began spreading slow, open-mouthed kisses down her neck, lower and lower. He thought she caught his drift about half way down her body when he looked up, a wolfish grin on his face just before he removed her panties and positioned himself between her thighs.

All arguments over age or stamina were soon forgotten and left behind the moans and gasps and throaty sighs that came from Lexi as he went down on her. It was a long time before they emerged for breakfast.

❦ ❦ ❦ ❦ ❦ ❦ ❦ ❦ ❦ ❦ ❦

Jake looked across the table at his girl who looked like the sexiest thing he had ever seen, sitting in his button-up shirt and nothing else. Just that knowledge was hard enough to deal with, but with her sending him her sexy glances every once in a while, he was a bundle of nervous energy.

He knew he needed to call Matt and find out what the latest was but he couldn't bring himself to care right now. At least for this minute, he wanted to enjoy it.

He think he finally got all those movies talking about needing the love of a good woman. She was definitely good. Sometimes she was good in a bad way, he thought with amusement, but he knew that she was everything good that he had never had in his life. He intended to keep it and the hell of it was he didn't know how, but he was sure of one thing. He would protect what was his or he would die trying. And Lexi was definitely that. *His*.

Chapter 17

Lexi was doing her best to stay up on the kiteboard, feeling frustrated that she couldn't get the technique down. Jake, for all his gruffness and surliness in the past was a surprisingly good teacher. He was patient and Lexi didn't know why. She felt like an extreme klutz every time she fell off the damn thing. They had mastered kiteboarding in the sound yesterday and it had been exhilarating feeling the wind whipping about and catching air every time the wind changed positions. It was more a skill of balance and centering. Lexi had only ever been on water-skis and she had been terrible at that. But, kiteboarding was something she had taken to as a natural according to Jake. Well, until now, that is.

Yesterday they had driven up Highway 12 to Canadian Hole, an area named by locals for all the Canadians that make the trek every year to come kiteboard on the Pamlico Sound and often the Atlantic Ocean as well.

That's where they were now. Lexi had been rather insistent about wanting to try her luck in the rougher waters of the Atlantic after their great experience yesterday in the sound.

She readjusted her bathing suit for the fifteenth time, now wishing she had listened to Jake when he told her she needed a different suit for what they were attempting. The bathing suit had been just fine for the tame waters of the inlet, but now here out in the ocean today where the waters were choppy and the winds much fiercer, she had almost lost her top to the waves at least three times.

Jake watched her fussing with her suit and he smiled to himself. God, she was cute when she was determined about something. She had a fierceness about her that he found surprised him. She was nothing if not stubborn. He watched the pattern of the waves, looking for the perfect set. He was looking for something a little more challenging than the small waves she had already mastered and a little less daunting than the wave that had knocked them both on their asses a few minutes ago.

They had both come up sputtering and she looked positively bedraggled looking with her thick blonde hair falling over her eyes. He had laughed so hard watching the look of shock wash over her features and she tried to smooth in her hair into some semblance of normal, finally resorting to dipping her head beneath the water to get it to behave. She wasn't a girly girl but she was pretty particular about her hair, he knew.

They had gone to dinner the night before and she had taken an exorbitant amount of time getting her hair just right, which was weird to him. He thought she looked beautiful right now with her sea-salt and windswept hair slicked back from her forehead. She wasn't wearing any make up and to him, she had never looked more beautiful.

His body tensed as he spotted the perfect set of waves coming up. "Get ready, Lex. Keep your feet wide, plant them firmly just like we worked on. Find that zenith, baby." He encouraged and was pleased when he saw her getting in the stance that would allow her to be able to stand up against the wave set which was quickly approaching.

The zenith was the focal point she needed to pay attention to right above her head. The kite needed to be in the frame directly over her head if she wanted to catch the tail of the wind. If she could line the kite up just right and find that and get her edge, she'd soar; he could almost feel it. He decided to sit this set out, dangling his feet on either side of the board. He willed the waves towards them, feeling in his gut that she was going to get it this time.

She stood up perfectly, planting her feet with just the right amount of pressure as the board lifted against the force of the wave and the kite lifting it just off the surface of the water. She caught a good twenty feet of air and he heard her whoop and he couldn't help but let out one of his own.

"Way to go, girl!" He called. He knew she couldn't hear him, but he said the words anyway. He was so proud of her. It had taken him at least a week to be able to kiteboard in the ocean and she had done it in less than a day.

He could see the look of intensity on her face and he knew the minute she over-thought it. Her balance swayed and the board flipped sideways and she tumbled into the ocean with a splash. He smiled as he paddled his way over to her, his kite dragging behind him in the water.

He paused for a moment seeing a flash of something white bobbing in the water and he grinned widely as he fished it out. She was going to be pissed, but he had tried to warn her about her choice of suit and how it was going to be pretty much ineffective against the forces of nature out here.

He finished paddling over to her and jumped off his board to get beside her in the water. She was sputtering and trying to get the hair out of her eyes. He held up the tiny scrap of fabric that served as the top to her bathing suit with two fingers, an obvious smirk on his face.

"Looking for something?" He teased and even in the bright sun, he could see her blushing as she bobbed in the water, her creamy white breasts made even lighter in the noonday sun.

Every once in a while as the waves ebbed past them, he got a glimpse of a bit more of her and it surprised him how much that aroused him. It had been four days since they had first made love and he couldn't seem to get enough of her. They had finally had to go get condoms; they were screwing at least five times a day, so it was stupid not to.

Lexi reached her hand out for her suit, coming up beside him in the water. "Did you see me?" She asked excitedly. She knew she was standing there naked from the waist up, but at least the water was hiding it for the most part.

"I saw you babe," he said as he pulled her close in the water, fixing the bathing suit around her. "You were great."

"Stupid bikini," she muttered as she reached up to tie it behind her neck and turned around so Jake could finish tying the one across her back.

He smiled as he finished tying off the suit and grasped her shoulders to face him. He smiled down at her. "I told you so," he laughed.

She hated the "*I told you so*" but she found that she couldn't be pissed at him with the look he was giving her after giving her suit back. "I know, but I really thought it would be okay. I need a new suit." She said smartly, winding her arms up around his neck, being careful to keep the cord to the kiteboard attached to her wrist.

He brought his hands up to her sides, his fingers skimming over her ribs, feeling her shiver beneath his touch. He wished it wasn't so damned exposed out here. He'd love to take her out here in the ocean but it was hardly practical with their boards attached to the both of them.

"I want you," he whispered as he brought his lips down to hers, not giving her a chance to respond, feeling extremely satisfied as she practically melted into him, the water surrounding them and lapping at their bodies.

Lexi moaned under his touch and his lips and as he told her his wishes, her body echoed that desire. She felt him growl against her lips and then just as quickly he pulled himself away, pressing a firm kiss to her forehead.

"We should get back to the house," Jake told her as he finally was able to drag himself from her embrace.

"Tease," she grinned at him but let him go reluctantly, but she knew he was right. Their session out here in the ocean had about worn her out. Her body was starting to protest from the punishment she had doled out in the past few days. Between the kiteboarding and their lovemaking, her muscles were fairly quivering from all the activity.

"Come on." Jake said as he waded through the water, trying to ease the board with the current going diagonal to the shore. The currents out here on the Outer Banks could be especially strong and Jake was ever watchful of deadly riptides. This area was known for it and he'd rather not tempt fate today if he had the choice.

Lexi followed him, sighing as they finally reached where the sea met with the sand, pulling the board beside her, rather than behind her. She had gone kayaking a few times with her family and had gotten smacked in the head by more than one wayward boat being propelled by the rough waves. After the first couple of times, she had finally learned her lesson. She sighed deeply as she breathed in the briny air.

"Can we call Laurel tonight?" She asked Jake as they plodded up the long boardwalk back to the house.

"Yeah," Jake replied, his tone turning serious. "I talked to Matt this morning. They are getting ready to move Laurel to a safer location tomorrow." He had been saving this conversation for later, not wanting to worry her, but since she had brought it up, now was a good time as any.

"Why?" Lexi asked, the alarm evident in her voice. "Did something happen?" She stopped in her tracks.

They finally reached the fence surrounding the house and pool on the ocean side of the property. Jake pushed it open and they quickly stored the kiteboards.

Jake handed her a thick towel and grabbed one for himself as they reached the steps. "Let's talk about this inside okay." He knew they were isolated here but he had begun to feel a little uneasy the past 24 hours. He hoped his instinct was wrong, but he kept getting the feeling that they were being watched.

He had glanced over his shoulder several times in the past day and had even run reconnaissance the night before, scouting the perimeter of the beach house as Lexi slept, needing to reassure himself that he was imagining things. He attributed it to the lack of sleep here lately. He and Lexi had been staying up pretty late, exploring one another and just talking and laughing until the wee hours of the morning.

He needed to get his shit straight, he thought as they entered the house, the cold air hitting their wet skin. Maybe they'd move tomorrow as well. It might be better to be safe than sorry.

Lexi turned to face him, looking impossibly small wrapped up in the giant towel and the worried look etched hard into her soft features. "Tell me."

"It's just a precaution. In fact, we might be moving our location as well." He didn't tell her that he had felt they were being watched, hoping to hell he was just being paranoid. He leaned down and pressed a kiss to her forehead. "It's not a big deal. I promise. Go on and take a shower. I'm gonna go call Matt," he assured her.

"Are you sure?" Lexi asked. She trusted him, but the thought of Laurel being in further danger felt like a dagger of ice cold dread piercing her stomach all over again.

"Would I have taken you kiteboarding today if there was something really wrong?" He asked her sensibly.

Lexi couldn't argue with that and she visibly relaxed as she took a step forward and felt some of the tension leave her body as his words sunk in and he pulled the towel from around her and wrapped them both inside it.

"No," she finally conceded. His words made sense and she couldn't fault him for trying to take her mind off of things.

Jake pulled her against him, loving the feel of her body pressed against his, their skin cool from the ocean but warming with their passion for one another. "Love you, Lex," he whispered gruffly. The words were still hard for him to say, but it got easier every time. He still couldn't believe that his admission had spilled out of him after they'd made love last night. They had definitely been caught in the moment but one thing was for sure, it was real. As real as anything he had ever felt.

"Love you too." She pulled away and smiled at him, following him down the hall to the bedroom they now shared; his. She had moved all her stuff into his room the day after they had first made love. It had been unnecessary before that for they'd barely worn clothes at all that first twenty four hours.

With all that, it was hard to not believe it. She marveled at the love they had for one another and it was hard to reconcile everything that had brought them together. She trusted that he would keep them safe.

Her, Laurel, him; all of them. He had become her protector, her lover, her confidant, her everything. She felt her heart soar inside her chest thinking about all that he was to her. Suddenly her entire life was wrapped up in Jake Jackson. And despite the circumstances, she had never felt more certain of anything in her entire life. She loved this man beyond anything she had ever felt for another person.

She thought perhaps every moment in her life had led up to this and she was grateful, so grateful for the opportunity to feel something bigger than the universe itself. Loving Jake had changed her. He had awakened something in her and now that it had been freed, there was no turning back. She didn't even want to.

❦ ❦ ❦ ❦ ❦ ❦ ❦ ❦ ❦ ❦

Lexi felt something pulling her from the sweet tendrils of deep sleep. It was someone shaking her awake. She opened her eyes, trying to adjust to the darkness of the room and opened her mouth to scream, finding that she couldn't because suddenly a hand clamped down over her mouth, rendering her mute. As the fear catapulted through her veins, she only had one thought. *"Where the hell was Jake?"*

Chapter 18

Lexi felt the rough hand clamping harder down over her mouth as she struggled against it. Some part of her had maybe thought it was Jake trying to wake her up, but only just at first. For she knew, from the texture of the palms and the foreign scents invading her nostrils, that it wasn't him.

She knew from the rough touch that it wasn't him. And most of all, the bile automatically rising in her throat told her that it wasn't him. She was trying desperately to remember her training and act on it, even as she had been awakened so abruptly. But when she felt the cold metal of a gun against her temple, she froze and tried to relax her body so her captor would know that she got his message.

"Now this is what is going to happen, Lexi." She cringed as she recognized the voice and fought to keep the tears at bay that were pricking at the corners of her eyes. Somehow Thomas had found her.

That could only mean one thing: he didn't know where Laurel was and he had gotten desperate.

Lexi tried not to cower as he came around to face her, his hand still clamped over her mouth and moving the barrel of the gun to point it at her forehead and Lexi felt sick as she felt the hardness pressing against her skin. There was something very sobering about knowing all it would take was one slight twitch of his finger and it would be all over for her.

Lexi had always thought if she were in this situation that she would think fast and get the gun away from the person. But in actuality, everything became crystal clear. It was survival mode and instinct just kicked in. Right now, her gut was telling her to listen to him and do exactly as he said. She already knew just what evil he was capable of, so she nodded her understanding, waiting for his words.

"I'm going to remove my hand and you're *not* going to open your damn mouth," he instructed her, his voice rough, pushing the gun a little harder against her forehead and she visibly flinched. She hated this lack of control, but she knew that the next few moments were crucial to her getting out of this alive. She looked up at him, his face a mask of rage, his skin having broken out in a sweat and his normally perfectly combed hair falling over his forehead.

This man was not the same person that Laurel had married. She didn't know what the hell he had gotten involved in to make him so crazed, but she had a pretty good idea on coming face to face with him. She had seen enough addicts enough in her life. She had never pegged him for a user, but it was becoming apparent that he was on something.

His pupils were pinpoint and the sweat coming off his body had that sickening sweet smell of an addict's telltale musk. Suddenly, a lot of what Laurel had suffered made perfect sense. *Laurel.* God, she hoped she was okay. She had just talked to her a couple hours ago so she let that thought assure her that at least her sister was safe, even if Lexi herself wasn't.

Thomas, good as his word, took his hand from her mouth and she worked her jaw back and forth. "Please Thomas," she pleaded as she looked up at him.

"I said not to open your damn mouth, Lexi." He bit out. "I already know it's your fault I don't have my Laurel right now. You're lucky I don't shoot you in the head." He spit the words at her and she trained her expression to remain impassive.

She knew Thomas's type and anything she said to him would likely incite further anger. He was like a literal ticking time bomb. One wrong move and he would explode, setting the worst kind of path of destruction in his wake. She hoped to God Jake was okay. She couldn't bear the thought of him in danger and she had to trust that he could take care of himself and she prayed to god that he wasn't already dead.

Lexi remained silent. "You're going to tell me where your sister is Lexi. I got all night and I'm all out of patience. We can make this easy or we can make this hard." Lexi glanced around her and Jake's bedroom. Where the hell was he?

"Your boyfriend?" He laughed with that evil glint in his eye. "I took care of him." Lexi really thought she might be sick at his words.

"You killed him?" She could hardly get the words out. If Jake was dead, because of her, she would never forgive herself.

"No, you stupid bitch. I didn't kill him. He's an ex-Fed. You think I'm fucking crazy? I got my reputation to think about. He's gonna be out for a while though." He tucked the gun into the front of his pants and rubbed his palm over the knuckles of his right hand.

"Fucker has a hard face." He remarked. "It was fun watching him go down with my stun gun though," he said as he patted his pocket. She had no doubt he would use it on her if necessary.

Lexi saw red then. He had already hurt one person in her family and god help her, she had come to think of Jake the same way. He was her whole world. Suddenly, she just couldn't stand the thought of him hurting anyone else who was close to her.

"I hope you broke your hand, you sorry sack of shit." She spit the words at him. She might not be able to hit him but at least she could tell him exactly what she thought of him finally. She ignored the warning voice in the back of her head, rational thought going out the window in the face of her pent-up rage.

"You are the worst kind of coward. Beating a woman? Raping her?" Her voice rose an octave and she expected him to stop her at any moment, but she was driven by her rage and he seemed to be surprised at the fight in Lexi.

She continued. "It's probably the only way you could get it up," she said, seething now. She bit out the words and even though he looked like he was about to come unhinged, she couldn't be sorry for saying them. He deserved to die for what he had done to her sister.

Thomas drew his fist back and drove his hand into her jaw, putting all his weight into the punch. Lexi's head snapped back at the force of the hit, her head reeling from the impact as she felt like her face was going to explode. She could taste that familiar taste of copper in her mouth and she reached up to touch her lip where it was split. As she pulled her hand away, she had a fair amount of blood dripping from her hand.

Lexi knew she was probably glutton for punishment but she honestly didn't care what Thomas did to her at this point. She could hope for Jake to wake up all she wanted, but she was in this alone and she could take care of herself. "That all you got?" She couldn't keep the venom from her voice. If he was going to kill her, she wanted to make her last moments count for something.

Thomas made to unbuckle his pants. "You wanna find out, goody two shoes. I know you already spread your legs for that goddamned redneck you've been shacking up with here. Let me show you what a real man feels like."

Lexi's eyes went wide and she suddenly wanted to pluck her words out of the air and take them all back. She had definitely underestimated him. She knew he was far gone, but not this far. She suppressed a whimper as he came at her, undoing his pants. It was too late now. She had incited a rage in Thomas and she knew he wasn't going to back down.

Thomas saw the fear in her eyes and his grin spread in malice and he pulled his hand back and slapped her hard across the cheek. Lexi cried out in pain as his hand connected with the same area he had just punched moments ago. The momentum of the hit sent her reeling backwards off the side of the bed. Thomas rounded the corner of the bed and was on her in an instant, straddling her hips even as he undid his pants the rest of the way and pushed them and his underwear down long enough to expose himself to her.

Lexi felt sick; he was going to rape her and there wasn't going to be anything she could do about it. He reached between them and ripped her tank top upward exposing her breasts to him and his mouth spread in a menacing smile.

He reached down between them and crudely cupped her between her legs, squeezing hard. When he began to fumble around to move her panties aside, her blood roared with adrenaline as she began to frantically kick her legs against his movements. The fight was not out of her yet.

She bucked against him with all her strength, but he outweighed her nearly double and he had his legs clamped on either side of her hips. He stopped trying to pull at her clothes long enough to look at her. She barely had time to register the look on his face as disgust before he reared back to slap her.

Lexi's head whipped to the side and she winced. He slapped her again, the sound of his palm cracking into her flesh resounding through the room. She whimpered and tried to clamp her legs shut but he pried them apart roughly, his fingers digging into the tender flesh there.

As he leered down at her, he licked his lips and Lexi shut her eyes tightly, resigning herself to her fate. Just because he was going to have his way with her, didn't mean she had to watch it happen. She willed her thoughts elsewhere, as if she could fly up out of this room and be anywhere but her own body.

Suddenly Lexi felt the weight of Thomas being lifted off her and she opened her eyes in surprise, relief flooding through her as Jake appeared behind him.

"Get your fuckin' hands off her!" Jake pulled him up and slammed him into the wall, Thomas' head making a sickening dull thud, but he still was able to get back up again. Jake was on him in an instant and wheeled him around to face him.

"He has a gun!" Lexi called out, wanting to protect him as much as possible. His right eye was almost completely swollen shut and he had blood dripping down his face onto his T-shirt. He had definitely taken a beating from the other man.

Jake spared one more glance at Lexi ensuring she was safe for the moment and that brief distraction cost him. As Thomas regained his balance, he initiated a punch, sending his fist slamming into Jake's gut.

Jake puffed out what air he had left in his lungs and moved to block Thomas' next hit, narrowly missing a fist to the temple, which would surely have brought him down after such a recent blow to the head having rendered him unconscious once already.

Jake cased his opponent, circling him. "You should have never come here. I'm going to fucking kill you, you piece of shit," Jake spat at him and swiped his arm up over his mouth, barely noticing the amount of blood coming off on his sleeve as he did so.

Thomas crouched and made as if to charge at Jake, but he anticipated the movement and dodged to the left as he wrapped his arm around Thomas's neck from behind, putting all his weight into the hold. He held his position until he felt Thomas crumple to the ground. Jake let out the breath he had been holding and checked his pulse. Stupid prick was still breathing and Jake was surely sorry for that, but he had to make sure Lexi was okay. He kicked him in the ribs one more time for good measure as he stepped away and realized with barely seething rage that it wasn't enough.

"Is he dead?" Lexi whispered from where she sat against the wall by the bed, her legs tucked up to her chest and her arms wrapped around her knees. Some part of her brain was screaming to run. Far away. The other part didn't even believe that this had just happened.

Jake crept over to her silently. She looked like she might be in shock and he didn't want to scare her. He felt a flash of anger as he saw her lip where it was split. It made him want to go back over and finish the stupid prick, but right now Lexi was his priority. She looked so impossibly small sitting there curled in on herself.

"Lexi, you're safe now," he whispered to her as he approached her, crouching down in front of her and putting his hand to her face. She leaned into him and closed her eyes and he sighed in relief.

His gun. Where the hell was his gun? Fuck it. He didn't care about going by the book on this one. He was wasting the guy now and they could ask questions later.

His decision made, he wheeled around and sidestepped the bed, fully intending to find his gun and finish him off once and for all.

He glanced back over to where Thomas was and felt all the blood drain from his head.

"Oh my God, Jake, he's gone." Jake looked back to the source of the voice, his girl, his Lexi, who was still looking to him for the next move.

He leaned quickly down, pressing a soft kiss to her forehead. "I'm locking the door behind me, Lex." He caught the glint of metal under the bed and quickly retrieved it, pushing the gun into her hand. "If he comes back, keep shooting until he ain't moving."

Jake took a breath. "But don't shoot me." He felt compelled to add that. "Don't open the door until you hear me say "all clear". Got it?" She was listening but she wasn't really responding, just letting the tears fall from her eyes. Jake reached out to shake her shoulders a bit and she finally looked up at him.

"I'm sorry," she whispered as the tears fell helplessly to land on her knees. He knew then that they were in big fucking trouble.

"Lexi!" He shouted at her, desperately needing her to hold off on whatever was going on inside her head. "I know what happened just now was awful. And I promise I'll make him pay. But right now, I don't know where the hell he went. And I need you to do what I tell you so we can get out of here alive. Okay, babe?" He placed his hands on either side of her head and rubbed his thumbs gently down either cheek, tracing the track her tears had made as if he could staunch the flow of grief. As if that would make up for the fact that he couldn't save her from Thomas.

He had the most awful weight that had settled over his chest and that pit of fear had grown roots in his stomach. But, for now, he had to concentrate on getting Lexi to safety. That was priority number one.

Lexi looked at him thoughtfully while she processed what he was telling her. "Go find him. I will be fine," she whispered.

Jake visibly relaxed when he saw a glimpse of his Lexi appear behind the frightened woman that sat before him. He pressed a chaste kiss to her forehead before he backed away. "Good girl. Remember the safe word. He reminded her as he slipped silently through the door, ensuring that the knob was locked before he turned away to find his target. He scanned the hallway and found the telltale drops of blood: his, of course.

But Thomas had evidently stepped in it and he could see a slight footprint with specks of blood going up the other side of the hallway. He followed the pattern all the way out the sliding glass door of the living area, looking around left and right. At the bottom of the steps just before the boardwalk to the beach, the trail went cold. Jake dug his flashlight out of his pocket, shining the light at the sand, looking for any trace of the bastard but the wind had already shifted the patterns in the dry sand making it impossible for Jake to track the bastard any further.

It looked like he had come in from the beach. Jake heard a dune buggy and saw the glint of aluminum reflecting from the moonlight and figured that was how Thomas had gotten here unseen. No matter now, Jake meant to get them the hell out of dodge, he thought, as he watched the vehicle speed off, heading north up the beach.

He raced back up the steps, taking them two at a time. He checked the entire house before going back to his room, all the doors locked up tight. He knocked at his door twice. "All clear, Lexi."

He heard a rustle from behind the door. "Jake?" Her voice was barely above a whisper.

"It's me, baby." Jake had a chance to catch his breath a bit and he thought he had a plan figured out. He knew Laurel was being moved in the morning. He and Lexi had talked about it last night. The word had come down that Thomas had headed back up from Florida where the fake trail had gone cold. Last they heard he was in Georgia but by the looks of it, that last piece of information had been false.

There was no way Thomas could have found them that quickly. It only meant one thing and it made Jake sick to his stomach. Thomas was greasing somebody's palm in their organization; *a fucking mole*.

He was getting Lexi out of town and the sooner, the better.

Jake let out the breath he had been holding when the door knob finally twisted and Lexi opened the door to him, the sheet still wrapped tightly around her body. As he walked in the door, she stepped back to allow him entry. He kicked the door shut behind him and opened his arms as Lexi fell into them, sobbing against his chest.

"Did you find him?" Lexi asked him through her tears. Jake picked her up in his arms, careful to keep the sheet around her. He sat down on the bed, keeping her in his lap, just feeling a bone crushing need to keep her as close to him as possible. There was no way in hell he was letting her out of his sight from now on.

"I lost the trail at the beach. Looks like that's how he came in." He pulled back slightly to look down at her. "He didn't-?" He found that he couldn't finish the sentence. If he had raped her, Jake knew he would not rest another moment until he hunted Thomas Garner down and cut his junk off him and fed it to him before finishing him off in the most unsavory way he could come up with.

He was a mercenary, for Christ's sake; how the hell had he let his guard down so much that the prick had been able to come within a mile of Lexi? He knew better and yet the answer to that question was in his arms right now. He'd let his guard down *for* her, had fallen head over heels for her, and wasn't that a hell of a quandary.

Lexi shook her head at Jake, looking up at him, her face etched with sadness. "No. But he-," Lexi couldn't finish the sentence as she sobbed again. This was so not like her to fall apart. She thought she might have an inkling of the powerless and shame that her patients had experienced when their trauma had happened to them. All she thought she knew about victim-blaming went out the window in the face of her own experience.

The thoughts came unbidden, unwarranted and untrue or no. *She should never have goaded Thomas; it was her own damn fault.*

Jake ran his hands down over her back, pulling her against him, trying like hell to absorb some of the pain that was evident in her breaking voice, the sobs wracking her body. Jake had never known how to deal with a crying woman, but this wasn't just any woman. This was his girl. He had never felt so helpless in his entire life and he was so pissed he didn't know what to do.

But for right now, he had to concentrate on one thing at a time. He held her close and whispered assurances to her, hoping like hell she could hear him over the sobs, but he thought maybe the whispered promises were more to himself than to her. Because he swore on his own life, he would never let anyone hurt her again. Not as long as he drew breath and Jake planned on being around for a long fucking time.

Chapter 19

Jake looked down at Lexi sleeping against him on the boat. She had finally stopped crying about twenty minutes ago, her sobs having slowed down to just a hiccup here and there. Her head was nestled into his side and he drove the boat one-handed easily.

He had taken his small skiff out instead of the Zen Goddess that they had taken to Ocracoke. That had been last week, but to him it felt like a lifetime ago. He knew it would be much safer to take the smaller craft, especially for the plan he had in mind.

Even after the heat of the day, the air on the Atlantic was cool as he drove the boat out beyond the shoals and turning it to the right. If Thomas had been heading north, then they were sure as hell heading in the opposite direction.

He then purposefully made a circuitous route to his destination, careful to watch for any evidence of a tail. He continued this strategy for the next couple of hours, making sure not to repeat any route twice. He knew where he was going, he had driven it many a time, sometimes in the worst of weather conditions. One time he had gotten this very skiff caught in a summer squall. It had been scary for a little while, but he had navigated the waters fairly well, thinking on his feet and somehow managed to avoid capsizing the boat.

Jake thought back over the evening's events while he wove the boat expertly through the choppy waters of the Atlantic. He had called Matt in the car on the way to the marina. They had kept it brief as usual, but Jake needed him to contact his company and let them know what was going on. Jake would do it himself but he knew it would require a lengthy explanation that he couldn't afford to have and risk being traced.

It was bad enough he had to call Matt. He knew his old friend could convey to them the gravity of the situation and assure them that he had things under control, even if he himself felt he didn't. In short, he trusted Matt with his life. He knew Lexi did too. He hadn't known her for long, but he got the feeling that she wouldn't work for someone she didn't trust.

Lexi knew Jake thought she was asleep. But for right now, it was easier to pretend she was. He had been sending her worried glances every few seconds ever since he had gotten back from looking for Thomas.

He had called Matt and let him know what went down, leaving out the part where Thomas had almost raped her. He had been purposefully vague stating that Thomas had "roughed her up a bit". She almost laughed at the absurdity of the phrase, but she didn't have the energy. She felt almost numb after all that had happened.

She kept reliving it all over and over again in her head. Every time she closed her eyes she saw Thomas's face, his eyes blazing, leering over her; then him taking his pants off and his hands on her.

Every time she thought about it, she wanted to vomit. She had already thrown up twice and she didn't relish the thought of heading into dry heaves, because she knew there was no way there was anything left in there.

Jake hadn't said anything at all, just held her hair back from her face, gathering it into a low ponytail and securing it with an elastic that he'd later tell her he picked up from their nightstand, just in case. He had then gotten a cool cloth and placed it on the back of her neck. Everyone knew that nurses made the worst patients. But this time, she knew she could not properly care for herself. She was grateful beyond words for Jake's silent, but strong, compassion.

She steadied her breathing carefully, not wanting to alert Jake of her consciousness. She didn't want to be awake. She wished she could just let her mind go and drift off to sleep; a dreamless kind where no one would be waiting in the shadows to violate her, no one would be shooting at her, or chasing her. Every time she tried to let go, she remembered waking up to *his* hand clamped over her mouth. She fought again for control of her breathing, finding that all of her training didn't do shit for her.

Lexi thought of all the phrases that people used to describe a rape or near rape event; *"it's not your fault"* and *"you didn't do anything to deserve this",* and though Lexi had used those dozens of times in talking with her patients and sitting on the witness stand during rape trials, they were hollow-sounding words now. They were nothing but simple platitudes, words strung together by someone who had never experienced the horror of the ultimate betrayal of trust.

She was trying hard not to draw parallels, because it didn't make any damn sense to do so. She sighed as she felt the boat begin to slow down. They had been driving for what seemed like hours now. She opened her eyes to see where they were. The soft grey light of morning was just beginning to make its presence known, the soft golden tendrils of dawn visible just over the horizon.

When Jake had skimmed over the truth about what all had gone down at the house with Thomas, a lie had never tasted so bitter. He had a hollow feeling in the pit of his stomach and he wasn't sure that there was ever going to be anything to make it go away short of rewinding time and not letting Thomas get anywhere near Lexi.

He was truly worried about her. He had seen a lot of shit in his day and in his line of work. His mercenary days had been rife with witnessed encounters like what had just happened with Lexi. He had thought himself to be jaded before, but he knew the truth now.

When something like that happened to someone you cared about, someone you loved, it was a whole different story. Seeing Lexi lying on that floor pinned beneath that spineless shit had felt like a punch to the gut. He swallowed hard, the image burning in the back of his mind, fueling his anger further.

Lexi stirred beside him and he turned his head to look at her. She shifted her position and sat up beside him, letting her hand stray to his leg where she rested it on his knee.

Lexi felt some inexplicable need to be touching him at all times. She didn't want to let him go and she was so glad they had reached the point in their relationship that she felt like she could touch him and he wouldn't shy away. Because right now that's what she needed. She needed to feel him close and know that he wasn't going anywhere. She just couldn't bear to be away from him. He made her feel safe and that's what she needed more than anything right now.

She rubbed her hand down over her eyes, the sandpaper feeling behind her eyelids long ago having been replaced by something more akin to flames, between all the tears she had shed and the lack of sleep.

Jake finally spoke. "You sleep any?" He asked her.

She looked up at him in surprise. "I thought I had faked you out," she said with a tiny hint of a smile. Sometimes he amazed her.

"Nah, girl. I knew you weren't really sleeping. Your breathing wasn't as even as it should be and whether you know it or not, your body feels different when you are sleeping. You are a lot heavier."

She smiled a little at him, but Jake noted that the smile didn't quite reach her eyes and he felt that lurch in his heart that she was in pain.

Lexi's smile had been something he had revered probably ever since he met her. To see that light dimmed even a little, extinguished in a matter of minutes, it kind of made him want to punch something. And cry.

It pissed him off, the whole idea of all of it. Jake hadn't cried in a really long time, but he thought right now, he probably could. But, he couldn't afford to risk that kind of emotion right now. A lot was at stake and he needed to keep a clear head if they were going to make it through all this.

Lexi was quiet as she looked around. It was hard to see where they were in the dim light of early morning, but she could make out the shape of an island in front of them on the horizon. They appeared to be in the sound and she caught notice of the channel markers lining either side of the passage they were taking through the water, their orange tops bobbing in the boat's wake.

"Where are we?" she asked curiously. Maybe if she spoke, she could block out all the thoughts that were screaming at her right now. It was like her subconscious demanded attention but she simply could not go there right now. It was just too hard to think about. She didn't know when she would ever be able to process it all. Right now, it was right foot, left foot, inhale, and exhale; repeat.

Jake smiled at her softly as he directed the boat into the inlet at the southern tip of the island. He reached over and rubbed his hand down over her hair, smoothing down the wayward strands that had gone frizzy from lying against him for so long.

"We're going to a very little known uninhabited island," he told her. He wasn't deliberately being vague. He was concentrating on where he pulled the boat through the narrow waters of the inlet of the small island. One false move and the boat would be sand-barred until the tide came back in.

He pulled the boat all the way forward into the slightly more marshy area of the island and shut down the engine. He hopped out quickly onto the shore and tied her off to a nearby tree, securing it tightly and testing the strength of the line, feeling fairly satisfied that it would be fine, at least for the time being.

There was a small company on the mainland that ran ferries to the island, but he didn't want to have to resort to that if his boat drifted out to sea. Besides the fact that he was trying to keep everything hidden so that no one could find them. *So that Thomas couldn't find them.*

Matt had told him the timeline of Laurel's move and then had moved it up in light of recent events. He figured they were probably already at their new destination by now. He hoped like hell they got somewhere safe. He had gone into the bathroom for a minute to relay to Matt his suspicions about a mole in his organization. Matt had said he would put out feelers.

To Jake, that was code for, "I'll take care of it." Matt was a stand-up kind of guy and he wouldn't tolerate any dirty dealings in any organization, especially one he so closely worked with like Special Ops Force. He was a play by the rules kind of guy and honestly it was one of the things that Jake liked most about him.

Where Jake had grown up with utter chaos and abuse of authority, Matt represented the good side of the law; the side of the law that Jake usually didn't believe in. It was hard to believe in a system that had failed Jake so epically for most of his life. But, he believed in his friend and that was enough for him.

"Deserted?" She asked him and he nodded. It all sounded very clandestine to Lexi, but if it kept her away from Thomas, she didn't care if they were going to the south side of the moon. Of course, she knew there were deserted islands, places not charted on maps even, but they kind of seemed like something in a fable to her until now. The sun was starting to rise as Jake began shutting down the boat's gauges and securing her for the time being.

Jake looked over at her. "Nobody has lived here since 1963." He informed her and relayed to her that the island had been inhabited up until the early 1960s when the last two residents had moved away, two spinsters, when the last male on the island had died. It had become such a trip for them anyway that it didn't make sense for them to make the trek every spring, so the town had been deserted for decades until it was later preserved by the state parks system as part of the nature conservancy.

The island was manned by park rangers, but he knew all of them and they knew he sometimes came here to fish. They left Jake alone and that's the way he preferred it. He kept his old camper parked on the other side of the island. His plan was to borrow one of the rangers' golf carts on the south point of the island to get from point A to point B and return the cart the next day.

"There's electricity on the island, but my camper isn't near any of the hook-ups. We're going to be roughing it for a couple of days. There is a shower house though, so we can clean up," he explained while she waited.

She just nodded, her eyes scanning the area and taking in the sights. He finished securing the boat and got back in it briefly to unload what few things they had brought with them. His camper was already stocked with plenty of food and water. They had just brought some clothing and towels and a few blankets. He set their belongings on the sand and held out his hand for Lexi to get out of the boat.

Lexi took Jake's hand and as soon as she was over the side he grasped her hips to set her on the ground. She wanted to lean against him and wrap herself up in his warm embrace and never leave this spot.

Jake looked down at her worriedly. He had never seen her with such deep-etched emotions on her face. He also had never seen her this quiet before. It was unsettling, to say the least. To his practiced eye, it looked as if she might break at any moment and he kept waiting for it, knowing he would have to find all the pieces and put her back together should that happen.

Jake grabbed their bag and hefted it onto his back and held out his hand for her. She reached for him and laced their fingers together and he gave her hand a little squeeze as they set out for the five minute walk to where he knew a golf cart would be waiting for them. The walk was quiet and he kept stealing glances at her, not really sure of what to say.

He didn't know how to broach the subject or if she wanted to talk about it. But he knew the value of silence; he had spent his life perfecting the art of silent communication, so instead of aggravating her about it, he watched for nonverbal cues. Right now, he could tell she was on autopilot, following along beside him.

They finally reached the golf cart, parked by one of the natural dunes on the sound side of the island. He breathed a little easier now that they were here. He had taken a circuitous route to get here, unsure if he was really being followed or not and he felt relatively certain that they weren't followed.

He usually trusted his instinct without question, but since everything that had happened, right now he wasn't so sure he still did and was second guessing his every move. He glanced to Lexi beside him and figured it was probably because the stakes hadn't ever been quite this high and that niggling anxiety just didn't want to settle in his gut.

Lexi watched as Jake found the key to the golf cart and placed their bag in the back. She climbed in beside him and leaned against him, that perpetual need for constant contact not ebbing away at all. Jake expertly wove the golf cart onto a small path that diverged from the one they had been traipsing over. He finally pulled up outside the bath house and Lexi nearly wept at the thought that she would finally be able to wash the scent of Thomas from her body and hopefully cleanse her skin from any traces of his hands upon it. She could smell him, a nauseating mix of addiction, rage and sadistic lust, coming out of every pore, even on her hair, like he'd become a permanent part of her.

After a brief ride, Jake pulled the cart in front of the island's only bathhouse. They both got out and he carried their bag in one hand, holding Lexi's hand in the other. After checking to be certain it was unoccupied, he turned the deadbolt on the sturdy wooden door and turned to get her shower ready.

Lexi sat down on the bench by the sinks while Jake adjusted the shower to the right temperature. As public bathing areas went, it was rather nice. Industrial style showers had been installed with thick tiled walls surrounding each stall, which were enclosed by frosted glass doors. There were toilet stalls and sinks on the adjacent sides of the bathhouse. The floors were cold concrete and their footsteps and movements echoed off the interior, but oddly enough, it wasn't eerie.

She watched as he laid out a couple of towels and got out their toiletries, setting hers carefully beside his, glancing at each one. It was amusing to watch really. She guessed he had probably never seen so much feminine stuff.

He held up the bottle of shampoo, reading the label. "*Vanilla Essence*. You use this?" He asked her.

She nodded and smiled softly at his open curiosity. "Yeah, it's my favorite."

Jake nodded and flipped the lid back and inhaled deeply. The now familiar scent of vanilla with flowery musky overtones filled his senses.

"Well now it makes sense." He murmured. She looked at him, clearly puzzled by his words. "Your hair." He remarked as he sat the bottle down and reached out to touch the object in question, weaving

176

his hand lightly through the thick blonde strands that were flowing over her shoulders.

"This is why it always smells so damn good." He looked wistful as he pulled her into his arms. "I know you're not okay, baby girl. What he did, it's not okay," he said simply.

Lexi tried very hard not to cry again at his sudden gesture of tenderness biting her lip as she felt the tears stinging her eyes. She really just wanted to get this shower done and go to sleep, in that order. But she nodded up at him miserably. "I know," she whispered, her eyes closing against the onslaught of emotion.

Jake wasn't sure where to start, but he knew she wanted to get cleaned up. "I'm probably going to suck at this," he told her. "I also know you probably want to be alone right now, but your cuts need tending to." He touched her lip softly, the blood still crusted on the skin at the corner of her mouth. She had another cut on her forehead. He hadn't inspected the rest of her yet. There was already a dark bruise spreading along her jawline and every time Jake saw it, he was filled with rage all over again.

"I *don't* want to be alone," Lexi whispered. She didn't know how to explain her sudden needy state. Jake looked slightly uncomfortable. The confidence he had with her had effectively gone out the window with Thomas' visit.

She reached down to strip her yoga pants from her body, letting them fall to the floor. It wasn't like she cared anything about them now. As far as she was concerned, her clothes could be burned.

Jake stepped closer to her glad that she had started the process because he sure as hell didn't know where to begin. He didn't know what was appropriate and what wasn't. He had undressed her dozens of times, but this was not even remotely the same thing. But she didn't seem daunted by it, so he wasn't going to be either.

Lexi lifted her arms above her head and Jake lifted her tank top over her head and handed it to her, which she promptly threw it on the floor beside her pants. Even though her instinct was to cover herself, she didn't make a move to do it. She somehow felt if she did, she would be giving Thomas all the power. Jake had seen her naked plenty of times.

Lexi reached down and stripped the last garment from her body, her panties, and nearly wept as they fell to the floor. She couldn't help the way her shoulders hunched in a bit. She couldn't help the sob that escaped her lips. She couldn't help the way her hair fell in her face. She couldn't help any of it and stood there for a second before finally Jake took her into his arms.

Jake stood there for a millisecond before his gut took over and thought for him. He pulled her to him, enclosing her in his arms and splaying his fingers over her back, clutching her closely. She sighed against his chest and he felt odd being fully clothed when she was so clearly the opposite.

She exhaled into his chest, a broken sob tearing from her throat, and Jake swore he could actually hear his heart breaking inside his chest. He would give anything in this world or the next to take away the hurt she was feeling right now. He didn't say anything, just held her until she finally stepped back and nodded to him, moving to stand under the warm spray, letting the water flow over her and smoothing her hair back from her face.

Even the sting of the water as it hit her split lip couldn't squelch the overall well of relief she felt in letting all signs of Thomas wash down the drain below them.

She stepped slightly out from under the water as Jake joined her in the shower. He had stripped down to his boxers and had brought over the shampoo, soap and washcloths. He took the cloth and wet it down, setting to work on removing the blood from her now swollen lip. She winced a little and he bit his lip. "I'm sorry."

"It's okay." She replied, watching his face as he worked on getting her cuts cleaned up. He rewet the wash cloth and wiped at the cut on her forehead. The initial spray of the warm water had taken the sting

178

out of that one before he got to it. It was just slightly sore to the touch on her forehead. She strongly suspected that she was going to feel worse the next day.

Jake turned her around in the shower, inspecting her body for any further injuries. His jaw tightened when he saw the slight telltale sign of a spreading bruise over her ribs. "Did you fall, Lexi?" He asked her tightly.

"Um," she started, thinking. "Yeah I did. When he slapped me, I fell backwards over the bed and landed on the floor." She brought her hands up to the spot he was skimming his fingers over and she gasped as he hit a much tenderer spot.

"Might have some bruised ribs here," he remarked. With every passing minute, Jake was wishing more and more he had finished the son of a bitch off. He fought for control over his anger. He had to help Lexi with this crucial step in the healing process. He was no psychiatrist but any idiot knew that a shower after something like that, could be the best thing.

He finished cleaning up her cuts and set to work on washing her hair. He inhaled deeply, loving the smell of her hair. He massaged the soap in gently and he felt her leaning into his hands. He guided her back to the water to rinse the soap from her hair. He handed her the washcloth after she finished rinsing. He waited for some kind of sign from her because he honestly didn't know what to do next. She looked up at him pleadingly. "Please don't leave me Jake. Go ahead and take your shower. I just-. I don't want to be alone."

Jake nodded to her. "I'm not going anywhere, baby girl," he told her firmly.

As they finished their shower, Jake having tended to his own wounds while she dressed, Lexi would glance at him from time to time. He was just watchful of her, but seemed careful to give her space. She liked knowing he was there if she needed him.

They finished their shower and left the bathhouse as tidy as they found it, shutting off the lights and closing the door behind them. She had to admit she felt a little better afterwards. Jake deposited the bag with her cast-off clothing in the trash can outside the bathhouse.

He glanced at Lexi for approval and she felt the tears coming again and nodded. He was simply the most beautiful man. It made her heart ache that this had happened to her. Just when she had finally found some happiness and found the love of her life, fate had cast her ballot for a bleak future.

But to Lexi, he was the only small light in her otherwise dim life. His instinct that she didn't want that clothing anymore was incredible and it made her fall in love with him all over again.

Jake helped Lexi into the golf cart and put their bag in the back, driving the cart out to where his camper was parked. He would move the camper to the beach later, but for now, it was hidden well behind the dunes. He knew no one would spot them easily where they were now. The island was actually only about 5 miles south of Ocracoke but with its remote location and virtual abandonment, it made it the perfect place to hide out.

They were hiding in plain sight; Thomas wouldn't think to look there. No one would. He was starting to wish he had taken Lexi here first instead of his beach house. Maybe Thomas wouldn't have found them and done what he did.

They walked up to the camper and Jake opened the door, glad they were arriving before the heat of the day so it wouldn't feel so much like the inside of an oven. Deciding to air the place out, he threw open every window. There was a nice breeze kicked up on the beach and it felt surprisingly cool even though it was one of the hottest summers anyone could remember in the South.

Lexi followed Jake into the camper. It was an old Airstream, vintage with all the original furnishings in perfect condition. She thought it had either been kept in a time capsule or Jake had gone through a lot of trouble to restore everything. She was betting the latter was true.

Lexi glanced around; it was small and a little cramped but to her, it was exactly what she needed. It was virtually the hole that she longed to crawl into right now, a small enclosed space where she could bury her face from the light of day and ignore the thoughts that were plaguing her mind.

The camper had a small kitchen on one wall and a closet on the other with a small bathroom. She walked into the bathroom, the space just big enough to house a shower and a sink with a small toilet tucked into the corner.

She walked over to the sink, testing the knobs even though she knew Jake had told her there would be no electricity out here. Which to her, most likely meant no running water as well. Something caught her attention in the corner of her eye and she glanced up to find the source, surprised when she found her own face staring back at her.

She didn't recognize the woman in the mirror. This person could not be her. Her hair, still damp from the shower hung limply over her shoulders. She ran her tongue over the split in her lip, watching as it traced the swollen flesh and wincing as it burned. She turned her head to the side to get a better look at her badly bruised jaw, the skin already purpling to near black though it had been mere hours since Thomas had attacked her.

She closed her eyes and tried to turn from the mirror but whenever she did, she saw Thomas as he crouched over her, holding her down. She let out a half gasp, half sob at the sudden image in her brain and felt her breathing quicken.

Suddenly, she couldn't draw enough air into her lungs and her heart began a staccato rhythm that seemed to thrum inside of her head instead of her chest. She kept exhaling hoping the pressure in her chest would abate, but found herself trying to draw more in more air in a vicious cycle. She could feel the blood draining from her head by the minute and was helpless to do anything except try to force air into her aching lungs.

Jake heard when it happened. The soft gasp and sob was unmistakable. Jake turned from where he had been preparing a quick sandwich before he set about getting Lexi settled on the bed at the back of the camper. He dropped the sandwich on the counter and quickly closed the distance between him and her. When he reached the bathroom door, he found her crumpled on the floor, her breathing rapid and labored.

He recognized the signs of PTSD immediately. He had the same symptoms for a long time after he had returned from his last trip to South America, his very last mercenary job on foreign soil ever. She appeared to be in the throes of a panic attack. He crouched down by her, wishing like hell she had collapsed anywhere but the tiny cramped bathroom.

There was no way to get himself in there and sit with her. He was going to have to try to convince her to leave the bathroom floor. But first he had to keep her from hyperventilating and passing out, although he knew if that happened, the panic attack would take care of itself.

The thought that the outcome would likely be the same either way helped calm him to do what was necessary. He reached down to her, scooping his arms up under hers and whispered softly to her.

"Lexi, I need you to listen to my voice. You are having a panic attack. You are safe, baby." God, this fucking sucked. Jake was getting sick and tired of receiving that blow to the gut every five seconds. It was wearing him down. He couldn't even imagine how she felt.

So far, her breathing had not changed one bit. "Honey, I need you to put your arms around my neck." This wasn't going to be easy, but he had to try.

Jake sighed in relief as he felt her arms come up to wind around his neck, just as he'd asked. "Now I want you to hold on tight. You don't have to do anything but that; hold on tight." He stood up and he felt her arms tighten around his neck. He pulled himself up and as Lexi rose a little from the floor, he scooped his arms up under hers and pulled her to standing, pulling her against him in the process. She was no longer gasping for breath at least, her breathing starting to settle into something that resembled normal.

He reached down and grasped her under her legs, swinging her up into his arms. Her body sighed against him and she buried her face in his neck. He could feel the wet warmth of her tears against his skin as he carried her the short distance to the bed. He sat down on the bed and arranged her on his lap. She leaned against him, the sobs now wracking her body. Jake didn't know how long they sat there. He didn't know how long she cried and he didn't care. He just let her go through it, whispering to her that he wasn't going anywhere. "I'm right here, Lexi."

After a bit, her sobs subsiding finally, she pulled away from him and she looked up at him with a pained expression. "Do you still love me?" She whispered, all that raw need evident in her watery blue-green eyes.

Jake felt it again, that stern fist to his abdomen and he exhaled the pain out as he responded. "Of course I do." He put his hands on either side of her face, going with his gut. He placed a soft kiss on her forehead and then the tip of her nose, just a soft brush of his lips against her skin. Then he kissed each cheek before he pulled away a bit. "I love you, Lexi. Nothing is going to change that." He wasn't sure what else to say but that and hoped that was enough.

Lexi nodded at him quickly, not trusting herself to speak and not sure what she would say anyway. She was overwhelmed by Jake's tenderness. It was hard to imagine the Jake that she had fought with so fiercely when they had first met. All traces of that surly man had vanished. The look he bestowed upon her now was achingly beautiful even as she saw the love there, she saw something else too.

Determination. She knew he was going to find Thomas and she wasn't even sorry for what Jake was sure to do to him.

Jake knew she needed to sleep and he had a small prescription of mild sedatives reserved for times like this. In his line of work you could never be too prepared. He shifted Lexi to sit beside him on the bed as he reached over and grabbed them out of the drawer beside the bed. He shook one out in his palm and handed it to her. "It'll help you sleep."

She shook her head. "I'm fine. I need to be in control at least a little bit." She smiled at him wanly as he put the pill back in the bottle and nodded in agreement. She laid down on the bed and pulled Jake with her, her need to be close to him winning out over any other emotion right now. She sighed and closed her eyes, willing her thoughts away and tried to concentrate on the perfect love she had right beside her, instead of the tumultuous thoughts that threatened to swamp her with sadness.

Jake laid down beside his girl, her head tucked under his chin and thought about all that had happened. He knew that there was no way he could have known that there was a spy in their midst, but the whole thing still made him feel a little powerless. That had been the whole point of his career as a mercenary; the feeling that he had some control over what happened in his life. Right now, he felt like everything was careening out of control and this girl in his arms was right at the heart of it all.

It didn't set well with him. This woman beside him was his whole world. He had to get his shit together so he could take care of her like she deserved or else his original fears were true. He didn't deserve her, not by a mile.

Chapter 20

Jake sat on the dunes and watched Lexi as she stood out looking at the ocean. It was late afternoon and they had been here on this island for five days already. Five days of a lot of silence. Five days of his girl contemplating recent events. Five days of him trying to figure out the best way to act around her.

It was so fucking hard sometimes, it made his head hurt. So far, he had just been taking subtle cues from her and it had worked out well. He wished like hell he had access to a therapist for Lexi like Thad did Laurel.

He had a feeling there was something more there than what met the eye where Thad was concerned. He had had a conference call with him and Matt yesterday and every time Thad said Laurel's name, his voice changed a bit. It was probably imperceptible to the untrained ear, but reading people was in Jake's nature and he made it his business to be able to read between the lines.

He hoped Thad knew what he was getting himself into. The guy was a freaking genius as far as his brain was concerned. He had come into their organization a few years back and at first, like always, Jake had been skeptical about him. But as time wore on and he had to spend more and more time with Thad, the more he had come to respect him.

To Jake's knowledge, Thad had never really had a steady girlfriend. Honestly, the kid really didn't have much game when it came to women, but maybe there was something really special there with the two of them. It sounded like Laurel was making great strides in progress and Thad had been teaching her basic self-defense.

Thad was a black belt in Taekwondo and word had it that he had a PhD in Martial Arts and Philosophy. When Jake had heard that, he was extremely impressed, but not all that surprised. He found it very Zen and that was something that had always secretly fascinated Jake, thus the name of his boat, Zen Goddess.

Jake glanced back at Lexi and saw that she was just toeing the sand and letting the water wash over her feet. He sighed deeply, wishing like hell he knew how to get her to open up. Thad had suggested that he let her talk about it. So far though, she hadn't wanted to. Thad had told him to be patient, but patience was not something that came naturally to Jake except when hunting and tracking.

All these new feelings that had invaded his heart and soul were strong and needed an outlet. But since Thomas had made his visit, Lexi had been so damn quiet, the silence was near deafening. And that was not like Jake at all. He had always been comfortable with the quiet and even the quiet moments with him and Lexi had been welcome.

But this was different. She wasn't shutting him out exactly, but she wasn't letting him in either. He wished there was some way he could help her get out of her head.

Jake thought back over the conference call with Thad and Matt. They had been coming up with a strategy as they did every day. So far there had been no sign of Thomas. Matt had been working on finding out who the mole was and they had a few suspicions. In talking with Jake about the events leading up to Thomas breaking into the house, Matt had made a careful observation that Jeb had most likely led Thomas right to them.

When Jake remembered how he had felt like someone had been watching them, it all made perfect sense. He was still mentally berating himself for letting his guard down so completely. No one knew where they were. Not even Matt or Thad. He used a disposable cell phone when he called them every 48 hours and he hoped like hell they would find the bastard soon. He didn't want to have to risk taking the skiff back to the mainland for supplies, but eventually he might have to. It wasn't something he wanted to even think about.

It wasn't like they could exist out here forever. It was a great hide-out for now, but eventually they would have to go back to regular life. His biggest fear was that this would all be over with soon and given what had happened to Lexi, she might just want to forget about all of it. And in the process, she might forget about him too. It wasn't rational thinking probably and he wondered if being stuck on this island was starting to mess with his head.

He hoped like hell that wasn't the case and if it were a couple of weeks ago, he would let her go without a problem. But now, with everything that had happened between them and the terrifying depth of which he loved her, there was no way he was going to let her go easily. Jake wasn't sure if that thought scared him or reassured him.

Lexi looked out over the water and dug her toes in the sand. She was just concentrating on the way the sand sunk a bit with each crashing wave, sinking her feet a little more into this stretch of beach, going over and over the events of last night, trying to change the outcome.

The thing about rewriting history was that you were rarely successful and as she stood there, trying to recreate the events of last night, she thought maybe it would be easier if she could just vanish into the sand, gone thick like mud. She could let the universe envelope her and fall down into an underworld valley, cocooned somewhere she didn't have to think about all the thoughts that kept tumbling about in her head.

She felt Jake watching her now and oddly enough, it didn't bother her at all. She liked having him close by. He had said that he wouldn't leave her; he had meant it. And she knew he would keep his word.

She sighed. She just didn't know anymore what the hell to think about things. When Laurel had met Thomas, he had seemed like such a nice guy and for the first year things had been wonderful for her. They had started talking about starting a family and Lexi was thrilled for them. She had been looking forward to finally having a niece or a nephew to spoil rotten. But then about a week after their first anniversary the fights had started. It had quickly escalated from there.

Lexi had talked to Laurel briefly last night and she had sounded so good. She sounded happy and Lexi was really happy for her. Although Laurel didn't say anything specifically, Lexi knew that something was happening between her and Thad. She had nothing but good things to say about him and she knew she had mentioned his name at least ten times in their conversation and every time she talked about all the things he was teaching her, her voice held a tinge of pride.

Lexi hoped she knew what she was getting herself into, but Laurel had a good head on her shoulders, especially now that she was away from her psycho soon-to-be-ex-husband.

Or maybe soon to be dead husband. Lexi really hoped for the latter and lately she often imagined she was the one sending him from this world to the next. Every time she thought about his hands on her, she rewrote what happened to her. It was a good tactic that she had used with her patients before. The survivor remembered what happened and when they did, they imagined it happening differently.

In Lexi's case, when she thought of Thomas when he forced himself on top of her, his pants down around his knees and the evidence of his sickening arousal pressing against her thigh, she imagined herself being able to bring her knee up into his crotch with whatever force she could muster. It would have bought her the time she needed. She knew that she had pretty much frozen up when he had been on top of her. But he had a gun and he outweighed Lexi by more than double. Still, she clenched her eyes tightly shut and willed herself to imagine getting in her crotch kick and squirming out from underneath him. Maybe when he was bent over nursing his injury she could grab for her gun in the nightstand.

She imagined herself standing over him and she never shot him in the back of the head in this scenario. No, she wanted him to know he was getting ready to meet his maker and be shipped promptly off to hell because that was where he belonged.

So, in her mind, she waited until he got up and turned around and then she just smiled evilly at him, no words, and pulled the trigger.

Unfortunately Lexi had had to kill enough people in her line of work that she could imagine very clearly the bullet hitting him square in the forehead. Just before that though, she would see the recognition in his eyes that he had just been bested. Lexi sighed. As crazy as the tactic sounded, it was working. She could feel herself begin to assert some control over the situation and thus her emotions surrounding it.

She really had to applaud Jake for being so patient with her. Even now, he was sitting on the dunes 200 yards back from the water. She knew if she turned around and motioned for him, he would come to her. It wasn't like she was getting some kind of power trip off of that.

He was giving her the space and time she needed. She knew he would do anything for her and he'd showed just how much in the silent resolve he had in sticking by her side the past few days.

Then too, he had proved the depth of his feeling for her, that fated night, when he had helped her get cleaned up right after the attack

189

and every moment since he had continued to show her how much she meant to him. For all the tender moments they had shared in the past few weeks, the one in the shower stood out in Lexi's mind the most. She had never seen such a look of devotion and love in his eyes since she had met him.

Lexi really liked this little island. They hadn't done much in the way of exploring besides to move the camper from day to day. The island was a lot bigger than she had thought it would be and a lot more beautiful than even the one they'd come from.

Lexi dragged her toes lazily through the sand, searching for hidden treasure. She liked knowing that there was no one on this beach but them. After all the ways this world had hurt her recently, she found she was at home here; like maybe she and Jake were the only two people left in the whole world. And it was okay.

She had never thought she would like the feeling of being isolated on a deserted island. Sure she used to joke about it all the time; everyone did. But now that she was here, despite what had brought her here, she was feeling more relaxed than she had in a long time. Her only complaint was the damn biting flies. They were vicious here. They had green heads and they were slow and fat and stupid, so you could kill them. But they landed very stealthily on your unsuspecting skin, so you only got to kill them after they had already bitten you.

Because of that, Lexi was starting to take a secret pleasure in murdering the pests. The days were hot here, but the constant breeze blowing on the barrier island cooled it considerably. The nights were pleasant and they had taken to sleeping with the windows open in the camper. The camper had a small generator that they used for the stove and refrigerator.

Lexi sorely wished for the days they had spent swimming in the ocean and learning to kiteboard. If this was ever over, it was something that she definitely wanted to try again. She had loved the adrenaline rush it provided and she loved even more that Jake was the one that taught her. She honestly did not know what she would be doing right now if it weren't for him. He had been her rock; her protector, and so much more. They of course slept together every night. There was only one bed in the camper and it was smaller than the one at the beach house but it was sufficient.

The only problem was the nightmares that plagued her nightly. She never slept well anymore. It had come to the point that she and sleep were enemies. She had a hard time falling asleep since every time she closed her eyes, she saw Thomas bending over her as he clamped his hand over her mouth. If, on the rare occasion, she finally settled her mind enough to drift off, she was awakened every single time with the nightmare that he was back.

She woke up crying and Jake didn't say a word. He just opened his arms as she pressed herself to his side and cried herself back to sleep and he just let her. Then, every morning when she woke up, he was there beside her, waiting patiently for her to open her eyes. The man was a damned saint for putting up with her and he deserved a medal for it. Maybe she would tell him that later.

Jake watched Lexi from where he sat and he was fighting like hell to stay seated. Her shoulders were starting to hunch over and he knew that meant she was about to break down again. He waited, ready to jump up if needed.

As he saw her step back from the water and drop to the sand on her knees, his heart felt like it snapped in two. He just could not stand to see her hurting like this. It was too damn hard. And he wanted to kill Thomas all over again. He was no longer sure that he could just hand him over to the authorities if and when they crossed paths again.

He was getting surer of the fact that he would probably kill him outright. He could make it look like an accident or self-defense and he was pretty sure the feds would be glad to look the other way since Thomas was such a scumbag. But for doing what he did to Lexi and to her sister, he thought he could probably kill him with his bare hands, without so much as blinking.

Going with his gut, Jake got up from where he was sitting and he made his way down to her nonetheless. When he had almost reached her she turned around and smiled up at him, her first real smile in nearly six days, and he couldn't help but return it, feeling relieved that it wasn't what he thought.

As he smiled at her, he realized that it felt damn good to finally smile about something and he didn't even know what it was that had her looking at him like that. He was just glad to see her face lit up like that almost like the old Lexi. Almost.

She held up her treasure, displaying it proudly. It was a whole conch shell, a little bleached from the sun but still retaining a bit of its original grey color. Lexi turned it over in her hands in awe and sat back on the beach, stretching her legs out in front of her. "It's whole. I've never found a whole one before." She breathed in wonder.

Jake sat down beside her and smiled softly in her direction, loving that she was enthralled with something as simple as a sea shell. It's one of the things that he loved most about her; her ability to find the beauty in every single thing, living or not. "I found a couple before but that one's pretty big," he remarked as she turned it over and over in her hands.

He watched in fascination as the wonder danced behind her eyes and she held it up to her ear, a light laugh escaping her as she rolled her eyes at him playfully.

He had to smile back at the almost child-like expression on her face. She closed her eyes as she listened for whatever it was she was trying to hear and hoped like hell this moment never ended. It was the first sign of Lexi, *his* Lexi, he had seen in days.

Lexi pulled the shell down from her ear and looked over at him with unshed tears in her eyes. There was a difference in these tears though. Her eyes didn't hold a tinge of sadness; instead she looked happy. He thought she was incredible and even though her face was a little red from the unshed from the tears and her eyes were all watery, she had never looked more beautiful to him.

Lexi held the shell out to Jake and he took it from her. She sighed deeply and took the first deep breath she had taken in what felt like days and it probably was.

"The conch shell is the oldest known musical instrument." She remarked. "I remember reading about it in my Philosophy class in college." She rolled her eyes then. "I know, pretty hippy dippy; but it was required."

She traced her fingers in the sand as she spoke. "Anyway, the ancients thought the conch to be a nearly reverent item and it holds a lot of symbolism. The one that always stood out to me though was the belief that the call of the conch shell is meant to be an awakening of sorts. That it is supposed to bring about a victory from suffering." Her voice broke then as she let the tears fall unbidden down her cheeks.

Jake's heart was aching but he let her continue, holding the shell on his lap while she continued her story. He knew she was making a point and he was anxious to see what it was, because whatever it was, it had changed something inside her. Getting to glimpse the old Lexi again was something that he had been starting to think he would never see.

"I have been asking for a sign from God for the past few days. A sign that I am supposed to continue. A sign that I can move on from this. That I can be okay again. And then I found this in the sand. I have never found a whole one Jake, never." She breathed, reaching up to wipe the tears from her face, knowing that she was going to get the sand stuck to her face when she did so, but it was important that he understand what she was trying to say.

"When I pulled it out and it was whole, it was like I had received my sign that I can come back from this. I think that I can maybe stop suffering and claim my life back. It's not going to be easy and I can't even imagine what it's been like for Laurel, but if she can get over what happened to her, then I can get over this. She is being so strong. I can be too." She finished.

Her voice was steady and sure and that determined spirit was back in her eyes as she spoke. There was something really beautiful about watching the old Lexi slide back into place and he wanted so badly to take her in his arms, but he waited. He was still taking his cues from her. They would get there eventually; he just had to be patient.

"I think you are the strongest woman I have ever known, Lexi." He told her and he meant it. She looked at him in surprise and her face warmed under the intensity of his gaze. "It's true. Here you are with something awful that just happened to you. Yet you put yourself in Laurel's shoes. I have never seen anyone as selfless as you," he said softly, letting his glance drift down to the sand where she was tracing circles in it.

"Oh Jake, can't you see? I think I am able to move on from this because of *you*," she said, her voice breaking again.

Jake opened his mouth to speak, but Lexi put a hand up to stop him. "No, you need to hear this. More than that, you need to believe it." Her voice was firm and her eyes were blazing with that fire that was pure Lexi.

"I am not going to forget all this. I won't be able to. But I can get past it as long as you are beside me. Jake, I don't know what I would have done without you in the past few days. I got to thinking that this might have happened whether I was here with you or not. It really was bound to happen sooner or later. I can't thank you enough for being patient with me these last few days. I know it hasn't been easy. But I want you to know that you are still everything to me. I still love you. I will always love you. So while I can't forget about all this, I wouldn't want to anyway. Because forgetting this would mean forgetting you too and Jake, I can't even imagine my life without you anymore." She stopped and hoped like hell she hadn't said too much. She didn't think she had. They had been through too much together and while the Jake she had first met would have cut and run when things got tough, she knew the Jake sitting beside her was not going anywhere.

Jake nodded almost imperceptibly as Lexi finished her speech, trying to choose his words carefully. But he knew that wasn't going to happen so he just opened his mouth and let whatever was in there spill out, trusting his gut like he always did. "Lexi I told you this before. I ain't never met anybody like you. God, Lex, I can't imagine my life without you either. And that scares the ever living shit out of me." He smiled at her and she laughed.

"But I don't care, because being with you has made me feel more alive than I have ever felt in my life. I'm not going anywhere and if you will have me, I'll be by your side every day. Just like I have been here. I still don't know what you see in me. I've done a lot of shit in my life I ain't proud of. But being with you has made me want to be a better person. You *make* me a better man. I don't think I could go back to my old life now if I tried." He finished and he would never admit it but he could feel the tears inching their way down his face. Something about this beautiful woman had broken him down and tore down everything he had built up around him his whole life. He felt raw and exposed and like he might lose control at any moment. But he had meant it; he felt more alive than ever." Finally having run out of words, he whispered. "I *love* you."

"Oh Jake, I love you too." Lexi said as she turned to face him, the sand shifting slightly beneath her. She leaned towards him and closed her eyes as she placed her lips over his. Jake didn't move a muscle and she could almost feel him holding his breath.

Jake closed his eyes as he realized that Lexi was about to kiss him. He hadn't kissed her in days and now that she was getting ready to initiate it, his heart was hammering in his chest. As her lips met his, he heard her sigh and felt himself sigh too. He let her lead the kiss. She moved her hand up to place it on the side of his face and she lightly rubbed her thumb over the stubble on his cheek as she deepened the kiss ever so slightly.

He opened his mouth under hers as he felt just the tip of her tongue slide into his mouth. Lexi angled her head slightly, their lips meeting continuously in short, soft, languid kisses. It was almost as if they were kissing for the first time again, except that their bodies knew differently. For Jake, it was like coming home again after a long absence.

Lexi broke off the kiss and leaned her head on his shoulder, both of them sitting on the sand and looking out at the ocean, neither speaking a word for a full five minutes.

Lexi finally spoke first. "Jake?" She whispered, her voice barely heard over the loud roaring of the ocean crashing against the shore.

"Mmmm-hmmm?" he murmured back, feeling as relaxed as he had felt in weeks. It felt good to not have to worry for a change.

"Do you think there is something going on with my sister and Thad?" She asked him, sitting up again, really wanting to stretch her legs. She had been sitting on the sand too long.

Jake shrugged. "I got the feeling there might be, but who knows." He stood up then and reached his hand down to help her up, almost as if reading her mind. "God I'm getting too old for this." He groaned, putting a hand to his lower back and Lexi couldn't help but giggle. It was times like this when the age difference between them was noticeable and she resisted the urge to tease him about it.

"You want to go for a walk?" Jake asked her, handing her the shell that had sat between them on the sand.

"Thought you'd never ask." She said with a wink, allowing him to pull her up to her feet. It was almost as if the attack had never happened. Almost. Jake knew no one else would know it, but he could see it in her gaze. Just a hint of darkness that had clouded those bright blues and made her smile slightly less brilliant. He vowed silently to do everything in his power to make certain that the full light of hope was put back into her eyes.

Lexi brushed the sand from her shorts and the backs of her legs and carried the shell in one hand and held Jake's hand with the other, their fingers intertwined, a fine layer of sand dotting both their hands.

They walked along in silence for a bit before Jake spoke. "You know, Melinda, that therapist. She has an excellent track record for helping women get over their attackers. Actually Melinda and Thad have worked together for years. She works on the mental and Thad works on the physical. The two of them together with their intense therapy regimen have gotten more women over sexual assault faster than some therapists alone can do in ten years or more." He paused for a moment kicking at a large stick on the ground, almost looking like a piece of driftwood.

He was always looking for driftwood on the beach. And sea glass. That was probably his favorite thing; to find a piece of glass on the beach, all the hard edges worn away and it being softly and slowly polished by the incessant tides of the ocean and sanded smooth by the coarse floor of the sea.

"I always thought there might be something there with them, but they've always been just friends. Then I found out later that Melinda was married all along. Her husband John is some famous author, can't remember what it is just now." Jake stopped. Lexi just nodded at him to continue.

"Now it kind of makes sense to me. Thad hasn't ever really talked about a girl before, but he couldn't shut up about your sister. Did Laurel talk about Thad?" He asked as he kicked the piece of wood back and forth, finally reaching down and picking it up, another idea forming in his head.

"Yeah actually she did. She couldn't shut up about him either." She looked at him, her mouth forming an 'o' of surprise. Her girlie heart did a little flip and suddenly she wished again fiercely that she could see her sister and they could just talk for hours about everything. About boys and clothes and make-up, instead of the life and death matters they were facing right now.

"You think they are together?" She stopped herself, unable to believe it. Her and her sister finding something wonderful at the same time. Well, it was just too much to hope for. She knew if Laurel was here with her, they would be heading off to the nearest corner to giggle and whisper for hours and hours. Just like the old days, she thought with a wistful smile.

Jake held out his hand as if to say he didn't have any idea. "I guess we'll find out when this is all over." He mused and Lexi nodded, looking down at the stick in his hand.

"What are you doing with that?" She smiled at him, amused.

"Actually, it's a secret," he said, winking at her. Lexi's heart flip-flopped at his words and the expression on his face. Never mind that him winking at her always sent her pulse racing.

"What is it?" She asked him, pulling on his hand slightly so he was right beside her.

"Well if I tell you, then it won't be a secret now will it?" He said, holding the piece of wood away from her. Why don't you explore over there?" He suggested pointing to the dunes to their left. "There's a bunch of those flowers you like." He knew how much she liked them.

Lexi looked at him uncertainly wondering what he was up to, but she nodded at him. "Okay, fine. Maybe I can gather a bouquet for the table inside." She said walking away from him to the dunes.

Jake made his way further down the beach towards where the waves were crashing. The tide was getting ready to come in so he was going to have to hurry. But he found a large smooth spot on the sand far enough away from the swirling tide and began working. When he finally finished, he stood back and admired his work, glancing back at the ocean making sure that it wouldn't wash away his message. Lexi turned from her spot on the dunes, having collected several Beach Morning Glories in her fingers. He motioned for her to join him by the water.

Lexi didn't waste any time in making her way back down to Jake. As she approached him, he had a self-satisfied grin on his face and it looked so good on him. "What's the surprise?" She felt like a kid on Christmas, as ridiculous as that sounded.

He was still holding the piece of driftwood and he used it now to point down to the sand. He had moved far enough away from what he had written so she could see every word.

Lexi looked down at the sand and it felt like something was trying to squeeze her heart right out of her chest but in a good way. She looked up at him, fresh tears welling up in her eyes, but the smile on her face was unmistakable.

Written in the sand was the simple sentence. *"Marry me, Lexi?"*

The morning glories were suddenly forgotten as she dropped them and the shell in the sand as Jake knelt down before her on one knee. He had never been more nervous in his entire life and that included the first time they had kissed and the first time they made love and all the moments like this in between.

But honestly they hadn't had a moment this serious yet. They had been living everything day by day, taking things one day at a time and figuring everything out together. He hoped like hell he wasn't making a mistake but the look on her face spurred him on a bit.

When he finally trusted himself to speak, he began. "Lexi, I love you. And I meant what I said earlier, I can't imagine my life without you. Don't even want to. I know that we ain't a likely pair, but I don't care. I know that people might have an issue with it. I still won't care. And I don't think you do either. You've made me feel things that I didn't think I would ever feel. Made me wish for a life that I never thought I'd have; that I never thought I deserved. But I was wrong. You have given me the best gift anyone could ask for. Your love. And if you give me a chance, I promise to spend the rest of my life proving to you that I deserve this. That I deserve *you*. Will you marry me, Lexi Green?"

Lexi looked down at this impossible man. This impossibly beautiful, complex man and she knew that words were not going to come for a minute or two, so she just held her fingers over her mouth, trying to hold back the happy sob that wanted to escape and nodded her head fiercely. "Yes! Yes, I will marry you, Jake Jackson." She said.

Jake got up from the sand and wrapped his arms around her neck and buried his face in that space between her shoulder and her neck, feeling like someone had just handed him the world on a silver platter. He breathed in that familiar scent of hers, the cloying mixture of vanilla and orchids and he knew he would spend a lifetime memorizing every essence of her, every curve, every dip, every smile she sent his way and he knew he would never take any of it for granted.

He knew what it was like to have nothing and no one. He would never go back to that because the woman that he never even knew he was dreaming of had just agreed to spend the rest of her life with him. He couldn't wish for anything more; he wouldn't even try.

Chapter 21

Lexi was dreaming again and the devil of it was that she knew that she was dreaming, but she couldn't wake up. She had gone to sleep with such sweet thoughts on her mind that at first it surprised her that she found herself locked in her ritualistic nightmare.

It never changed; Thomas always clamped his hand over her mouth, she still said all the things to him that she probably shouldn't have, he still pinned her to the ground, his heaviness weighing her body down and the knowledge of what he was about to do weighing her mind down to the point that she couldn't think of a way to wake herself up.

She screamed as he pried her legs apart and she felt herself shatter then, her subconscious coming awake finally and her eyelids fluttered open. Jake was whispering her name. "Lexi. Lexi, *it's ok. You're safe.*" It was what he said every night this happened.

She opened her eyes to find that Jake was sitting back at a safe distance. He knew from experience that her hyper-vigilance at night time often had her coming up swinging when she finally woke up. She thought that maybe part of her would always have this love/hate relationship with sleep now; like part of her subconscious was now irrevocably damaged.

She looked at Jake, the misery radiating out from her eyes. He wished like hell there was something he could do to keep her from waking up like this every single night. He didn't mind the waking up; it's just that his heart splintered every time she woke up out of breath and that wild and frightened look in her eyes just before consciousness slid back into place.

She threw herself into his arms, just like she did every night. Sometimes they had to go outside and get some air. This looked like it might be one of those nights. He pulled her closer as she settled her head against his chest, tucking her head under his chin. He wrapped his arms around her tighter and took her lead, as usual. After a few minutes, her sobs finally subsided and her breathing evened out. He thought maybe she had fallen back asleep. That happened sometimes too; he would just lie her down gently beside him, keeping his arms around her. His arm always fell asleep, but he didn't care. She was safe and that was all that ever mattered to him.

He was mildly surprised when she pulled away from him and wiped her tears from her face with the back of her hand. He reached up on the shelf and handed her the box of Kleenex they kept there. She looked up at him.

"Thank you." She whispered as she took a handful of tissues and blew her nose none too delicately. Jake felt the corners of his mouth turn up. He often would get her laughing when she was done; her nose was always shiny after she cried and if she blew her nose too hard, it would resemble something like a fog horn. It had been a sorely needed source of comic relief during this whole thing.

"It's no problem. You know that." Jake murmured with her still in his arms. Even after crying, she looked impossibly beautiful. They always turned off the generator at night time and it was pitch black on the island at night. Tonight though, the pale silvery light provided from the moon cast an ethereal glow on Lexi's face as it streamed through the skylight directly over their bed. She looked like an angel sitting cross-legged in front of him.

Lexi looked at Jake sitting across from her. He had repositioned himself where they were both sitting cross-legged with their knees touching. Lexi tentatively leaned forward and placed her palms on his bare knees. He was wearing his boxers like he did every night. After that fateful night they had gone back to sleeping in light pajamas or underwear.

Lexi had gotten an idea last night before they finally fell asleep. They had fallen asleep in each other's arms, whispering about their future. She had been overcome with love for him and she had thought that maybe what she needed was a good memory to replace the bad one. She didn't have the nerve then, but she thought she did now.

She knew that she enjoyed making love with Jake. She knew that she loved him. It was just a matter of getting back on the proverbial horse. She didn't know exactly what she was ready for but she knew she was ready for something besides this deep pit of emptiness inside her. She had just convinced herself that this was what she needed. She needed to be reminded of the pleasures physical touch could bring.

Jake looked up in surprise as she placed her palms on his knees and squeezed ever so slightly. She looked up to meet his eyes and was completely caught unaware by the gentleness she saw there. It wasn't that he never looked at her that way, but normally when they were intimate, his expressions tended to stray more towards unrefined desire. The one thing that she didn't want to see when she looked at him was pity reflected back in his gaze. She knew that was not something that she would be able to handle.

She knew that was true of him when she saw the scars on his back. It was raw; it was pain; it was the gut-wrenching feeling that you didn't want to feel as different as you did.

It suddenly struck Lexi that this was yet another thing they had in common. His past and her present; they meshed together as proof of what horrible things people could do to one another. She thought that maybe, just maybe, she had been what he needed to leave some of his past behind and to face his demons at last. She knew right now beyond the shadow of a doubt that he was exactly what she needed now for all the same reasons, even if the circumstances were different.

Lexi cleared her throat before speaking and telling Jake her idea. "I was thinking that maybe we could find some good memories to replace the bad ones?" It was a question, not a statement. He had to be okay with this. She knew it had been hard on him restraining himself from even kissing her. It wasn't that she didn't want to kiss Jake or make love with him. It was just that her brain was so full of the bullshit behind what had happened that there wasn't room for anything else. But now, she thought she might be ready to try again. Her heart was thrumming in her chest waiting for his reply.

He thought for a moment and he did move his hand then to worry his teeth over the spot on his thumb. "'Alright. We do this one way only though." He said. He was willing to give her all the control, except on one thing. If he thought she was breaking apart again, he was going to stop it. He could not have her risking all the progress she made. And he knew that his heart could not take witnessing her shattering into a million pieces again.

"Okay, I'm listening." She said. She kind of knew what he was going to say before he said it. She knew he was restraining himself because he didn't want to hurt her in any way. And she knew that he wouldn't. But she waited for him to say his piece.

"If it looks like you ain't handling things all that well, then we stop." Lexi cast her eyes downward. He reached out and took her chin in his hands. "I mean it. We stop." He said gently. "And I want you to put your eyes right here." She looked into his eyes and knew what he meant.

She nodded at him. She took a deep breath and steadied herself. It wasn't exactly what she had in mind for what she needed but what he was suggesting made better sense. It wouldn't do either of them any good if they just tried to pick up where they left off in the bedroom. It was almost like they were starting all over again. Lexi was okay with it and she knew Jake was too by the suggestions he had made. She knew that as much as he enjoyed the physical aspect of their relationship, he wouldn't want to do anything that he thought might set her back.

She also knew what it had taken for them to get to the point that they could be physical with one another. She almost cried in frustration at the hand fate had dealt them. Whatever doesn't kill you makes you stronger or something like that, she thought, taking another deep breath to steady her nerves. She nodded at him again. "I get what you're saying. It makes sense." She said.

"Hey." Insisted Jake. Lexi looked up at him.

Jake made a gesture with two fingers denoting his wishes. "Eyes right here, remember?" He said softly. "And one more thing." She looked right into his eyes and willed him to answer her.

"I love you." He said simply.

She resisted the urge to close her eyes and absorb what he was saying. "I love you, too, Jake." She whispered, her hands splayed out over his muscular thighs, feeling the coarse hairs there. She didn't take her eyes off of him. It was a whole lot harder to look intensely into someone else's eyes, but she found it to be more powerful than she had thought it would be.

She knew that she had always heard the eyes were the windows to the soul and she wondered why people didn't look at each other this way more often. Despite the fact that she felt exposed and raw in looking into Jake's bright crystal blue eyes, she had never felt more loved. She had never felt safer than she did in this moment. It strengthened her resolve that they were making the right decision.

She moved her hands achingly slow the rest of the way up his thighs and her palms came to rest on Jake's hands. She leaned forward slightly and tilted her head up towards him and then thinking better of it, leaned back again. "Guess that means we can't kiss huh." She said.

Jake nodded at her. "I think it'd be best if we save that for later. Can't keep eye contact if we get all lost in our kissing like we usually do." He said and he couldn't resist the way the corners of his mouth turned up and the spark of humor in his eyes.

Lexi smiled back at him. "How'd you get to be so smart?" She said teasingly.

"It ain't being smart. It's just logistics. You can't kiss and keep your eyes open at the same time." He said simply.

Lexi nodded at him as she moved her hands over his and moved them, one on each of her hips. She knew what he meant about the kissing. It wasn't something that bothered her and he was right in saying that they could really get caught up in the moment if they weren't paying full attention to what was going on. She moved her hands back to his chest and splayed both hands over his pecs, her eyes on his the entire time, just ghosting her fingertips over the hard, smooth surface of his skin.

Lexi realized that Jake wasn't moving his hands on her at all. "It's okay Jake. I'm not going to break."

Jake mulled over Lexi's words. She was wrong about her not breaking. That was precisely what she had done this past week. She had broken and he knew she wanted to be fixed. He supposed that was what he was; what this night was for. The superglue that could piece her back together. He was honored to have the job, he thought as he splayed his hands over her hips, his thumbs resting in the hollow on each side and rubbing lightly back and forth. "Is this okay?" He asked her, looking into her eyes.

"Yes." Her voice was barely a whisper.

"Good" he murmured. As he continued to move his thumbs gently over the tender flesh over her hip bone and then splaying his fingers out and bringing them up to her waist.

"How about this?" He whispered.

"Yes." She breathed, her eyes never straying from his as he moved his fingers up to grip her waist. What she saw reflected there was the most tenderness she had ever seen in him. It almost hurt to look at him this way and to have him stare at her so intensely, but when she looked at him all she saw was love and hear heart felt like it dipped a bit inside her chest.

He hummed his appreciation for the softness of her body as he skimmed his fingers up her waist just slightly under her tank top.

Jake saw the moment she started to lose control. He had been afraid of it and that's why he kept asking if every move he made was okay. She had shut her eyes tight and then opened them again immediately, looking at him with the tears making her eyes just a little too bright.

He moved one of his hands from where it had been lightly gripping the hem of her tank top. He brought his hand up to rub away the tears that were finding their way down her cheeks. He brushed his thumb right over her cheekbone. "You wanna stop?" His voice was barely above a whisper and he felt close to tears himself watching the anguish wash over her features. It just looked out of place on her normally smiling face.

Lexi didn't speak this time. She just looked at him and shook her head and then smiled at him again, taking a shaky breath and piece by piece, under a hooded gaze, she removed all of her clothes and sat before him. "This is easier." She said simply and reached for his boxers.

He caught on fast and slid his boxers from his body as she straddled him. She just wanted to feel him moving inside her, as if his presence there could scrape out everything bad and she could become a new person with him again, like nothing bad had ever happened to her.

Jake smiled at her softly. "I think it's a perfect idea." Of course, what else could he say when she was impaling herself on his length, her heat enveloping him and caressing him. This was exactly what he had wanted. For her to decide what she needed. Right now, she didn't need anyone undressing her or cajoling her. She needed to be in control.

"You're so goddamned beautiful." He murmured watching her struggling against letting her eyes fall closed as she rocked herself over him. And it was true. He had never seen anything more beautiful than this girl, this warrior, riding him and proving to them both what she was made of. Steel. Something stronger than he himself was crafted of, he thought.

Jake took in the sight of her, drinking in every detail like a man dying of thirst. She began to move her hips up and down in a slow, lazy rhythm, rotating her hips with every third or fourth thrust, effectively pushing him as far inside her as he could go. Lexi brought her hands up to his shoulders, her fingers searching for purchase as he moved his hands down to grip her waist, his thumb resting above the curve of each hip as she moved up and down.

"Yes. Jake. Yes." She whispered, the intensity of her gaze boring into him. His breath was coming faster and faster as she created a delicious friction between them, their lovemaking driving them both to the breaking point.

Lexi once again lost herself in all sensation, driving herself to that precipice and holding back again. Every move, every pulse of her body over his, was making her body scream for more. It was exactly what she needed. There was no one else here. No monsters, no bogeymen, only her and Jake and this need between them both, burning up the night.

"I'm close baby girl." Jake's voice was gravely, signaling his imminent release. But she was close too and he held off a little longer, feeling her walls gripping him harder as her orgasm rolled through her. His fingers came up to splay across her back, holding her to him, as if to press her more firmly where their bodies were joined.

Lexi flew apart at the seams as her release finally found her and it didn't stop. It just kept coming and finally, she felt Jake give in too. He held her tightly against him as she came undone.

"I love you Lexi." He said and together they rocketed off that precipice together, soaring into the night until they finally came to rest against the other, chests heaving, their sweat-slicked skin sliding together as they fell back to the bed, breathless.

"I love you, too." She breathed with a helpless little giggle coming out at the end.

They stayed that way for a minute, letting their breathing return to normal and floating back down from the cloud of emotion they had been riding for the last hour. Lexi pulled herself off him and collapsed beside him.

"What's that smile for?" He said affectionately as he pulled her back into his arms and she rested her head on his chest. The smile looked damn good on her. It had been too fucking long since her face had been this relaxed.

"That was incredible." She breathed. She raised up from where she was resting. "It was almost like it was our first time", she remarked, her eyes all soft.

He looked at her tenderly and brushed his lips across hers. "With you, it's always like the first time." He always knew the exact right thing to say, she thought.

"We didn't use anything again." She wrinkled her nose at him. It wasn't like they had time to get condoms before they came here.

"Yeah, I ain't worried," he shrugged and she looked up at him in surprise. It was the last thing she thought he would say.

"You're not?" She asked, her voice barely a whisper now, not wanting to believe what he was saying.

"Nope. You agreed to marry me right? Or did you change your mind?" He asked her and Lexi raised her head up again to look at him in wonder.

"No I didn't change my mind. You can't get rid of me now." She teased.

He turned and propped his head up on one hand. "Honestly Lexi, I never thought I would feel like this but I am ready for anything life throws at us. If that's a baby because we are less than careful, then so be it." He said simply. "Yeah, we should probably be more careful sometimes, but if it happens, we'll handle it."

Lexi smiled at him, awestruck by what he was saying. He was saying he wanted a child with her, at least that's what she thought he was saying. "So you'd have a baby with me?" She whispered, her voice breaking a little as she said the words.

"God Lexi. I would do anything you asked me to do. If you wanted a baby, I'd give you a whole damned houseful." He looked at her, his voice oozing confidence that he'd never before felt.

She smiled and laughed even as she felt tears of joys welling up in her eyes. "Well not yet." She admitted. "But someday." She said, resting her head against his chest again as she stifled a yawn. She had no idea what time it was but it felt like bedtime now, the nightmare that had awakened her a dim memory.

"Yeah, someday". And he was looking forward to all the somedays they were going to have. Jake sighed as he felt her rest against him, knowing that sleep would claim her soon. He was tired too. The lack of sleep since they had gotten here was starting to wear on him.

"I can't wait to become Mrs. Jake Jackson." She said sleepily as she splayed her hand on his chest and rested it there. He reached down and pulled the thin blanket over both of them. He could feel his heart flutter at her words. He felt her body relax as she drifted off into a hopefully dreamless sleep.

He thought he had experienced the full gamut of emotions where Lexi was concerned but this night had topped every moment they had ever had together. It had been raw and passionate and tender and every single thing that represented the love they felt for each other.

When she mentioned their lack of birth control, it was like for the first time in his life, he had received the blueprints of what he was supposed to do next. Somehow in the space of the last few weeks, fate had paved the way to happiness. It was a foreign feeling, but one that he was becoming accustomed to. With Lexi, it just couldn't be helped.

As he closed his eyes and drifted off to sleep beside the love of his life, he knew he had meant the words he spoken to her. He really was ready for whatever life threw at them. He couldn't wait for her to become Mrs. Jake Jackson either. He never thought he would want conventional things like marriage and babies. But she had irrevocably changed him; for the better. For her, he would do anything. For Lexi, he would walk to the end of the earth and back and be glad for the journey.

Chapter 22

Jake couldn't believe he was dancing with Lexi on the beach. Some part of him knew that it was corny as hell. The bigger part didn't really give a damn. When he had heard the song, he had recognized it. Back at home, they played it all the time on the radio. But when he heard it with Lexi sitting there in front of him, he just knew beyond anything that song was meant for the two of them.

Every single word described their relationship perfectly. Every single word described how Jake felt about Lexi. Jake had never been the hearts and flowers kind of guy. And if anyone had told him a few months back that he was going to be doing half the things he was doing with this girl, he would have told them to go to hell. He would have laughed first, but yes, he definitely would have told them they were crazy.

He figured that he had never been a romantic before because he had just never met the right girl. He hadn't met this angel in his arms, so hauntingly beautiful and brave. It amazed him really. That she could love someone like him. That a girl as beautiful and good and kind as Lexi Green had agreed to marry him, Jake Jackson. A nobody, nothing from a no-name backwater town in the middle of Georgia.

He tightened his hold on her slightly as they swayed to the music, the song getting ready to come to an end. And he was sorry for it.

As the song came to an end, they pulled away from each other. Jake kind of felt funny about his impulsiveness. Maybe she was going to think he was a dork. Fixing a picnic for her and slow dancing with her all in one day. Yeah, he probably had lost his mind. He kicked at the sand and walked back to their blanket so he could begin cleaning up the mess before dark.

Lexi stared after him as he sulked away. He was *so* exasperating sometimes! She watched as he piled everything back into the bag he had used to carry everything out in. He glanced up at her then.

"What?" Jake asked. She was staring at him now, hands on her hips and she had that *look* in her eye. The same one she had on her face that first day they had fought and he'd pinned her against the wall and kissed her. Looking at her now, he knew he was in trouble. And he even knew why. He knew it was crazy. He knew she loved him. And yet something like him impulsively pulling her into his arms made him skitter backwards a few steps. It was stupid and he knew it.

Lexi saw the defeated look on his face and it pretty much broke her heart and pissed her off all at the same time. She finally crossed the sand to where he was standing, holding the empty wine bottle and staring at it as if it was the most interesting object out here. She walked over to him and gently took the bottle from his hands and sat it down in the sand. She pulled at his hands with her own.

"Jake look at me." She insisted, squeezing his hands and feeling him squeezing them back. He finally raised his eyes to hers. "You have to start believing that I want this. That I want to be with you. I want to marry you. I want to have your babies, you jackass." She couldn't help but smile at the last part. She saw the corners of his mouth curve into a slight smile.

"I just ain't used to all this is all," he said, unable to find the right words.

"Well, you're going to have to *get* used to it." Lexi insisted.

"I've never done any of this before, Lexi. I've never had a girlfriend. Never had anybody care about me before. I know Jeb cares in his own way, but most of the time it's to suit his purposes. Lexi, you're the only person besides my Ma who has ever cared about me and loved me just for me. I guess I just keep waiting for something to happen to make you change your mind about me. That I might *do* something to change your mind," he glanced down at her IPod, packed on the top of the bag. He looked away then, afraid he had said too much. For the life of him, he just didn't know the most right things to say sometimes. It's why he was so quiet most of the time.

Lexi stepped forward then, dropping his hands and putting one hand on either side of his face. "That's what this is about? Because you did something on the spur of the moment and danced with your fiancé?"

His eyes went wide then. "Yeah, that's right, I said it, your fiancé," She kept her voice firm but gentle. "If we were not in the middle of this mess, we'd be having an engagement party. And then you'd have to dance with me anyways. The fact that I didn't have to ask you to tells me a lot. It tells me that you are a romantic at heart," Lexi paused and put her hand up as Jake started to speak.

"Let me finish." Lexi admonished him. "I know that with your past and in your line of work, you've always had to be a certain way. You've had to be the tough guy." Lexi put her hands down at her sides, giving her words time to sink in.

Jake nodded at her, sighing deeply. She wasn't wrong and it was almost disconcerting how accurate her words were.

"Jake, you don't have to be that guy with me. Be yourself with me. Be the guy that fixes picnic dinners. Be the guy that sweeps a girl off her feet. Be the guy that slow dances with his *fiancé* on the beach though the world around them has gone to hell." She looked at him pointedly on the last one, hoping her words were penetrating his thick skull.

Jake knew he had no argument for her. He hadn't had one from the beginning of this conversation. Hell, if he thought about it, he should have known he was in big trouble that day he met her in the bar.

He smirked at her. "You ever tell anybody I ain't the bad-ass everybody thinks I am, I'll deny it."

Lexi smiled saucily at him; she saw the twinkle in his eye. "So what's next on our agenda, Romeo?" She teased, unable to help herself.

"Oh, now I'm Romeo. That would make you Juliet. That ends tragically, you know." He said, tickling her gently while she laughed and simultaneously pressed herself to his side.

He sighed. "It's time to call Matt. You ready?" Lexi nodded, excited. They always called Laurel when they called Matt. She knew she would only have a few minutes to speak with her, but she was going to do her damnedest to pull the truth out of her about her and Thad.

Jake reached into his pocket and pulled out the cell phone, turning it on and glancing at his watch simultaneously. Matt answered the phone on the third ring. "Lincoln."

"It's me. What's the status?" He asked his friend. He had to admit it was good to hear his voice.

"Hey." Matt answered him, lowering his voice as he spoke. "Somebody saw him in Atlanta today. Thad thinks he might be giving up."

Jake knew he was talking about Thomas, but something didn't sit well with him about it. He knew types like Thomas; it wasn't likely that he would just give up and he said so to Matt now. He could feel the beginnings of dread starting somewhere in the pit of his stomach.

"I know, I don't think he has either," Matt said echoing his thoughts. "Source says that it was almost like he wanted to be seen. Something feels wrong," Matt admitted.

"Should we leave here?" Jake asked, suddenly worried for Lexi's safety.

"Not until we know what we're dealing with. Be ready to go just in case. Stay in touch." The cell went dead in Jake's hands. He cracked it in two and added it to the bag of stuff they needed to carry inside the camper.

He looked to Lexi who was wrapping her arms around herself, the wind having kicked up in the last little bit. Jake looked out over the choppy waters of the Atlantic, seeing the bright flash of lightning far in the horizon.

She deposited the cell phone he had given her to call Laurel back in the bag.

"How was she?" Jake asked.

"She didn't answer." Lexi shrugged.

Jake contemplated that. It wasn't unheard of. They could call again in a few minutes. "Well, right now we gotta get this stuff inside. It's getting ready to storm. It looks like it might be rough," he said as he glanced up at the dark clouds quickly rolling in. Summer storms on the Outer Banks could be violent and devastating. They didn't call them barrier islands for nothing.

Tiny islands like these that dotted the coastline of the Outer Banks were the only protection against the stormy seas, especially during hurricane season.

Lexi knelt down and started gathering everything together. The wind was picking up and blowing everything about. She suddenly remembered the blanket on the other side of the camper. She had left it there when Jake came and got her for their picnic.

Jake called out to her as she turned to go get the blanket. "Come on, Lexi. We gotta go." He yelled. The urgency in his voice had Lexi moving faster than what the sand would allow.

Jake had already packed everything in a hurry. It was starting to shape up into a nasty thunderstorm. They had to get off the beach. It was far too dangerous. These storms often kicked up waterspouts and deadly lightning. In addition, if the tides got too high, it would swamp the camper and they'd be sand-barred until help came. He got in the driver's seat as Lexi sat down beside him. He drove the camper slowly over the rutted path, steering towards the cabins he knew to be two clicks north of where they were now.

He pulled up in behind the dunes, surveying the area before getting out. The cabins were part of the island's life-saving station, the buildings situated far back from the beach. The hexagon shaped cabins built on high stilts were going to be their only hope for weathering this storm.

Jake knew they were often unlocked because practically no one knew about the island's existence in the first place. He knew the other side of the island sometimes had a lot of fishermen trying their luck off the waters of the inlet, but those were mostly day-trippers from Ocracoke Island. People rarely came to this side of the island and he was now very glad of that fact.

The waters of the Atlantic in this region were treacherous and ships would often wreck right off the coast. Back in the old days when the life-saving station was the only thing they could think of to keep ships from crashing into the coastline, the men who worked the station would monitor the shores for signs of distressed vessels and would swim out and bring any survivors to safety. The cabins they were headed for were part of that station. Then some years later, when lighthouses were built up and down the North Carolina coast, the life-saving station had been phased out much like the town had later on that century.

They got out quickly and Lexi grabbed up the bag of stuff from their beach picnic and her duffle from the back. Jake grabbed his bag and some of his gear and met Lexi in front of the camper. The skies opened up then and the rain pelted at them, the large drops making splotches in the sand. They finally reached the steps up to the cabin. They took them two at a time and dropped everything at the top right before the door to the cabin Jake was going to try. They were drenched from head to toe from the sudden deluge.

Lexi sputtered and wiped ineffectively at her face, trying unsuccessfully to wipe some of the water from her cheeks. She looked to Jake who was drenched as well, but he seemed completely unfazed by it. She supposed it had something to do with his work before. He was probably used to the elements. He fiddled with the lock on the door and finally eased it open. It was slightly stuffy inside from being enclosed in the heat of the day, but not completely miserable and at least in here they could stay dry.

Jake crossed the room and opened the windows slightly to air the place out. The cabins were very rustic and just basically functional. There were two bunk beds on opposite walls of the main part of the cabin. It went into an L-shape beyond the beds and contained a kitchen equipped with propane gas, a solid oak table and eight chairs around it.

Lexi sneezed delicately as the dust was stirred up while Jake went around and flipped the furniture covers off everything and stacking them neatly in the back corner.

"Bless you." Jake said automatically, looking up at her finally since they had gotten inside safely. "You okay?" He said, his face a mask of light concern as he lit the propane lantern he had carried with him from the camper. It cast a soft pale yellow glow about the room, the shadows cast upon the walls in mysterious dancing ghosts.

"Yeah, just allergies," she explained, smiling softly at him. It was funny the little thing her heart did when he said bless you. Silly really that she would be all giddy over something as mundane as that, but it thrilled her nonetheless. It was always the simple things that struck her where Jake was concerned. Sure, the romantic gestures like proposing on one knee on the beach and slow dancing with her to a song that inspired him; she was pretty sure she fairly melted on both those occasions but it astounded her that the simplest things could give her such joy. For the first time in a week, Lexi suddenly felt lighthearted.

He stood back and surveyed the cabin. "Well it'll do. We can hole up here for the night and hope like hell the camper is still standing in the morning." His face was doubtful as he looked out the window, the darkness punctuated every few seconds by a nearly blinding flash of lightning. He didn't mind the storm; his concern was for Lexi and it honestly would suck if his camper got washed out to sea. He didn't think that would happen but it was highly probable that it would be half buried in the sand in the morning. He turned back around to face Lexi, thinking he would just figure it all out tomorrow.

She was going around the room, exploring the new territory, her hands alighting on an object now and then as if she was somehow memorizing it for later. He stood back and silently observed her. It wasn't very often that he got to just stand and watch her without him catching her. His breath hitched in his chest, the air just not quite coming as it should.

She was at the table now, her back facing him. He swallowed thickly as if seeing her for the first time. Her shorts, which had been loose at the beach, were now clinging to her in all the right places. His eyes traced the curve of her hips, down over her backside and down her long legs, the slickness of the rain glistening on her pale skin in the glowing light cast by the lantern. He followed the lines in her body all the way back up over her back. She was wearing a white tank top and nothing else and he suddenly knew when she turned around, the fabric would be sticking to her and her nipples would be plainly outlined. He felt himself grow hard and he wondered briefly if he was always going to feel this way about her physically. He was never sated it seemed. He pretty much figured he would spend the rest of their lives making love to her every day.

Right now he wanted nothing more than to walk up behind her and pull her against him and kiss the back of her neck and nip the flesh there, knowing the response it would likely bring. They were still trying to be careful of the physical side of their relationship, constantly assuring that Lexi would not take any steps backwards in her progress. He moved then, busying himself with finding something for them to dry off on. He dug in his duffle bag and came up with two towels. He silently walked it over to her.

Lexi had been thinking about what might have happened in the cabins before. She turned when Jake appeared in the corner of her eye. She smiled as he handed her the towel, relieved that she would finally be able to wring out the sopping mess that was her hair.

She moved to do just that and almost missed the look that Jake was sending her as he watched her. It reminded her so much of when they had first met; his stolen glances when he thought she wasn't looking.

Just that one look hit Lexi like a freight train, right in the center of her chest and simultaneously felt a tiny chill as her muscles shuddered a bit. Her eyes caught his and the intensity of his gaze made her gasp a little. In that one moment, it reminded her all over again of the first time he had kissed her, the first time he had made love to her, the first time they had been able to intimate after the assault, the first time he had told her he loved her. All their firsts were contained in the gaze he was now bestowing upon her, equal parts desire and love.

Making a sudden decision, Lexi placed the towel on the table and crossed the distance between them, standing on her tip-toes, winding her arms up around his neck and placing her lips on his, her body pressed into him, molding herself to his hard form.

Jake took a deep breath as Lexi took the initiative. For the first time since the attack, she seemed like her old self. He held his breath a bit until her lips met his. Though they'd made love the night before, it hadn't been like this. Not with this urgency, this passion. This unbridled desire she was displaying, the urgency of her kiss made him stumble a bit and he pulled her with him until they were leaning against the table, his backside pressing firmly against the sturdy wood of the table.

He skimmed his fingers up her arms, tentatively at first, just ghosting over the surface. He felt her tongue probing at the seam of his lips, teasing them open. He opened his mouth willingly and gave himself over to the kiss, letting her tongue lap at his. She pulled away slightly to nip lightly at his bottom lip.

He gasped and was nearly breathless with the insistence conveyed by Lexi in every touch and every kiss. He pulled back to look at her, breaking the kiss and he heard her whimper.

"Lexi." It was a breath, the air escaping from his lungs, having been held in too long. He looked into her eyes and where he expected to see that tiny niggling piece of uncertainty laced with absolute trust, all traces of doubt were gone. Instead there was only trust and a burning need reflected back in her eyes. Her mouth was slightly parted, her breathing a little ragged in that way he knows she gets when she is finally ready.

"Jake, please just let me." She insisted as she tried to tell him with her body what her words just could not communicate. She brought her lips to his again, teasing him slightly, pulling back and meeting his lips in a teasing rhythm, before finally reaching up and gripping his shirt in her fists, pulling him against her. She wanted him and she wanted him now.

Suddenly she was tired of tip-toeing around her anxiety. She was tired of being a slave to the panic and the fear. Even if it was only for tonight, she just wanted to feel everything with reckless wonder.

Jake looked at her, her eyes half-lidded with smoldering desire. He knew exactly what she was saying. He took a deep breath as her lips began flirting with his again in a teasing kiss. He wanted so much to flip them around and bend her backwards over the table and have his way with her. He pulled back once more.

"You're sure?" He asked her. He had to be absolutely certain before they gave themselves completely over. Jake would rather die himself than to hurt her for an instant.

Instead of answering him, Lexi un-fisted her hands from his shirt and reached for his own which had stilled on either hip. She needed him to touch her like he used to. Like he wanted to memorize every curve and valley; like he would never be able to commit every inch of her to his memory. She pulled his hands up to her breasts and pushed them against his palms.

"Take me here." Her words fell on his ears as if she had whispered the desire of his heart; to take her as he wished, against the table.

He looked at her in wonder, whipped her tiny shorts from her body, pushed her panties aside and did just as she asked. While the wind and rain howled outside, they made their own quieter storm inside. Two bodies, one rhythm, riding out the night together.

When they finally pulled themselves up from the table a considerable amount of time later, Lexi sat up suddenly, listening keenly for a minute. The only sound in the cabin besides the storm was the sound of their breath trying to return to normal, but then she heard a faint ringing. She was confused and then she remembered calling Laurel.

Jake sat up suddenly and looked at her. "Lex, didn't you turn the phone back off?" He asked her as he moved to find the device, stumbling over the chair in the process.

"Oh no, I think I forgot!" She watched as he reached down into the bag for the phone.

Pulling it out and glancing at the display, dread settled over him as he recognized the number. It was Lincoln. As he flipped the phone open to answer it he had two simultaneous thoughts. Why the hell was Matt calling them? The other was that they needed to get the hell off this island and fast.

Chapter 23

"What the hell is goin' on?" He knew without asking that something had to have happened. He held the phone awkwardly against his ear as he grabbed a pair of shorts from his duffle and slipped them on.

"Jake, it's Matt," Lincoln' voice came across the line. Jake had thought it was him but with the strange circumstances, he had wanted to be sure before he identified himself before he gave away his name. He suddenly noted the fact that Lincoln used his given name instead of his surname; this was personal. That couldn't be a good thing.

Jake felt the dread pooling in his stomach and sat up ramrod straight, reaching for his pack of cigarettes, lighting one quickly and taking a quick drag. He sat beside Lexi, who had found one of his shirts and buttoned up the middle three buttons. She made a sight sitting there in his shirt, especially with the knowledge of what he had just done to her. She sat down on one of the chairs at the table. She was watching him a mixture of guilt and terror. He sat down on the chair beside her and reached over and squeezed her knee, hoping that would be reassurance enough until he got off the phone.

"Talk," Jake clipped out.

Jake heard Lincoln take a deep breath on the other end of the line. "Laurel and Thad got here an hour ago. They left their safe house this morning after getting a tip that Thomas was in the area. Now, that don't make any goddamn sense because, as you know, someone saw Thomas in downtown Atlanta this morning as well. There's no way he could have been in upstate New York and Atlanta at the same damn time." He finished.

Lexi was mouthing "Is Laurel okay?" He quickly nodded to her and watched as her posture visibly relaxed in relief.

"He's got a decoy somewhere," Jake concluded. "Son of a bitch," Jake bit out. If he was going to that much trouble, it likely meant that he was getting ready to make a move.

"So what's the plan? We got to get the girls someplace safe," Jake looked to Lexi. He didn't want to break her confidence but he really felt like Matt should know what happened at the beach house that night. He searched her eyes. She knew what he was asking her without him asking. They had learned the extreme power of nonverbal communication since that night.

He could see the quiet resignation in her eyes, along with a fierce determination. She looked so damned vulnerable sitting there, he pulled her into his lap, extinguishing his cigarette on the table. Right now, Lexi was the only drug he needed. Holding her in his arms was all he needed to feel like the world might be an okay place to be, so long as she was in it with him.

"Listen, Matt, I gotta tell you something important." Jake paused for a moment before spilling everything to Lincoln, looking to Lexi one last time. Her face was passive and she nodded at him.

Lexi wound her arms tighter around Jake's neck, needing to feel him close. In his arms, she felt safe.

"I'm listening'." Matt replied. Jake could hear the concern in his voice.

"Thomas did a little bit more than just 'rough her up'." It actually hurt Jake to say the words. Telling it was almost as bad as having seen the immediate aftermath. If he was having this strong of a response, he couldn't even imagine how Lexi felt. He could feel her breath warm against his neck. But she wasn't crying and Jake thought that was somethin', maybe even progress.

"Son of a bitch. Did he rape her?" Matt bit out the last two words, feeling like poison on his tongue.

"No, but he tried." Jake felt the rage building in him again as the image of that bastard lying on top of Lexi filled his brain. "I should have killed him when I had the chance. I can't stand that he touched her. If he had done that-" Jake seethed, not even able to finish his sentence.

Lincoln was very quiet on the other end. Too quiet. "What are you thinking?" Jake asked him. He was usually contemplative, but on the phone he was most times succinct.

"You love her, don't you?" Matt said quietly.

Of all the things he had expected Lincoln to say, that was definitely not one of them. Jake thought of all the ways he could answer that question but the only route that seemed true to his nature was to admit it. Sure, he was surprised that he was so transparent, but he supposed Lincoln knew him better than anyone else.

"Yeah I do. I love her." Jake said quietly, looking to Lexi as he did. Her head had snapped up in surprise.

"It's okay, Lexi. Matt will understand," Jake reassured her.

Jake heard Lincoln let out a breath on the other end of the line and something that sounded suspiciously like a chuckle. He chose to ignore it.

"So what's the plan? I gotta tell ya, I feel pretty sure my camper is sand-barred. Probably the same with the skiff," Jake blew out a little puff of air. "I'm pretty much fucked unless you have a helicopter I don't know about." Jake knew he had connections with the Marshals office but this wasn't government business just yet. It would be when people knew about Thomas and his shady business dealings and murderous intent.

Jake had always felt strongly if Thomas was removed from the face of the earth, at least eight inner city drug and prostitution rings would shatter.

Matt chuckled low. "No, but where's your boat?" Matt said the words carefully, hoping he wasn't about to get his ass chewed for it. Jake was a little particular about a couple of things in his life. One was his boat and the other was his motorcycle. And let's not forget his crossbow. He never used the thing but the way he was always cleaning it, Matt wasn't sure where he stood if Jake was supposed to choose between his friend and the weapon.

"She's parked in the marina at in the village. Extra set of keys, starboard side, taped to the inside of the storage cabinet. How long do you think it'll be before you get here?" Jake glanced about the cabin. With as far away as Matt was, he estimated it would be noon the next day before he could get there. It wasn't like they had any choice though. Jake sighed in resignation. He wasn't used to having to sit and wait like this but he figured another half a day wasn't going to hurt anything. It really wasn't like anyone knew where they were.

"Well it might be helpful to know where ya are if I'm expected to come and get ya," Matt quipped.

"Smartass," Jake muttered then rattled off the coordinates.

"Jackson?" Matt stopped him from hanging up.

"Yeah?" Jake had never known the man to linger at the end of a phone conversation.

"Don't let her out of your sight." Matt said seriously.

"Fat fuckin' chance of that." Jake added before hanging up.

He let out the breath he had been holding since the beginning of the conversation.

Lexi pulled back to look at Jake, their faces nearly even with her perched on his lap, their towels bunched between them. "We have to leave? What happened?" Lexi asked.

Jake took a deep breath. "Matt's pretty sure Thomas is getting ready to make a move. A dangerous one." He filled her in on the details, Lexi taking it in. It was refreshing to be able to talk to her about all this. Given her background with Matt, he didn't have to stop to explain certain terms to her.

"So Matt is going to come and get us?" Lexi asked, thinking that it was going to be all kinds of weird being with Jake around her boss. "In your boat?" Lexi looked at him puzzled. "Just how good of friends are you?" Lexi eyed him suspiciously. Something didn't add up; she knew how closed off Jake could be, but here he was letting Matt drive his boat.

Jake chuckled low. "Okay, so I might know him better than I let on." Jake admitted. "Let's just put it this way. I'm Carl's godfather." Jake looked at her, smirking as he watched her jaw drop open.

"No way!" Lexi actually hated that phrase, it was so overused but she figured it fit here better than anywhere else.

Jake actually laughed at Lexi Green completely caught unawares. "Why? What's so surprisin' about that? I've known Matt forever. He and Vivian and I grew up together. I was at the hospital when Carl was born. We've lost touch here recently in social circles. Though God knows he's tried to get me over there," Jake had evaded more invitations this past year than he could count. They were a very social couple, Matt and Vivian, and always wanted to unite everyone.

But after everything with Maria, Jake had withdrawn himself from lots of society and that included cook-outs and kids birthday parties. Dropping by on a Sunday before football with a big present in tow; that was more his style of god-parenting and he knew Vivian and Matt were okay with that.

Jake's line of thought reminded him of Matt mentioning someone that he wanted him to meet. He would always try to do it on the sly, but to Jake it always smacked of a blind date and he definitely wasn't about that. He looked to Lexi suddenly the thought hit him. It was almost too obvious.

"How is it that we haven't ever met?" Lexi breathed. She supposed she had been so busy here lately. Matt and Vivian had invited her over for various functions lately but she had been so busy with work and with figuring things out for Laurel, she had declined.

More than anything, Vivian had been pestering her to double date with her and Matt insisting that she had the perfect guy for her. When Lexi looked to Jake, waiting for his answer, she realized that he was looking at her with a surprised expression. As realization dawned on her face, her mouth formed a little 'o' and she gasped softly as her mind made the connection. Soon after, her heart stitched itself into the idea and she felt her breath catch.

"Did Matt ever try to fix you up with somebody?" Lexi was almost afraid to say it, afraid of what it might mean and thrilled at the same time.

Jake just nodded, unable to speak as the enormity of what they had just realized. He might have met her months ago if he had given in to just one of Matt's demands. He cursed himself for not being willing to take a chance.

Take a chance on her like he was now. All that wasted time was an infinity too long. He reached out to her then and pulled gently on the lapels of his shirt she wearing corralling her in his embrace, his arms completely encircling her and his hands splayed out over her back. He could feel her warmth, drawing every bit of it in. It was like it was meant for them to be together.

When he thought about how long he had fought it, how long he had told her that it would never work and under all the circumstances, it kind of seemed like the man upstairs might be trying to tell them something. It startled Jake that he thought in these veins at all; he thought he had stopped believing in a higher power a long time ago.

But something about Lexi and all the things that he felt about her; the way his heart clenched when she was near; being overcome with passion when he was with her, soaking in every word she spoke, every glance she sent his way, every touch, every kiss; Lexi had restored a faith in him that was so much further reaching than he had ever even suspected.

He felt like he had suddenly come full circle at the realization that this girl, this beautiful girl, was somehow his salvation, his shelter in a storm. She had saved him in every sense of the word. Now beyond anything, he had to save her right back. He was overcome in that moment. He drew in a ragged breath as he gasped a bit at the force of affection that he felt wash over him again and again and he sent up a prayer, whether anyone was listening or not. *"Thank you".*

She had molded herself completely to him, overcome by the realization of what had just transpired. Overcome by Jake pulling her into his arms, and now completely and utterly overcome with emotion at feeling this strong, beautiful man shudder in her arms. When she heard him whisper, *"thank you"* Lexi wasn't sure if she breathed for a full thirty seconds after.

Lexi pulled away from Jake and looked up at him. His face was still moist from the impulsive moment. "Jake, we were supposed to meet all along." She marveled.

Jake nodded. "Yeah, I got that." He rolled his eyes at her playfully even as he shook his head at the situation. Somehow without him knowing it, she had stowed away into his life and woven herself in to where it was hard to tell where he ended and she began.

He let her see him. Really see him. And what was more, she got him. She was the only girl who had ever gotten to know the real Jake Jackson and didn't turn tail and run. Whether they met now or they eventually gave in to Vivian's and Matt's repeated requests, it was always going to come down to this. Just this unbelievable love with a girl who had unbelievable faith and hope.

"Sounds like one of those books you were reading last night." Jake quipped, referring to the paperback romance she had resting on her lap last night. He tugged gently on her hair, playing with a long lock of it, now drying from the downpour.

"Don't do that," Lexi admonished him with a soft smile and a playful nudge.

"Do what?" But he knew. It's what he always did. Deflect a serious moment with humor. Another Jackson family trait, he mused.

"*You know*. Don't joke about this. God or fate or the universe or whatever; wants us to be together. Don't you think that's beautiful?"

Lexi looked at him with the most open expression of hope and belief in all that was good, his heart actually ached. He wanted to tell her yes, that he agreed with every word of it, but instead gruffly whispered. "I think you're beautiful."

Lexi blushed under his gaze. He had seen her naked and she had done the most daring and thrilling things with him, even right down to this night when he had taken her on the very kitchen table they were sitting at. But hearing him say that she was beautiful under the canopy of what they had just realized, it sent a warmth spreading all through her body in a whole new way.

"You told him you love me." Lexi breathed, referring to his candid conversation with Matt. Her face was awash with admiration.

"Don't see any sense in keeping it from anybody." Jake shrugged. "People are gonna know soon anyway, right?" He looked at the puzzled expression on her face. "Because you're marrying me?" Jake tapped on her forehead for effect, the teasing glint back in his eyes.

Lexi laughed. "Oh yeah that." She teased back, unable to help herself and he pretended to be offended.

She looked at him then, taking in the sight of him. The rest of the entire world faded to grey and she just knew that she wanted him on top of her, inside of her. She reached out and skimmed her fingers up over his arm, his biceps tightening under her feather-like touch.

Jake saw the change in her expression. He saw the passion there but there was just that hint of something else there; that something that looked like doubt. Jake stopped her hand on his arm. "What's wrong," He gently prodded.

"I just want you to replace every single bad memory with a good one," She said looking into his eyes, her blue-green ones slightly watery in the conviction of her request.

Jake nodded. He knew what she meant. "We can do that," he said. "We have a whole life time to do it." He smirked at her then.

"No, I mean now, Jake," She said as she shook his hand off and moved her hand down to the waistband of the shorts and skimmed lower to the opening of his shorts, the loose fabric giving her hand ease of access. She gripped him then and pulled her hand upwards, watching for his reaction.

Jake watched Lexi, her eyes meeting his as they always did these days and his own eyes narrowed as he saw the unmistakable desire, black bleeding into blue-green. As she reached for him and took his hardening length into her hand, he drew in a sharp breath.

"Now?" he was mesmerized by the look in her eyes.

"Yes, now, make love to me now." Lexi breathed, running her tongue lightly over her bottom lip.

Jake slanted his head over hers and brought his lips to hers, ever so slightly, just the barest hint of a kiss, so feather light that his heart felt the same.

He stood up then, answering her question the only way he knew how. He bent down to scoop her into his arms and carried her over to the bed, laying her gently back and as the night faded into the soft grey-yellow light of morning, Jake made love to Lexi over and over again, sometimes softly and tenderly, other times rough and tangled in each other's arms. One factor remained a constant; their love for one another and the knowledge that somewhere up there, a higher power than themselves knew what was going on and for this moment in infinity, they had to believe that everything was going to be okay.

Chapter 24

Matt glanced over at Jake again. They had been driving for the past hour after docking the boat at Shores Marina in Atlantic, North Carolina. They were headed inland now to the new safe house in a very small town, barely even a dot on the map, about an hour southeast of Raleigh. Lexi had fallen asleep in the back seat almost as soon as they had gotten in the car. The ocean had been pretty choppy and the sound hadn't been much better. Lexi had been sick from the time they got on the boat until right before they got in the car. She never threw up but she looked so miserable, both men had felt sorry for her.

Jake looked at Matt, noticing his calculating gaze. "What?" Jake asked, never really having seen the exact expression on Matt's face before.

"So did you figure it out yet?" Matt asked him, unable to hide the smile on his face.

Jake turned to look at Matt and leveled his gaze at him. "You mean that you and Vivian had been trying' to play matchmaker?"

Jake chuckled a little. "Yeah we figured it out last night. Sorry I was so stubborn. Why didn't you say anything' before? You knew we were gonna be alone all this time." Jake shook his head at Matt who was laughing now.

"I was afraid if I said anything, you'd back out of the whole thing. I figured fate knew better n' me and Vivian ever did. She's gonna be happy she was right." Matt replied. His face softened then. "She okay?" He gestured with a nod of his head towards the back seat.

Jake's eyes narrowed then and he lowered his voice, "It was rough there for a while, but she is doing a lot better now." Jake glanced in the backseat. She was still sleeping, her arm thrown up over her head. He had been worried about her on the boat. She hadn't looked good at all, but then she seemed pretty okay after they got back on dry land.

The silence in the car was pierced by a phone ringing. Matt reached on the seat between him and Jake glanced at the display before answering it. "Thad." He informed his friend.

"Lincoln." Matt said into the phone.

"Hey Matt, it's Thad. I just got a video call from headquarters. They think they might have found Garner. We've been told to stand by until further notice." Thad rushed it all out. He knew they could only stay on the phone for a very short period of time.

"Thanks Lee, that's good news but I'll believe it when I see it I guess. Everything okay there?" He asked, inquiring about Laurel.

"Yeah, we're good. See you when you get here." Thad hung up and Matt placed the phone back on the seat.

"They found Garner. They'll be making their move in the next hour." Matt let out a long breath. "God, I hope this is finally about over." He rubbed one hand over his face.

"You're telling me. Course when all this is over, we have a wedding to plan." He looked at Matt sideways, gauging his response.

Matt looked at Jake, the realization slowly dawning on him. "You're getting married?!" Matt shouted excitedly and then caught himself.

"Yes, big mouth," Jake muttered as he looked in the backseat. Too late, Lexi was stirring.

"Didn't have you pegged to be a hopeless romantic, boss." Lexi said groggily as she sat up and rubbed her eyes, the sleep heavy in them.

"Welcome back to the land of the living, Green," Matt said good naturedly. "So what's this I hear about you getting hitched?" Matt never had been one to beat around the bush, she thought.

She smiled at him in the rearview. "It's true, he got down on one knee right out on the beach and everything." Lexi looked to Jake, hoping she had not overstepped, but he had turned around to look at her and the only thing she could see in his expression was love.

Matt leaned over and playfully bumped his shoulder against Jake's. Lexi thought it was cute really. Had she ever seen them interact before, she would have been able to immediately tell that these two shared a lot of history. "You got game, bro." Matt teased.

"Nah, she just hasn't figured out what she's gotten herself into yet." Jake smirked at Lexi then.

"Tell me about it." Lexi rolled her eyes mockingly.

"Whew, wait until Vivian hears about all this. She's gonna be thrilled. Don't be surprised if she wants to throw you both an engagement party." Matt laughed then.

For the last 10 minutes they had been driving into a heavily wooded area and the road had gotten rougher and rougher as they bumped along in Matt's black SUV. Now as they turned the corner, Matt turned down a dirt road, barely perceptible from the road. They continued on this road until they reached a clearing where there was a two story log cabin; very modern looking but still seeming quite at home here deep in the forest.

They pulled up in front of the cabin and they all got out and stretched for a bit. The sun was starting to set now, the orange ball low on the horizon.

The front door to the log cabin opened and Laurel came running out, taking the steps down to the yard two at a time.

"Lexi!" Laurel was smiling from ear to ear.

Lexi rushed forward, falling into her sister's arms. They were wrapped up in each other's embrace and he didn't know about Matt, but Jake didn't understand one word of what they were saying. They were both laughing and crying at the same time and he wasn't even sure the unintelligible garbles coming from the two women were actually English.

Thad stepped onto the porch, his hands stuffed in his pockets, looking down at the two girls, clearly happy to see each other.

"I missed you so much Laurel." Lexi said, sighing and drying her tears. Suddenly remembering, she let go of Laurel searching for Jake. He was standing off to the side, watching her. "Come here, Jake." She held out her hand and he walked over to her and took her hand in his.

"Laurel, you remember Jake." Lexi looked back and forth between the two of them.

"Yes, I'm sorry I was such a mess when we met the first time." Laurel extended her hand and Jake dutifully shook it.

"It's no problem. You look much better," Jake remarked.

"Yeah, I'm doing much better, thank you. I owe it all to Melinda and Thad." Laurel turned to find Thad watching her from across the way, smiling at her. She smiled back.

"Let's go in the house and have this reunion without the worry of being spotted by someone." Matt suggested and they all agreed.

Matt and Jake grabbed their bags and they all headed inside the house, Lexi and Laurel desperately clinging to one another again.

They walked into the cabin. It was a very modern home and was contemporary yet functional; lots of chunky overstuffed furniture situated around a fireplace, but no television, Lexi noted. The kitchen was attached from there and had a large eat-in café style maple table with matching ladder-back chairs. A winding staircase spiraled up into the rafters, leading to the bedrooms she supposed and she wondered briefly how long they were going to have to stay here.

Lexi and Jake took a seat on the love seat while Laurel, Thad and Matt sat on the sofa across from them.

"Laurel, Jake asked me to marry him. And I said yes." Lexi said without preamble then turned, looking in wonder at Jake. She could hardly believe that she was going to get to spend the rest of her life with this beautiful man.

Laurel actually squealed before running over and pulling her sister into her arms. "I'm so happy for you Lexi." She looked over Lexi's shoulder to Jake.

As Lexi pulled back away, Laurel stepped in front of Jake and bent down and kissed him on the cheek. "Welcome to the family. I'd tell you to treat her right but I can see that you already do that."

Jake swallowed hard then. No one had ever been this nice to him, at least not without there being something in it for them. "Thank you, Laurel." He nodded at her.

"Okay time to get down to business," Matt informed the lot of them.

They all sat down in the main living area, spread out over three different sofas in the room. "Any more word on Garner?" He directed his question at Thad, but he just shook his head.

As if on cue, Matt's phone rang then but he didn't recognize the number. He motioned for the others to be absolutely silent. "Lincoln."

Matt breathed a sigh of relief when he heard it was only Gibbs on the other line. "What's up?"

"I'm not sure if it's true, but I just got from a very reliable source that Garner is not in New York. He was seen in Atlanta this morning and they think they have his location pinpointed." The other man said. "They are making their move very soon."

"I hope we can apprehend him before it comes to that," Matt replied.

"Tell Jackson, he's off the hook. The girl too." Gibbs added.

Matt breathed a huge sigh of relief. "They finally figured out they had nothing to do with those two cops getting shot?" He looked to Jake and Lexi and nodded at them.

Gibbs let out a derisive snort. "They knew all along the bastards. They were just trying to draw Garner out. Instead it's made him do the goddamned opposite. I pray they get that S.W.A.T. team in there and apprehend the asshole. They don't catch him this time, they may miss their chance. Word is he's come unhinged in the last two weeks since his wife disappeared."

"Makes sense to me. That would be a trigger event for him. It's not surprising he spiraled out of control and now, hopefully, he'll slip up and get caught," Matt mused.

"I got a call coming in, Matt. I'll call you back if anything changes." Gibbs said and then the line went dead.

Matt closed the phone and laid it back down. He turned to face the group. "S.W.A.T. is a go in the next 15 minutes or so. They got him." Matt let out a puff of air and looked to Jake.

Jake nodded thoughtfully. Something was bugging him but he couldn't put a finger on it. It seemed too easy, a guy like Garner with all his resources and it was almost like he had led him there on purpose and was now thumbing his nose at them. He almost said as much to Matt and Thad then, but Matt's phone rang again.

"Lincoln," Matt bit out, a little impatient. This situation was making him nervous and he usually didn't get nervous.

"Matt, bad news," Gibbs was breathing heavy and his voice was hoarse. "The whole fucking place just blew up. S.W.A.T. was getting ready to go in and the sky lit up like fourth of July. No one has seen Garner. They saw him leaving the building right before the explosion happened."

Matt hung his head and tried hard to not throw up. "How many casualties?" Matt said and right now he just wasn't able to meet anyone's gaze. Jake and Thad had gotten up and walked over to where he was sitting. "Give me the coordinates and I'm on my way."

"Too many to count, right now man. We had thirty guys ready to go in and we can only account for 11 of them. Karen's one of the missing," Gibbs's voice broke on the admission.

"I'm sorry brother. I'm sure she's okay." The words sounded hollow even to Matt.

He heard Gibbs draw a ragged breath on the other end. "Boss man says you gotta stay there now. Too risky." Gibbs hated to tell him this. He knew he wasn't going to like it. "We'll have someone call Vivian and under the circumstances, we'll send a car over."

Fear laced with guilt burned its way down into his stomach. "Son of a bitch. Like hell I'm stayin' here. That's my wife and kids." Matt got up and began to pace the floors of the cabin.

"Lincoln, you know if you leave there now goin' after them, you're just gonna draw attention where it isn't needed." Matt knew Gibbs was speaking the truth. Everything he said made sense, he knew it better than anybody, but it didn't make it suck any less.

Matt sighed deeply. "Just be sure they're safe, Gibbs."

"You have my word." Gibbs assured him.

"Keep us posted." Matt said. "And Gibbs?" Matt stopped him from hanging up.

"Yeah?" Gibbs muttered.

"Karen will be okay. She's a fighter. You know that," Matt reminded him gently.

"I know, you're right. Talk to you soon Matt." There was a click on the line and then he was gone.

Matt turned from where he had been pacing and faced the others, dreading what he was about to have to tell them. "The building where Thomas was just exploded. He got away before it went up." Matt took in their surprised expressions.

Lexi and Laurel both gasped. Lexi brought her hands up to her mouth. "Was anyone hurt? Karen?" She had heard Matt's voice when he mentioned Gibbs's wife.

Matt shook his head. "She's MIA right now. They'll find her." Matt wasn't sure who he was trying to convince at the moment.

Matt sat back down and the others followed suit, none of them really sure what else to do at this point.

Jake checked the locks on all the doors before rejoining the others in the living room. He knew the whole thing had been too good to be true. Sometimes he hated being right all the time. He sat back down next to Lexi and took her shaking hands between his, squeezing gently. "I know a lot of people on S.W.A.T." She looked up at Jake then. "I guess we all probably do."

"How the fuck did all this turn into such a heaping pile of shit?" Jake asked Matt.

"I have no clue, brother. They just need to fix this and fast." Matt was tempted to start pacing again but he knew it wouldn't do any good. He had to trust that Gibbs would get the right guys on the job and everything would be okay.

Now that Thomas was missing again, he didn't know what to think. He wished he had a magic wand to make all this disappear. It was times like this when he really questioned his career choice. Then again, he wouldn't have met Lexi. There was no use going over all the what-ifs in his mind now. The only thing they could do now was sit and wait.

Laurel stood up then and Thad did too. "I'm gonna go upstairs and lie down for a bit," Laurel said softly.

Lexi nodded to her sister. "We'll catch up more later." Lexi smiled at her as she turned to leave the room. Lexi couldn't miss the way Thad placed his hand on the small of Laurel's back directing her out of the room.

Jake felt around his pants pockets and then patting his shirt for his pack of cigarettes and a lighter, forgetting that he didn't have any with him.

Matt reached into his jacket and pulled out a pack of Marlboro Lights. Jake looked at him in surprise. "You still carry a pack?" Jake muttered, taking the pack from him.

"Yeah, man, you know I hate hearing you whine about not having a smoke." Matt teased. Matt had been carrying a pack around just for Jake for as long as he could remember. Matt had never smoked a day in his life but he knew all too well what could happen when Jake was having a nic-fit.

Jake took out a cigarette and stuck it between his teeth, fishing for a lighter. Finally finding one, he lit it and drew deeply, pulling the smoke into his mouth and the back of his throat, feeling the burn. As he sucked the smoke into his lungs, he could almost feel the tension slipping from his shoulders. He looked to Lexi who was staring at him intently, an amused expression on her face.

"You know they cause cancer right?" Lexi teased.

"Yeah, yeah, they're bad for me. I get it." He waved her off, instead taking another drag.

"You should probably quit before we get married." Lexi was smiling sweetly at him. Though she was beautiful, it made him uneasy. He had a feeling he wasn't going to like where this conversation was headed.

"Why?" He was taking the bait, knew he shouldn't but he did anyway.

Matt was watching all this with a slightly amused expression, looking back and forth between the two of them.

"Well for one thing, it will make your swimmers slow." Lexi looked at him pointedly, laughing at the expression on his face.

Jake sputtered, nearly sucking the ash down his throat. "What the hell, Lexi?" He looked to Matt but he was just laughing, a deep silent chuckle. Jake's face softened then. He looked at Lexi, his expression a mixture of exasperation and affection.

"It's true, ya know. And if we're having a houseful, then you might want to think about that." Lexi couldn't keep the teasing out of her voice. She really did want him to quit though. The nurse in her couldn't just let him smoke and not say something, even though damn him he looked hot as hell sitting there with a cigarette dangling between his fingers.

Jake eyed her thoughtfully and put the cigarette out in the ashtray on the coffee table in front of them. He turned to face her, well aware that Matt was watching the whole thing. He could almost hear him biting back a smart-mouthed remark.

"Shut up Lincoln. You might want to leave the room. I'm fixin' to kiss my girl." Jake murmured as he brought his lips to Lexi's in a soft, tender kiss, then pulling away. "Bossy thing, ain't ya?"

Lexi just laughed, looking up into his face. "Better get started now if I want my nagging housewife award by next year," she teased.

He ran his hand through her hair before finally releasing her. He looked at Matt who was grinning like a Cheshire cat.

"What?" Jake demanded to know.

"You're in so much trouble. I saw this coming from a mile away, but you've been blindsided. Yep, so much trouble." He looked so smug that Jake would have slapped him if he wasn't so sure he was absolutely right. He was in trouble, but it was the good kind. The Lexi Green kind. And he couldn't wait to make this little slice of trouble his in every sense of the word.

But first things first; they were going to get Garner, if he had to see to it personally. Then they could start their life together. For the first time in his life, Jake Jackson was looking forward to what came next.

Across the road, a pair of eyes were watching them, the scope on his gun serving the purpose perfectly. He only wished he could pull the trigger and off the lot of them, but those weren't his orders. He was there to create a distraction and get the girls out alive. Any other casualties were fine with the boss, but he was clear about taking the girls alive. Said he had plans or some shit.

Levi didn't care. This was a big fuckin' payday for him and it was about time something good happened to him. Plus as pretty as these girls were, maybe he'd have a little fun himself, he thought wickedly. He fingered the trigger of his rifle affectionately, caressing the gun and waited to make his move. It wouldn't be long now.

Chapter 25

It was decided with no other news coming through at the end of the evening, they would all just go to bed and pick things back up in the morning, hopefully with a better outlook and a much better plan. It wasn't very often that Jake wished for his old job back, a mercenary but he almost did now. Somehow it had seemed easier at times. Figure out what shit needed to be done, go in, do it and get out. No bureaucracy, no red tape, no following an endless revolving set of rules. Most of all, there hadn't ever been someone he loved more than life at stake before.

Jake sighed as he reached the landing at the top of the stairs. Lexi had already gone up an hour ago, pleading leftover seasickness.

Jake turned the doorknob of the room they had been given, trying to be as quiet as possible. If by some chance Lexi had fallen asleep, the last thing he wanted to do was wake her up. He eased the door open, wincing when he heard the telltale squeak of the hinges. He stopped just inside the room, allowing his eyes to adjust to the dark. The moon wasn't giving much in the way of light tonight. He had always liked nights like this, had always found it was the best kind of night to go on reconnaissance. The moonless night provided just the right amount of stealth needed to get the job done without being detected.

Jake reached for his gun at his side when the lamp beside the bed suddenly flicked on. He breathed a sigh of relief to realize that Lexi was the culprit.

"Shit, Lexi, you scared the hell out of me," Jake breathed as he approached the bed. She still looked a little pale, but much better than earlier.

""M sorry," she drawled sleepily, arching her back and stretching, her breasts straining against the fabric of her t-shirt.

He leaned down over the bed and pressed a kiss to her forehead. He stepped back to look at her, wondering at her beauty. He wondered if he would always feel this way. Like he had been punched in the gut whenever he looked at her. He wasn't sure if he ever wanted to feel any differently, but it sure made it damn hard to concentrate on regular life stuff.

"Didn't mean to wake you," Jake undressed quickly down to his boxers and slipped under the covers that she was holding open for him, smiling as she scooted closer to curl herself against him.

"It's okay. I wanted to wait up for you, but I couldn't hold my eyes open. Everything okay with Matt?" she yawned and God help him, Jake even found that sexy as hell.

"Well, not okay really but at least he didn't look like he wanted to kill somebody when I left him just now. He's all kinds of pissed that he can't go home to Vivian. Worried sick about her and the kids."

"Can you blame him?" Lexi asked him, cuddling closer to him in the bed. She couldn't imagine how she would feel if she were separated from Jake, let alone if they had children too.

"Nah." Jake breathed. He was silent for a moment and Lexi pulled away to look at him. His eyes had gone all serious.

"Thing is I can't imagine how I would feel if I couldn't get to you and I knew you were in danger. I think it'd make me crazy." Jake said gruffly, his voice strained and thick. "Anything ever happened to you, I'd-" Jake looked at Lexi helplessly. He had never needed anyone before. He had never been afraid of anything before. But he was afraid now. It scared the hell out of him how much he loved this woman. Thinking about her being in harm's way like when Thomas attacked her, made him sick at his stomach and enveloped him in bone-crushing sadness.

Lexi didn't let Jake finish his sentence. She sat up and brought her lips to his to silence him, bringing her hands up to cup either side of his face. She poured every bit of tenderness she held in her heart for this man into kissing him, her lips pressed to his as a tiny sob escaped her mouth. "I love you so much Jake Jackson." Lexi breathed as she pressed her forehead to his. "I'm right here and I'm not going anywhere."

Jake let out a ragged breath and put his arms around her and crushing her to him. "I love you too, Lexi. Makes me crazy sometimes how much I love you."

She looked up at him and he was looking down at her in awe and wound her arms around his neck, leaning back to look at him. "How did I ever get so lucky?" She beamed at him.

"I think I'm the lucky one." He snorted.

"How about we're both lucky?" she whispered then, her eyes dropping a little.

"Deal." Their whispered assurances to one another did little to calm his fears though. It was a long time before he was finally able to fall asleep, worrying about what danger might be lurking out beyond the safety of this house.

Levi waited. That's what he had done his whole life. Wait for his dad to finally leave his mom so they could be happy without him. Wait for puberty to hit so he could finally become the bad-ass he knew he was meant to be. Wait for everyone he went to school discount his intelligence so he could climb the ranks of the police department. Wait for all those high and mighty assholes drive past him in his cruiser going even one mile above the speed limit. Wait for that night he finally got Amy away from her bossy older sister Andrea. He smiled to himself at that one. That night had been well worth the wait. Their fling had been brief but he had scratched the itch that needed taken care of and moved on.

And now Levi was waiting again. For the house to go dark and to make his move. He already had his distraction planned, hoping to draw the idiots outside and leave him ample opportunity to go in and get the women out. He had waited his entire life for this night. If everything panned out like he hoped, a big payday was ahead plus he knew he'd become the boss's number one. Garner made a hell of an enemy but an even better ally. Levi had fought to get this close to him for the past several months, moving up in the ranks of their loose association in the various rings they traveled. Everything he had ever wanted in life hinged on this one night and Levi wasn't about to let anything fuck it up.

His partner would be there any minute to help facilitate the process. Randall was new and young and impressionable. Levi had spent the last six months grooming him for just this type of situation. He was smart and a quick thinker and what he lacked in confidence, he would gain tonight. Tonight his fortitude would be tested. It was make or break time. He heard three taps on the trunk of the black sedan he had stolen for the night. It had a large trunk perfect for concealing two unconscious women.

Levi exited the vehicle and met Randall at the back of the sedan, which was well hidden in the outcropping of trees he had parked it in. His cell phone buzzed in his pocket and he quickly retrieved it. "Walsh." He bit out roughly.

"It's me." The voice was harsh and immediately recognizable. Garner.

"Thought I was supposed to call you after I got them," He hissed into the earpiece.

"I call the fuckin' shots, you sniveling shit," Garner bit out. "I want to call you, I'll fuckin' call." Just like that, Garner's voice transitioned from rough to smooth as honey. "Wanted to make sure everything is going down as planned. That S.W.A.T. shit was too close for comfort."

"I assure you, everything is under control." Levi willed the words to be true.

"You trust the guy you got to help you?" Garner asked.

"Yeah, no worries there." Levi glanced at Randall who was dutifully watching the house.

"Any troubles with anything and you know what to do. But the girls come to me alive. Even Laurel's sister. I got a special kind of hell reserved for that little bitch and her redneck boyfriend." Garner's voice dropped menacingly on the last statement.

"Got it. Looks like it's go time, boss." Levi said, hoping to get off the phone.

"Call me when you have 'em." Garner bit out and then hung up.

Levi placed his phone back in his pocket and reached for his pistol, clicking the safety off. He nodded to Randall and they moved towards the house, crouching low to the ground as they reached the back door and heaved the package Randall had brought with him through the window, effectively setting off the alarm. They retreated to the bushes that lined the back of the property and waited. It wouldn't be long now.

☙ ☙ ☙ ☙ ☙ ☙ ☙ ☙ ☙ ☙ ☙

Jake heard the sound of shattering glass from somewhere in the house and was on his feet in an instant. He dressed hurriedly, glancing to Lexi who had sat up beside him. "Stay here." His voice was low. He pulled on his boots, tying them quickly.

Lexi had only heard his voice with this stern tone one other time and it was only on a subconscious level that she even remembered it. It had been when Thomas had left the beach house that night and he had gone after him. Lexi was silent as she dressed in a pair of yoga pants and t-shirt, slipping her shoes on as well. He motioned for her to follow him as he grabbed his gun off the nightstand, tucking it into his waistband and grabbing his hunting knife for good measure.

He reached behind him as he eased the door open, pulling Lexi closer behind him, whispering over his shoulder to stay close.

Lexi had grabbed her gun too just in case and held it at her side while Jake checked the hall. They were met with Thad, Laurel and Matt looking just as shell-shocked as they felt.

Matt took command. "Thad, you take Lexi and Laurel and hole up in the bedroom. Me and Jake are going go see what the hell is up. Thad called it in to the guys up top. I got a bad feeling about this."

"Garner?" Thad's eyes were wide but confident.

Matt deferred to Jake. "Seems like somethin' he'd do." Jake said carefully. He would be lying if he didn't admit to the fear that had inched its way into his brain and was seeping down his spine at the moment.

Lexi came out from behind him and joined Laurel, who looked positively terrified. "It's gonna be okay." Jake whispered in Laurel's direction, catching her eye.

Thad held out an arm for Laurel to grab onto and she clung to it. Lexi could tell she was barely keeping her emotions in check. She followed Laurel and Thad to the back bedroom, glancing over her shoulder at Jake. "Be careful, baby." She whispered.

Jake nodded at her, not wanting to speak. He walked away and joined Matt on the stairs. Jake nodded at Matt, "Let's go, brother."

They crept down the stairs and hovered at the bottom, listening for any signs of life.

Matt motioned his intent of directions and that they would meet back up after sweeping the house. Jake nodded at him and headed to the right, sweeping through the dining area and into the kitchen, every muscle in his body rigid with the adrenaline that coursed through his veins.

There was a package on the tiled floor of the kitchen, shards of glass surrounding the area. A note was attached to the top and Jake glanced around to make sure it wasn't a trap. It didn't look like a bomb, but he still kept his hands off it to inspect the message.

"*She is mine*." Was all it said.

It was chilling and Jake felt an icy jolt of fear surge through his body. Matt appeared in the doorway. Jake got up from where he was crouched on the floor, hearing the crunch of glass beneath his feet as he shifted his weight and moved toward the door as Matt had indicated.

They exited the house and scanned the perimeter. Matt heard a sound off to his right and they headed in that direction, staying in formation. The sound picked up again further out and closer to the tree line. They inched forward slowly. Jake glanced back to the house, feeling uneasy for some reason. They heard it again, a faint crunching sound, like footsteps. As they got closer to the tree line, the sound just disappeared and they heard nothing. Radio silence. Matt turned back to look at Jake and that's when they heard the unmistakable sound of a retreating car engine.

Jake dropped into a run and Matt followed after him. They rounded the front of the house just in time to see disappearing tail lights. Everything seemed to happen in dream sequence for Jake after that. He saw that the tires were slashed on all of their vehicles as he approached them. He looked back to the house and saw the front door standing wide open. He nearly collapsed at what that might mean, feeling the first tendrils of real fear inching their way along his spine.

They ran back into the house and the first thing that Jake noticed was Lexi's pistol laying in the entryway. Jake glanced up at the curse that came from the top of the stairs.

"The bastard got me. He has Lexi and Laurel." Thad held his hand to his head, blood trickling over his knuckles. He made his way down the stairs.

"What the hell?" Jake screamed. "Who?" The questions tumbled out of his mouth about as fast as the thoughts were tumbling out of his head, desperately trying to process what was happening.

"Levi Walsh. Guess he was the mole all along. Said he's been working for Garner on the side for months." Thad looked like he might throw up. "He's taking them to Garner. Lexi and Laurel."

In all his years of working with Thad, Jake had never seen him show any hint of fear. But he looked terrified now and if it was anything like Jake was feeling, he was in good company.

As the realization that Lexi was gone settled in, the fear unleashed a pit of cold acid that was buried so far within him, he felt if he moved a single step forward, the whole thing might tip over and burn him alive.

A bone crushing weight settled in where his heart thudded away inside his chest and he knew that it wouldn't lift until he got her back. But for the life of him, he couldn't remember what the hell he was supposed to do next. He supposed that this was where the phrase "paralyzed with fear" came from.

The fear edged off as it was replaced by an emotion that Jake was more familiar with: rage.

Matt caught his breath. "Did you get to call it in?" He looked to Thad, hopeful.

Thad just shook his head sadly. "Didn't have time, man. Sorry." He pulled his hand away from his head. "We gotta get movin'." He glanced from Matt to Jake, the latter of whom looked like he was about to come unglued.

"What the fuck you pansies standin' there for?"

The three men turned to the source of the voice belonged to none other than Jeb Jackson, standing in the doorway behind them.

🍒 🍒 🍒 🍒 🍒 🍒 🍒 🍒 🍒 🍒

Lexi could feel a pounding at the base of her skull, hammering really and she reached up to see if she could hold the pieces of her head together long enough to figure out what to do about it. She realized then that her hands were bound behind her back. Her eyes flew open instantly, adrenaline kicking her senses into high gear and she realized with a fresh stab of fear that she was also blindfolded.

She rolled a little to her left, meeting with a cold hard edge of a metallic surface. She felt another white hot poker of fear flash in her chest followed by acid gathering in the back of her throat as she realized they were in the trunk of a car. She took a deep steadying breath and rolled back to her right, meeting with a firm resistance.

"Lexi?" Laurel whispered.

"Laurel." Lexi breathed and instantly on hearing her sister's voice she felt the acid settle back into her stomach. The fear was still there, churning, but she felt at least some semblance better that Laurel was okay. They were alive; at least, they were alive *for now*.

Suddenly Lexi had a flood of memories rush at her. Levi coming to the door of the bedroom. He had lied, telling Thad that Special Forces sent him to retrieve them all. As soon as Thad had let him in, the weight visibly lifted from Thad's shoulders, Levi had turned on Thad, hitting him in the back of the head with the butt of his gun.

Another guy had come through the door after Levi and grabbed Laurel. Lexi had reached for her gun at the same time Levi reached her and clamped a cloth over her mouth and nose, the smell sickly sweet. She knew instantly what it was and she held her breath and watched helplessly as Laurel slipped to the floor under the grip of the guy helping Levi.

Lexi had the thought that he looked barely older than a kid as she finally had to succumb to her aching lungs. She made a final kicking attempt to free herself before she slipped into blissful darkness.

Now, Lexi wiggled her wrists experimentally, but they were tightly bound, the rope fibers biting into the tender flesh there. Still, she tried to work it loose. What was a little skin, when the rest of your body was in such grave danger?

"It's okay Laurel. They will find us. Thad and Jake will find us. Matt too." Lexi knew they were big promises and she hoped like hell they were going to be fulfilled.

Given the conversation that she and Jake had earlier in the evening, she could only imagine what he was feeling now. Suddenly the argument that they had all those weeks ago came to the forefront of her mind and she was haunted by her own words. "I know you look at me and see another dead girl's face." Lexi nearly choked on a sob. She regretted saying those words and the thousand other words that she hadn't. She worked at the rope on her wrists, flexing and extending as much as she could, now determined more than ever to prove that statement false. This couldn't be how things ended. She wouldn't let it be.

Chapter 26

Lexi listened carefully as she felt the car slowing and coming to a stop after driving over the bumpiest road she had ever been on. Of course that could have something to do with the fact they were riding inside the trunk, her and Laurel. Their captor had been driving for hours now and Lexi wasn't entirely sure that she hadn't fallen asleep during part of the ride out of sheer mental and physical exhaustion. The car came to a halt which was almost immediately followed by the sound of the car door opening up and someone's boots crunching on gravel, walking first to the passenger side of the car and then back to the trunk again. Lexi braced herself and nudged Laurel so she could do the same. The trunk popped open and Lexi and Laurel squinted at the flashlight being shone in their faces.

Two pairs of hands came at them, hauling them out of the trunk, one by one, and righting them on their feet, depositing them on the gravel driveway that led to what looked like a wide expansive beach, but from this angle you couldn't see any bodies of water.

Lexi almost fell but was able to regain her balance by leaning back a little. It was hard to maintain balance when one's hands were tied behind their back, she thought. She tried to look around to see how Laurel was holding up, which earned her a sharp jab of a gun in her ribs.

"Don't even fuckin' think about it, bitch." The voice said. She recognized it as Levi's.

"Levi, whatever he has promised you, it isn't worth it." Lexi tried to speak in a soothing tone as possible even though her voice was shaking. She addressed him by name, her formal training coming into play in her mind instantly.

Lexi felt a palm flattened on her back and shoving none too gently. "Don't you presume to know about what I need, *baby girl*," he sneered the last word. Lexi felt a shudder at realizing that at some point or another Levi had been listening in somehow. She also realized that she really didn't want to know when it was. Chills spread over her whole body at the thought of him listening in while she and Jake had sex. She had a second thought that actually made her sick at her stomach. She wondered if he hadn't really been watching them. Somehow that was an even worse thought.

They were led to something that looked like a dune buggy that seated four people. How perfect, Lexi thought wryly. This whole thing was starting to feel like a set-up. They had gone to the new safe house and almost immediately Garner's goons had arrived. Lexi didn't think for one second that any of this was coincidence.

They rode for what seemed like an eternity over the sand and craggy dunes and Lexi had to squeeze her eyes shut for most of the ride since she couldn't cover her face to keep out all the sand blowing at it. She and Levi were sitting in the front of the thing and Laurel and their other captor were sitting in the back. Lexi still hadn't been able to get a good look at him and so far he hadn't spoken a single word. Smart guy. Less likely anyone would be able to identify him later, provided they made it out of this alive and didn't end up at the bottom of the ocean with boulders tied to their ankles.

She shuddered at the thought and forced her thoughts on the situation presently at hand. Sometimes, Lexi hated her pragmatic mind in times like this.

They finally came to a stop outside a two story house positioned far back from the beach just like the houses on Hatteras. Thinking of that beach house reminded her of two things simultaneously, Jake and Thomas, and that thought just about was her undoing. She took deep calming breaths as memories threatened to overtake her.

They were herded to the door which opened upon approach and Thomas was standing in the doorway, a sickening smile on his face. "Well, well ladies, we meet again. Come here wifey." He motioned for her captor to release Laurel into his custody.

Laurel was shoved forward where Thomas received her roughly and since Levi was busy watching the exchange between Laurel and Thomas, she was able to glance over and see who had hoisted Laurel up out of the trunk. She was shocked to see it was Randall Evers, a guy from their hometown.

Laurel had gone to school with him and he had been in her grade even. "Randall?" Lexi looked at him hoping to spark some kind of familiarity with him. He might be their only hope of getting out of this thing alive. Thomas looked positively insane, his hair completely disheveled and his clothes dirty and in disarray. As Lexi was shoved into the entryway of the house, she could smell a strong odor of alcohol permeating the air around Thomas but his pupils were pinpoint and seemed unfocused. He was high as well, it seemed.

Randall would not even meet her eyes. Instead he pretended that she hadn't spoken to him so she repeated it, this time even softer, working to steady her breathing. "Randall, it's you, I know it is," Lexi nearly whispered it.

Lexi noticed Laurel glancing at her but Lexi didn't meet her eyes, lest she attract too much attention from Thomas who seemed oblivious to the conversation happening under his nose.

They were led into some office in the back hallway of the two story house. All thoughts of engaging Randall were lost as they were led to sit down on the sofa. Levi moved quickly behind her and Lexi braced herself for whatever blow was about to befall her and instead felt the tension release on her hands as he cut the rope that tied them together. She brought her hands in front of her, barely sparing her wrists a second thought but rubbing them absently as she surveyed the situation. No one else appeared to be here besides Randall, Levi and Thomas.

"I trust no one saw you enter the driveway?" Thomas directed his question at Levi. Laurel was seated on his left on the love seat and she looked positively terrified. She looked at her sister now and met her eyes and Lexi tried to send her the most encouraging look possible without giving away anything else.

Levi shook his head, "No boss, no one saw us. Stupid fuckers fell for the plan hook, line and sinker." Levi chuckled a little but then looked uncomfortable when Thomas didn't laugh at his joke.

Thomas looked to Randall and then Levi. "Gentleman, I think I'd like a moment alone with my wife and her sister. We have some catching up to do." He rubbed his hand over Laurel's thigh and back up again, his hand kneading her leg. The expression in Laurel's face became one of determination and sheer rage.

Levi and Randall walked over to the sliding glass doors and walked out onto the deck, which presumably led down to the beach.

Lexi had not seen this look on Laurel's face before. It was like something just snapped and the old meek, frail Laurel was replaced by someone stronger and fierce. The face of a survivor.

Something clicked inside Lexi in that moment. She was sick and tired of the Green girls playing victim to this asshole. Clearly, Thomas had not counted on the fact that Lexi was stronger now than ever and his poor meek wife, Laurel had been trained for the last several weeks by a black belt.

She looked to Laurel and gave her a barely perceptible nod and her sister blinked her eyes slowly in understanding. Lexi felt pride swell up in her at the knowledge that her sister had just crossed an important threshold in her recovery. She was taking charge now and Lexi would too. All they had to do was wait for the right moment.

All three pairs of eyes turned to look at Jeb still standing in the doorway all of them too dumbfounded to speak. Jake had barely had time to process that Lexi was gone and now here was Jeb, his brother.

It was too easy. Jake felt a rage towards his brother like no other and charged at him, knocking him into the wall of the entryway and pinning him against the wall with his arm trapping his head in place just beneath Jeb's neck.

"Where is she you sonofabitch?" Jake spat out. He was being driven by a blind rage and he didn't know if he could control himself even if this was his flesh and blood he wanted to tear limb from limb but Jeb had to somehow be connected.

Jeb held up both hands and Matt noticed he was sending out a distress call. He looked to Thad and nodded at him, then they both stepped forward and pulled Jake off of him. Jake bucked against their hold, kicking backwards and trying his best to throw punches, Matt and Thad effectively restraining him.

Matt got close to Jake's ear and whispered so only he could hear him, "I know you're hurting brother. But Jeb looks like he's here to help. He didn't have anything to do with this." Matt waited to see if what he was saying was settling into Jake's grief-addled brain. Jake relaxed a bit in his arms and Matt continued, flicking his head in Jeb's direction. Jeb rubbed his neck and eyed the three of them warily, keeping silent.

"Now I'm gonna let you go. And we're gonna hear Jeb out. Got it?" Matt said gently. Jake nodded and Matt released him.

Jake straightened up and went at Jeb stopping just short of where he stood, glaring at him. "This better be good." Jake took several steadying breaths and tried to find his center just like all his training had taught him but none of it was worth a goddamn right this minute. All he could think of right now was that Lexi was in the hands of a madman. The thought was making him deliriously crazy and he paced back and forth, not trusting himself to stand this close to Jeb.

Matt nodded to Jeb. "Alright, say your peace."

"Now, you know I'd never do anything like what you just accused me of little brother," Jeb said. "I may have my faults but I've never purposely put a lady in harm's way." He looked at Jake pacing back and forth and Jake turned to look at him.

"You showing up here was awful damn convenient if you ask me," Jake bit out.

"Well yeah, why you think I disappeared all the sudden. I was tracking Thomas too. Been following him for months now. I put my ass on the line for this job. And I ain't gonna let you mess it up now. We almost have him." Jeb took a look at the three of them. "What I'm about to tell you can get us all fired, the whole lot of us." Jeb sent a warning glance at men.

"I don't think you have to worry about us gossiping like some hens in church." Thad said wryly.

Jeb laughed. "I guess not," He conceded and reached in his jacket pocket, which had all three of them drawing their weapons and pointing them at him. "Jesus, *relax*, people." Jeb said, laughing as he pulled out a badge reading "D.E.A."

Jake looked at him and all the facts just clicked into place. It all made sense. He nodded and he felt a little bad about accusing him now of having anything to do with Lexi's kidnapping. He hated to even think about it. He took a deep breath and listened to what Jeb had to say.

"Thomas's involvement in the heroin world is the focus of the D.E.A. and has been for the last two years. He has the fastest growing drug ring in all of the east coast. I don't know what that man does to incite loyalty but he has turned some mighty fine cops into his lackeys and it's just getting worse. But I can fill ya'll in on all this on our way."

Jake looked at him confused. "Where are we going? You know where Thomas is?"

Jeb smile widened then. "Course I know where he is. Well, thanks to some deep digging, I know where he's *going*," Jeb corrected himself. "It's been my job to know where he is at all times. We've been waiting for this opportunity for months. This whole thing with his wife has made him come completely unglued. And that has made him pretty sloppy. We received word a little while ago that his car was heading north. Can you get to your plane, little brother?" He looked to Jake then.

For the first time since he had walked back into this house, Jake felt a surge of hope. "You bet your ass I can."

"Good, because we're goin' flying boys." Jeb grinned. "So suit up, we pull out in ten." Jeb looked at the three of them still standing there looking at him.

"Get your ass movin' son. You want to go find your girl, don't ya?" Jeb prodded.

They all moved at once then, setting plans into motion and gathering all the guns and ammo and other supplies they would need. Jake stalked out to his SUV, a new purpose in his step now, popped open the hatch and lifted the spare out of the back. He pulled at the carpeted surface and popped the panel off that he had specially installed for moments just like this one. All the sudden, all his training as a mercenary came back to him, like it had never even left. He had a mission and it was time to get ready.

He pulled out the empty backpack stored in the back and began filling it with grenades and various other explosive devices. He hoisted the pack onto his back and reached further into the compartment, pulling out his crossbow. It had been a couple of months since he used it but he slid the strap over his shoulder, relishing the weight of the weapon as it bounced gently against his back. He walked back into the house to retrieve the rest of what he would need to go after Lexi. Thomas had taken his family, something he had never in his whole life thought he would have. Jake vowed that as soon as Lexi was safe, he was going to kill that son of a bitch. Slowly and with pleasure.

Chapter 27

Jake checked the gauges for what seemed the fiftieth time in the last minute. He had a ton of nervous energy and he had thought that focusing on the flight would help quell the some of the fear that had settled into the pit of his stomach, come to rest like an old friend come home. He hadn't felt this much anxiety since all those years ago, a world away in the rainforests of Central America.

When he and Maria had been running from the goons in that rainforest, he had felt this same fear but that fear had soon turned to dread and then despair.

No, Jackson, he thought, that was *not* going to happen this time. There was much more at stake now. He knew he had loved Maria but not to the depth that he loved Lexi. He loved her more than he liked to draw breath. And if Lexi were gone from this world, then Jake no longer wanted to be in it either.

He rubbed a hand over his face and realized too late that he had smeared camouflage paint all over his face, knowing that it was important now more than ever to hide himself as much as possible when they hit the ground. Jeb had filled them in on Thomas's likely whereabouts. They thought he was most likely holed up in the northern part of the state and that was where they were headed now. Word had been passed down from higher ups that Thomas had acquired some property in the last couple of years as he had moved up through the seedy heroin rings he had circled around before taking them over.

Thad was sitting behind him and Matt beside him; Jeb was acting as co-pilot, having flown back when he was serving Airborne in Fort Benning, Georgia. He glanced to Jeb now who was listening to Thad rattle on about Laurel and all the things she had told him about Thomas over the past several weeks. It was obvious from the tone of his voice that he really loved her and he was as desperate to get Laurel back as he was to get to Lexi.

"Something about this so-called safe house where Thomas is supposed to be seems too damn easy," Thad began.

Jake brought his thumb up to his mouth, absently chewing on the tip. "You think we're headed in the right direction, Jeb?" He needed to know now. They were quickly approaching the rendezvous point where they would pick up the Jeep that would take them on up to where Thomas was.

"It just seems wrong," Thad paused for a moment. "Laurel talked about a place Thomas was having renovated right before she finally left him. Supposed to be super hard to get to. There's no access from main roads and it's right on the beach way up the coast, almost in Virginia. Some place called Coronova, Cardoba?" Jake glanced back at him.

"Corona! That's it. Anyway, Laurel was saying that Thomas bought it awhile back but he was super secretive about it. I looked it up back at our safe house and the deed is not registered to him. It'd be perfect if you ask me. It's inaccessible by car where his house is located. We'll have to go on foot," Thad looked to the rest of the group.

Jake watched as Jeb swiveled his chair around and looked to the rest of them and studied Thad thoughtfully. "Why didn't you mention this before, man?" Jeb said.

"Better change course little brother. My sixth sense is damn near vibrating." He chuckled to himself. "Set a course due north. I know the area Thad is talking about. It's hella remote and it'd be a perfect place for this sonofabitch to hole up."

"Thad knows what he's doin' Jeb." He didn't know how the hell his brother could be so flippant when Jake's whole world had been turned upside down. He was still reeling and if he thought too long on what Lexi might be enduring at the hands of that bastard, it turned his stomach. He had to concentrate instead on how good it was going to feel to snap Thomas's neck in two with his bare hands. The fear was about the only thing keeping him upright and fueling his blood with rage that he could do little about it.

If he gave into the despair, he knew he would be absolutely no good on this mission. He had to distance himself from the situation and treat it as any other reconnaissance mission; go in, extract the target, kill the perp, and get out. Simplifying things in his mind was going to keep Lexi alive. Jake punched in a few things on the panel and the plane shifted direction ever so slightly.

"You sure we're doing the right thing? Do I need to radio ahead to the ground team?" Matt said in a low voice.

"Nah, we'll check this place out. It'll be kind of like killing two birds with one stone. Our ground team can concentrate on the other location while we scout out the digs Thad here has been kind enough to point us to." Jeb finished smoothly.

As much as Jake sometimes detested his big brother Jeb and all the shit he gave him, he was now extremely grateful for his help. His big brother, a DEA agent. He would have never thought it, but now it all made sense.

Jeb, who had spent most of his teenage years hopped up on every drug known to man and some he peddled himself was now bringing the knife down on big operations like this one.

When the old man had kicked Jeb out when he turned 18, he had gone rogue for a while and no one had heard from him. Jake, still a kid at the time by the world's standards, had figured Jeb had gotten himself killed. And then a couple years later, they had received word that Jeb had been injured in combat. He was coming back to the states and Jake had hitchhiked his way all the way to Fort Benning just to see for himself.

He had been shocked by the change in Jeb. But as all things with Jebediah Jackson, it hadn't lasted long. Ever since Jeb was in his twenties, he had been in and out of trouble. Now Jake wondered if it wasn't all a cover for his real job now with the DEA. He guessed some things with his brother would always be a mystery and that included the strange relationship Jake himself had with him. It was just the Jackson way, he guessed.

As the plane was started to descend on the course he had charted, his fingers started twitching just like they always did when he was heading into a mission. He prayed silently, something he hadn't done in ages.

He sent a silent prayer up to a deity he didn't even know existed anymore; but just in case he was putting in his special request.

"Hey God, I don't know if you're takin' requests these days, but if you could just help me out this one time, I ain't gonna ever ask for nothin' again. Just please let Lexi be okay and let me get her back. It's all I'm askin'." Even more than wondering if any higher power existed, Jake wondered if he ranked high enough on God's list that he was worth listening to. He hoped like hell he was.

Because while Jake hadn't ever been a praying person, he was praying now. And he was fairly certain that even if he himself didn't merit an answer to prayer, Lexi did. She was about the closest to a saint there was in his book.

Every nerve ending jangled as the plane made final descent onto the tiny air strip that ran parallel with the beach. It was go time, now or never. He braced himself as the plane touched down, the landing a bit rougher than he would like but after a hitch, the Cessna took to the ground like it was meant for it instead of the skies.

The plane came to a stop, resting at the top of the deserted runway and Jake shut off the engines, not even bothering to do a post-flight check. Lives were at stake; lives that mattered to him more than any ever had before and he meant to save them.

At the end of the day, Jake was just a man in love. Willing to do whatever it took to get his girl back.

Lexi lifted her head from her knees and looked to Laurel again. Thomas had back-handed her when she had come back at him after he was berating her for leaving him. The man was clearly delusional. Hearing her sister describe Thomas beating her was one thing. Witnessing it was quite another. Lexi thought something might have broken inside Laurel because she wasn't fighting back anymore.

He'd moved them to a tiny room with no windows, but from what she could see the door in the back of the room had to lead to the outside. She could easily see him killing them in there and dragging their bodies out to the beach to dispose of them.

She was just silently sobbing, knees drawn up to her chest and her head resting there like she had been defeated. Her shoulders shook with the sobbing and Lexi longed to go to her and comfort her but she needed to stay strong and not show any sign of weakness towards Laurel. She knew from all her training that it would only make things worse and add fuel to Thomas' sick fire.

She spoke calmly, as she would to a wounded animal. "Thomas, Laurel didn't come with me because she wanted to. I kidnapped her; it wasn't like she really had a choice. So go easy on her." Lexi kept her tone low and even.

Thomas was pacing back and forth in front of them. He and his goons had moved them to a different room and bound their ankles and hands again. He stopped pacing at Lexi's words. "That right, Laurel?" He crouched down in front of Laurel and his face was awash with mental anguish. Lexi knew it was only a matter of time before he came completely unhinged. It was like being in the room with a ticking time bomb and Lexi had no idea how to keep it from detonating.

Laurel looked up at Thomas, her eyes watery. "Yes, Thomas. I didn't want to go with her, but she made me." Laurel sniffed and her eyes flitted to Lexi's briefly.

Lexi nodded at her. This could actually work. They just had to distract him long enough so they could make their move.

Thomas reached out and smoothed a stray tendril of hair behind Laurel's hair, a tender gesture from anyone else but even Lexi could see Laurel flinch when Thomas touched her. Lexi winced as Thomas ran his hand down Laurel's face and caressed her neck, his thumb pressing in at the base of her throat.

"Right here, this pulse point," Thomas breathed, his lips very close to Laurel's ears. "This right here is where I can take my knife and slice your artery open, letting the blood spill everywhere," he was whispering now and Lexi shuddered at his words. Laurel, to her credit, was not moving a muscle and the tears just flowed down over her cheeks wordlessly. It was obvious that Thomas was not buying the kidnapping act.

Thomas drew back and stared at Laurel for a long second, the time dragging out and Lexi was afraid to draw air lest it incite him to do whatever was going through his mind right now. He looked to Lexi then.

"So, little blonde bitch, you think I'm supposed to believe that? I've been watching her and her little boyfriend." Thomas looked at her smugly then as if he knew something that no one else knew.

"Thomas, please, he was just trying to help me. He doesn't mean anything to me." Laurel pleaded now, the terror evident in her voice.

Shit, shit, shit, thought Lexi. This was not happening. Could not be happening. He was going to kill them now. Lexi knew it.

She thought of Jake and how it was going to destroy him when she was gone from this world. She regretted now more than ever telling him that she was just another dead girl to him. She wished she could take those words back. She wished she could tell him one more time how much she loved him.

Thomas turned to Laurel then and slapped her hard across the face. Laurel reeled for a second and then righted herself. Lexi winced as Thomas pulled her forward by her shirt, hearing the fabric rip as he did so, exposing the top of Laurel's bra. "You know, I'm going to make you pay for spreading your legs for that piece of shit, Thad Lee," Thomas spat the words at Laurel and then threw her backwards against the wall.

He got back up to pace again. "Ya know, I think I'm going to make both of you pay." He tapped the knife in his hand against his thigh.

Thomas looked to Lexi then and Lexi knew she had never seen evil manifest itself so completely as it did just then in Thomas's face. "We'll play a little game. First I'll have a taste of you, little blonde bitch." He nodded to Lexi, the leer in his stare at her breasts not even remotely disguised. "Then I'll have my wife. And I'm so generous that I'll let both of you watch the other. The one who screams the loudest when I make them come gets to live. How's that sound?" He grinned maniacally then, nodding to himself.

A cold wave of new fear washed over Lexi then and she remembered how it felt to be pinned beneath his disgusting sweaty body. Her stomach turned and threatened to heave up its contents. She strained her wrists against the ropes as Thomas came at her. Thomas pulled her up roughly to face him.

"I think I'll let you go first, little bitch. We'll see how Laurel likes it when I'm fucking someone else like I had to watch her." He held her close and the awkward way Lexi was bound made it hard to stand up but she tried to face him as best as she could.

Thomas turned her around. "Now I'm going to untie you, Lexi," Thomas breathed against her neck, making Lexi's skin crawl. "And you're going to be real good or I'll make it hurt. Then it won't be any contest at all. I'll have to kill you first while your sister watches. And that won't be any fun, now will it. You gonna play nice?" Thomas whispered, raising all the hairs on Lexi's neck.

Lexi nodded mutely and Thomas pulled her backwards against him, her hands now free and she rubbed at her wrists. He bent down quickly to cut the rope binding her ankles together.

Lexi knew it was now or never. She might not get another opportunity. As Thomas moved to stand back up behind her, running a hand over her ass as he did, Lexi took her chance. She waited until he was standing and used her whole body to throw her head backwards, feeling a sharp pain in the back of her head as it collided with her target, Thomas's nose.

He cursed as Lexi turned on him and she used the brief moment of surprise to shove him to the ground. His knife fell and Lexi lunged for it but Thomas was too fast.

Sensing her move before she made it, his fingers closed over the knife's handle and he brought it up and Lexi felt the sting of it slicing her arm. She glanced at her arm briefly, a bit of blood welling to the surface. Nothing more than a flesh wound, just nicking the surface and she knew she had to make her next move count.

Lexi leaned back and brought her leg up, delivering a kick with the top of her foot, feeling the satisfying thud as it collided with his ribs, driving her whole body into it and quickly following that roundhouse kick with a front kick to his solar plexus, effectively catching Thomas by surprise and watched with a moment of satisfaction as he hit the ground again.

The moment was short-lived however as he recovered quickly and reached forward for her ankles, pulling on her right one in just the right place, forcing her to the ground on top of him. She struggled over him for a moment, trying to wrest the knife from his grasp. He threw it to the side, for whatever reason and it landed near Laurel. He pinned Lexi to the ground and she never saw it coming. Thomas reached for the hair at the top of her head and yanked her up, slamming her head backwards into the tiled floor. Lexi felt a searing pain in the back of her head, saw a flash and then slipped into nothingness.

Chapter 28

Jake crept silently across the sand leading up from the beach to the house, the only house for a mile either direction that had lights on. He crouched down lower and caught movement on his right, knowing it was Matt. Thad and Jeb had gone around to the front after their long hike from the runway to the house. It had to be at least three miles but they had covered a lot of distance, the mission present in the forefront of all their minds.

He inched himself forward on his elbows, feeling the sand rubbing against his skin and not caring whether it hurt or not. He gripped his assault rifle in his hands and felt the weight of his crossbow on his back.

He motioned to Matt as they neared the house now, conveying the need to stop and assess the situation. He spotted one guy on the back deck of the place, lighting up a cigarette. Jake shook his head. If the guy was one of his trained soldiers, he would have his ass for lighting up on the job. It made him stand out like a sore thumb on the unlit beach.

Anyone with half a brain could spot him from a mile away. Jake eased his bow off his back and got it into position, pulling back on the bowstring and cocking it until it clicked into place. He aimed carefully with the guy still in his sights and pulled the trigger until the bolt disengaged from the bow and sailed steadily to pierce the target's neck, dropping him like a fly, the smoke from his cigarette still swirling in the air above where he had been standing.

He motioned for Matt to move forward and they crept silently toward the deck and eased up the stairs and flanked either side of the sliding glass doors. Jake heard distinctive voices from inside, some scuffling and then he heard the most beautiful sound he had ever heard.

Lexi. "Thomas, you know she doesn't mean any of that." Jake heard her say. She was alive. His Lexi was alive. He felt relief wash over him but he didn't even let himself revel in it for a moment. If anything, it strengthened his resolve to get the job done.

He looked to Matt and knew he had heard it too. Matt nodded at him and Jake reached over and tried the door finding it unlocked. He slid it open moving the vertical blinds silently to the side as he slipped inside the cool darkness of the room. The voices had come from the left and he headed that direction now, feeling Matt behind him. They fanned out on either side of the door that led into the hallway. They had taken down the one guy and that meant Levi was still somewhere close by. Jake knew Lexi was talking to Thomas so that accounted for everyone. Suddenly there was a shot from the front hall.

Jake crouched down and eased around the corner to the hallway and peered out toward the door, looking on in horror as someone stood over Thad's body. Thad was trying to crawl away, his arm outstretched and blood dripping down onto the carpet from thin rivulets on his arm, down the fingertips.

Jake cocked his bow back again and released another bolt into the perps head, hitting him right in the temple. He fell forward and Thad narrowly missed being pinned by him. Jake moved forward, pulling Thad back against the wall and propping him up, just as Levi rounded the corner.

"What the fuck was all that?" Levi cried as he reached his comrade's body, the arrow still sticking out of the side of his head. "What the hell?"

Jake pulled his pistol from the holster fastened around his calf and pointed it straight at Levi's head. "Don't move, asshole," Jake said in a low voice.

Levi raised his hands up at his side as Jake removed his weapon from the waistband of his jeans. Stupid prick, didn't even know to not turn his back on an unsecured room.

"No need to get all excited, brother, we can talk about this," Levi laughed mirthlessly.

Jake snorted derisively. "Number one, I ain't your brother. Number two, we ain't got nothin' to talk about." With that, Jake reached down and pressed his fingers in at the two pressure points on his neck and shoulder, keeping the muzzle of the gun pressed against the back of his head, and watched as Levi slumped to the floor.

"He dead?" Matt murmured as he glanced about, watching for any movement that might alert them to the presence of anyone else.

"Nah, just put him to sleep for a bit," Jake whispered gruffly as he pulled a length of rope from his back pocket and made quick work of binding Levi's wrists to his ankles behind him. Hog-tying worked for more than just pigs in his line of work.

He then crept back to the hallway, motioned for Matt to follow him and wondering what the hell had happened to Jeb and who the guy in the hall he had shot with the crossbow was. Jeb had mentioned Randall and Levi and no one else.

He waited outside the door for a moment before motioning for Matt to open it, hoping like hell he wasn't too late to save them.

Laurel had never been more scared in her entire life. She watched Lexi struggle with Thomas and for a moment her heart soared when she thought Lexi had kicked Thomas down and he might stay down but he just kept getting back up again. It was like watching one of those horror movies that Laurel liked so much.

The bad guy always got back up, the boogeyman always came back, the serial killer had to always get in one more kill before he finally was put to rest. But watching the intensity of Thomas's rage rivaled any plot line Hollywood's writers could cough up onto the big screen.

As Thomas threw the knife to the side, Laurel had worried for a moment that it might collide with vital tissue on her leg but instead it landed at her feet. For whatever reason, Thomas had not bound her hands behind her back and now Laurel was grateful for it. She reached for the knife and placed it between her legs at her knees, letting them grip it in place as she moved the binding rope tied tightly around her wrists back and forth over the upturned blade, making quick work of freeing her hands and then quickly cutting the rope at her ankles. By this time, Thomas was getting back up.

He stood over Lexi's body as she lay lifeless on the floor and Laurel was terrified that she was dead. She wanted so badly to go to her but it would have to wait until Thomas was taken care of. She didn't waste time in trying to get up lest she call unnecessary attention to herself and turned the knife around and aimed it upwards towards Thomas. After he caught his breath, he turned towards Laurel and didn't see the knife until it was nearly too late. He leaned to the left but not quite far enough to miss the blade that pierced his shirt, going through to skin.

Laurel felt the sickening collision of knife against bone and sinew, felt the pressure as she slid it in further and felt it catch a bit as she pulled it back out, because no way was she letting the knife stay in him. She instinctively knew that if Thomas was not injured enough that he would turn the knife on her.

She felt the blood, sticky and thick, flowing backwards down the hilt of the knife to the handle and settle on her palm. Thomas looked up at her in surprise as he clutched his right side where she had just stabbed him. He was bleeding, but not profusely and Laurel swore under her breath. She had missed hitting anything vital or else he would have collapsed by now.

Knowing that she had the element of surprise still on her side momentarily, Laurel threw the knife far out of Thomas's reach. She thought it better to fight him hand to hand and she knew keeping the knife herself would likely get her killed if he got it away from her. Laurel lunged at Thomas then, knocking him onto the tiles with a grunt and Laurel stood over him, ready to kick him in the ribs when she heard a stirring behind her on the floor.

"Laurel?" Lexi murmured from the floor and Laurel sagged in relief but the dip in focus cost her. Thomas was on her in an instant, shoving her to the floor and straddling her, his legs on either side of her and he brought his hands down to her neck.

"You stabbed me, you bitch! I thought you loved me, Laurel. I thought you loved me." Thomas was angry but you could hear the anguish in his voice, his disbelief a palpable presence.

"Loved you? I could never love you, you monster. I can't believe I ever thought I did." Laurel spat at him.

"Laurel-" Lexi tried warning her sister. The last thing they needed was Thomas even more pissed off than he already was. He was bleeding from his side and she wondered how it had happened. She wondered how long she had been passed out. She sat up and rubbed the back of her head, wincing as she felt the knot that had already formed there.

Thomas brought his hand out to the side and backhanded Laurel, the crack of palm against skin hanging in the air. He did the same thing to the other side of her face and to her credit, Laurel barely flinched. Lexi got up somewhat unsteadily and shook her head to clear the dizziness. She knew she most likely had a mild concussion, but she didn't let that stop her from getting to her feet and heading in Thomas's direction.

"Get off her, you bastard." Lexi started to pull Thomas off her sister but stopped as she felt a cold hard object pressed firmly against the back of her head.

"Fuckin' move and I'll blow a hole in the back of your pretty head." The voice whispered.

Lexi sunk back to the floor and held her hands up in a defensive gesture.

Thomas got up off Laurel again and motioned for her and Lexi to line up on the wall in their original seated positions as he caught his breath and smoothed his hand over his hair, which had become downright disheveled since they had arrived at the house.

"Thank you Levi, it's about fucking time you got in here. Where's that no good shit Randall?" Thomas said as he bent over to retrieve the knife Laurel had thrown out of the way. He rubbed his hand down over his shirt, feeling the blood seeping through.

"Bitch stabbed me." He murmured nodding in Laurel's direction.

Levi nodded. "Need me to take Lexi outta here?" He asked. He knew he wouldn't mind a little alone time with the blonde. She reminded him a lot of Amy. He had already heard her with the stupid redneck, Jackson and knew she was a firecracker between the sheets. He could feel his dick twitching inside his pants thinking about bedding that one. But that was only if the boss man gave the okay. He wasn't going to even let his horniness get in the way of him getting what was coming to him, not even for a good lay.

"No, I told you, I got plans for them both." Thomas turned to Laurel then. "I'm going to forget for a moment that you cheated on me with that Thad guy. I'm even going to forget about you leaving me in the first place. But stabbing me? Laurel? I really thought we were better than that." The anguish was apparent on Thomas's face and if Lexi wasn't so disgusted by him and hated the day he was born, she might have felt sorry for him.

"Better than what Thomas?" Laurel breathed, her voice barely above a hoarse whisper. "Better than you beating the shit out of me every day?" Her voice gained some strength. "Better than you throwing me down the stairs when I became pregnant with our child?" Laurel's voice broke a bit then and Lexi gasped.

Laurel glanced at Lexi then, her eyes apologetic. "Better than you raping me? Did you do that to your other wife?" Laurel felt despicable for saying the words, but Thomas had pushed her too far. Too far to turn back now.

"Laurel," Lexi's tone was meant to be a warning but instead it came out as a strangled plea. She cringed as Laurel let Thomas have everything that he deserved and more and prayed with everything in her that he wouldn't make her pay for her words.

Thomas's first wife and child were both killed in a car accident some years ago. "Thomas you know she doesn't mean any of that." On the one hand, Lexi couldn't believe she was actually refuting her sister's words and on the other, she knew what happened when you pushed Thomas too far. Lexi knew that Laurel had just taken it way too far.

Suddenly there was a gunshot from the front of the house and Thomas looked to Levi. "Go see what the hell that was," he barked.

"On it, boss," Levi assured him, striding to the door and closing it with care behind him.

Thomas rounded on Laurel then, pulling her to him and bent over Lexi, pulling up on her hair again and slamming her head against the wall. She watched in terror as Laurel came running at her attacker and jumped on his back to aid her sister's defense.

"Get off my sister, you fucking prick." Her sister's eyes were twin pools of rage as she began to deliver hard blows to the side of his head. His arm came out to block her and Laurel leaned down and fastened her jaws over his shoulder. Thomas let out a piercing yell before bowing his back, rearing up and sending his elbow backwards to land with stunning accuracy in her sister's solar plexus. She went down like a stone in the wake of the blow, air forced out of her lungs on a dull cry.

Thomas grabbed her up from the floor by her hair, and Laurel didn't even bother to scream. Her eyes were unfocused with anger and fear as he wheeled around, facing Lexi who was still watching all this from the floor, against the wall, cradling her head in her hands, thankful that this time she didn't lose consciousness.

Thomas leaned down, his breath hot on her throat as he spit out. "Don't fuckin follow us or I'll slit your sister's throat."

He yanked open the back door, the warm beach air rushing in for a brief moment before he slammed it behind them, and then they were gone. Her sister was just gone.

Jake listened outside the door where he figured Thomas was keeping the girls and Matt flanked the other side.

He leveled his bow on his shoulder, six bolts locked and loaded, pointing it to the center of the room as Matt threw the door open, his gun raised and pointed in the same direction.

But the room was empty. Except for a small blonde figure staring at them as they opened the door. She was sitting against one wall, rubbing the back of her head.

"Lexi." He barely even could breathe her name he was in such disbelief that she was right before him and within reach. Jake dropped his bow to the floor and crossed the distance in a matter of seconds, pulling her into his arms and crushing her against his chest. He felt some of the tension slip from his shoulders as he held her tightly against him.

Lexi couldn't believe he was here. "Jake, I didn't think you'd find me." Lexi could barely finish her sentence as a relieved sob escaped her lips.

"Shh, I'm here now," Jake murmured against her hair.

"Are you okay?" He pulled back to look into her eyes, needing to see her and feel her and know that she was truly alright.

"I'm okay, he slammed my head against the wall, but I'm fine." She smiled up at him weakly then and his heart melted.

Lexi pulled away from him, her motions frantic. "Laurel!" Lexi breathed, a look of fear creeping back into her eyes. "He has her. Thomas has her. He's going to kill her, Jake." Lexi's voice threatened to crack then, but she strengthened her resolve. That bastard had her sister and she would get her back or die trying. She allowed Jake to help her to her feet. "I think I dropped my gun somewhere." She looked to Jake then.

Jake reached into the pocket of his camo vest and handed her the pistol she had indeed dropped back at the safe house. "Thought you might be looking for it when I found you," He smiled at her warmly.

They moved to the door of the room and back into the hallway, finding no sign of Thomas or Laurel anywhere. Glancing into the hallway, Jake was satisfied seeing Levi was still slumped over on his side.

He called to Thad then, "We're going to get Laurel. Thomas has her. You okay there?"

"Hell no, I'm not okay," Thad said as he got to his feet, gingerly avoiding any undue pressure on his right shoulder. "But I'm still going with you get her back," Thad declared, joining them as they approached the sliding glass doors. "They went out the back." He whispered in Jake's general direction.

"They went to the storage shack out by the dunes." Lexi breathed. "That Randall guy was going on about it on the way out here. Said Thomas kept his stash there." Lexi said knowingly. His stash was most likely his main hub for the steady supply of heroin he doled out all over Atlanta.

He likely got it in from a runner right off this very beach, she thought, looking out to where she could hear the Atlantic crashing against the shore in a steady rhythm, the wind and sea drowning out all other sound. She tried not to think how easily it could hide someone's screams for help.

They all fanned out as they reached the beach and crept steadily toward the ocean. Lexi hoped Laurel was okay and holding her tongue. She hoped Thomas would hold it together until they got there. She suspected that while Thomas had probably started out selling the drugs, he was most likely now using them too and if his actions were any indication, he was in deep. He had completely come unhinged over the last couple of days, it seemed and that was a very dangerous thing. He seemed on the verge of a psychotic break, if it hadn't happened already. She needed to get to her sister. Fast.

A cold knot of fear had settled itself deep in her belly from the moment Laurel was dragged out of that room by Thomas and it had not lessened any. If anything, it was worse than ever. The key was going to be not letting that fear win and Lexi girded up her strength, drawing on every bit of training she ever had and on every memory she had of her sister to raise the determination she needed. She was going to get her sister back and Thomas Garner was going rue the day he had ever crossed the Green girls.

Chapter 29

Lexi followed Thad, Jake and Matt across the sand as they approached the shack. As they got closer, they could hear Laurel's screams and Lexi felt her blood run cold and if she weren't so angry, fear would have won right then. She was so finished letting Thomas hurt her sister and this had to stop here and now. Tonight. Even if she had to kill him. Screw protocol and doing things by the books.

Right now, she was not a U.S. Marshal; she was Laurel's kid sister and hell would have to freeze over before she would let that bastard hurt her anymore.

She feared they might be too late as they rounded the corner of the shack set on stilts up off the beach and they heard Laurel scream again. The shack had a long ramp that led up to it from the front and a ladder from the back. Matt and Jake looked to one another and she could see the silent communication there. It was the kind that came after years of working together. It seemed to be her fiancé's preferred method of communication and it served him well. Jake had revealed more things to her in glances and stares than he ever had by speaking to her.

Jake looked to her and Thad and motioned for Thad to go with Matt and for her to follow him. Matt and Thad rounded the back side of the structure and began to ascend the ladder. She looked to Jake and his lips were mouthing numbers, counting off to some internal clock, and suddenly he motioned that they were going in.

When Jake kicked the door in, he went in with his bow cocked and ready. Thomas predictably used Laurel as a shield. The terror was evident in her face as he held a gun to her temple.

"Drop the gun, Garner," Jake growled.

Thomas smiled sardonically, his teeth baring white in the bright white light of the overhead lighting of the shack. Lexi glanced to the sides and briefly caught a glimpse of large crated containers stacked on top of one another, alongside each wall. She looked back to Thomas, her pistol drawn and cocked.

"Not a chance, you derelict redneck." Thomas bit out. "This is my wife. I will do with her what I please."

Lexi swallowed a lump of bile that rose in her throat. He really did see Laurel as a possession; it was often that way with abusers. She tried to keep statistics of these domestic situations and how they ended out of her head as she spoke with authority she barely felt.

"You may as well surrender, Thomas. The feds are on the way," she lied smoothly. She kept hoping the cavalry would ride in and save the day, but that usually only happened in movies and television. This was real life with real guns and a real bad guy right in front of them and her sister was right in his clutches. For all intents and purposes, *they were the cavalry*.

By the time their other people got there, it would likely all be over and Lexi could only hope that the odds were in their favor and right now, it was really not looking too promising.

Lexi felt a sudden cold pressure at the back of her head. She lowered her weapon automatically when she heard the voice. "Drop it bitch," Levi's voice was low, right by her ear and she shuddered involuntarily as a wave of sickness washed over her.

Jake bit out a curse as he realized his mistake. He should have killed the bastard when he had the chance but he had been playing this by the rules.

He felt the swirling pit of acid settle into his stomach again as he saw Lexi being held at gunpoint. He saw red and all he wanted to do was kill every son of a bitch that stood in his way. He breathed in slow and deep, trying to steady himself. It wouldn't do anyone any good if he went off half-cocked with a move that would get them all killed.

"Let's just calm down. Let's talk about what we can do to solve this," Lexi said smoothly. Matt had just entered the back window, holding a finger over his mouth, begging silence. It was dimly lit but she caught his movement. She could only pray that no one else noticed. "Everyone just take a deep breath and we can all come out of this in one piece." She was lying through her teeth now, but it didn't matter.

What happened next occurred in a flash and Lexi just ended up going with instinct and training instead of any set plan inside her head. Matt came up behind Thomas at the same time that Levi noticed him and he took the gun from the back of Lexi's head aiming at Matt.

Lexi, anticipating the momentary distraction as her only chance, tipped her head forward slightly, standing on her tip toes and brought it back with force against the lower part of Levi's face, earning a grunt from him and she herself literally saw stars as his face connected with the already tender place on the back of her head.

287

She shook herself mentally and rounded on him, watching as he scrambled to get his gun, having dropped it when he fell. She caught a glimpse of Jake out of the corner of her eye and saw him go down. Her heart fell as she watched him land on his shoulder a few feet away and he cried out in pain.

Not even stopping to think about what she was doing, she bent down and picked up her pistol that she had dropped, drawing it around to where Thad was struggling with Thomas and Laurel was huddled in the corner with both hands over her ears. She had blood running down the side of her face and Lexi wasn't sure if it was hers but she appeared to be okay physically so she rounded back on Levi, looking around in surprise when she didn't find him.

Matt was laying on the floor not too far away, nursing his hip where he evidently had been shot. Thankfully it didn't appear to be too serious. He was getting to his feet when Lexi felt a kick to the back of her knees, sending her careening to the floor, the force of the fall sending a searing pain from her ankle all the way up to her knee.

She brought her arm around in a sweeping motion and brought Levi down beside her and as his head hit the floor, she crouched over him and brought her elbow down hard on his nose, feeling the sickening crunch of bone and feeling the blood as it spurted over his face and splashed onto her arm. He brought up both hands to his nose and then to her neck as he tried to strangle her, flipping her over in the process and kneeling above her, he began to squeeze harder, cutting off her oxygen.

Lexi felt her vision graying at the edges and she fought with everything she had to stay conscious. He was really strong and his hands were wrapped tightly around her neck, rendering the rest of her limbs useless since they were presently without blood flow.

Lexi fumbled around on the floor, finally finding her gun and just when she thought she was going to go under, she brought her gun up to his forehead and pulled the trigger. Everything went dark for a moment as his body slumped onto hers, quite dead weight at this point. She used what strength she had from the adrenaline pumping through her body and flung his body off of her own.

She grimaced as she brought her sleeve up to her face and dragged her arm across it, bringing it away and she stared at the amount of blood smeared there.

Red.

Everywhere, bright red blood.

Jake had watched from the floor in horror as Levi knelt over Lexi and put his hands to her neck. Even from his position, Jake could see that he was strangling her to death. Fury welled up within him and he rose from his feet just in time to hear the gunshot and for one sickening, deafening moment, he thought that his life was over.

Not because he had been shot, but he was sure that when the gun went off and with Lexi's expression, that she was forever lost to him. He barely was able to release his held breath as she threw Levi's body off her and ran her arm up over her face, the fresh smears of blood spreading over the pale white of her cheek.

She struggled to get to her feet as she watched Jake walking towards her and their eyes locked. He was favoring the shoulder and held his arm back from his body almost behind his back. Jake suddenly stumbled backwards as Thad was hurled in his direction by Thomas.

Thomas's nose was bloody and his eye was swollen. Thad appeared to have really worked him over and Thad was not without his own injuries. His face was covered in blood and he was gasping for breath as Jake tried to steady him. Laurel was still sobbing uncontrollably and Lexi looked to her again just in time for Thomas to lunge at her again. Laurel's eyes went wide as Lexi just saw red.

"Just stop it." Lexi screamed at the top of her lungs and she didn't even recognize her voice. She aimed her gun straight in the air and fired it as she screamed.

They all turned to look at her, their expressions a mirror of shock as Thomas dropped his gun on the ground.

"Now kick it to me," Lexi demanded, her voice steady but her hands slightly shaky as she held the gun out in front of her. Thomas did as he was told and raised his arms in surrender.

"Now walk away from Laurel." Lexi didn't take her eyes off Thomas for one moment. Thomas moved towards Laurel and Lexi tried to gauge his expression and he almost seemed to be smirking at her. Anger welled up in her then.

"You think this is some kind of fucking game?" She screamed at him. She knew she was losing control and she didn't care anymore.

She pulled back on the hammer of her pistol and took aim. "Any final words, asshole?" She said as she smirked right at him.

"Lexi," Matt and Jake both called her name at the same time and she didn't spare them a glance, just held Thomas's cold stare. She wanted to see the light go out in his eyes when he went down.

"I'm going to finish him, Matt," Lexi hissed from between her teeth.

"You don't want to do that, Lexi." Matt used the calmest voice he possessed, though everything he was feeling belied his words. He had seen this happen to many an agent in his days. This situation was too personal for her and he should have protected her better.

Lexi just shook her head. "You're wrong," She breathed, holding Thomas's gaze. "It's the only way I can know he won't hurt me again. Won't hurt Laurel again. Won't hurt *anyone* again." Her fingers were shaking badly but she tried not to let it show.

Jake moved closer. "Lexi, Matt is right. He's unarmed. It doesn't look good. And besides it'll be far better letting him rot in prison for the rest of his miserable life," Jake said, his voice hoarse with unshed tears, hoping like hell he could get through to her. She was not a federal agent right now. She was Lexi Green, assault survivor. She was her sister's keeper. She was acting on instinct and emotion, a deadly combination in their line of work.

"I don't give a shit how it looks, Jake," Lexi bit out and brought the gun up, her arm getting steadier. "I need to do this."

"Think about us, Lexi." Though he didn't want to, he used the only thing he knew he had left in his verbal arsenal.

"I need to keep everyone safe. Especially us," Lexi breathed.

Matt looked on the scene, swearing to himself and holding his breath at the same time, unable to do anything lest the whole precarious situation tip out of balance.

Jake saw that he was getting through to her and he held his breath as he said the next words. "You put that gun down, I'll make sure he can never hurt anyone again, I promise you that," Jake said gently.

Lexi finally lowered the gun as Jake skirted around her and Matt followed, moving to grab Thomas. Thad had gone over to Laurel and drawn her into his arms and she was now seated in his lap and he was tending to a large gash on her arm, which was bleeding steadily. Thad's own shoulder was bleeding through his shirt at the moment.

Matt had Thomas's hands behind his back and was reaching for his cuffs, "Thomas Garner, you have the right to remain silent…" Matt pulled his cuffs from his back pocket and just as he was about to fasten them around Thomas's wrists, they heard Jeb's voice from right outside the shack amid gunfire.

"Get out here, we got rapid fire comin', Jake." They heard commotion from out on the beach, distant sounds of rat-a-tat that were growing steadily closer.

"Jeb." Jake bit out a warning, a question, he was not quite sure, looking to Matt.

Jake and Lexi moved outside, leaving Matt to tend to Garner. Thad and Laurel stayed put. Neither of them were going to be any good right now to anyone in their condition.

"Matt!" Jake called out.

"I'll be right out!" Matt called going back to what he was doing, fumbling with the cuffs, but the distraction outside had caught all of them unawares.

"You have the right to remain silent, anything you say," he began again and then stumbled backwards as Thomas's elbow connected with his solar plexus, taking his breath away. He gasped for breath as Thomas rounded on him and sucker punched him, his head reeling back and felt all the muscles in his neck pull. But as much pain as he was in and despite the fact that Thomas exiting the shack from the back window, the only thing Matt was thinking was that he had to get out there and help.

He yelled out then as he made to push the door open. As it was, it was hanging on the hinges where Jake had kicked it in.

"Garner just went out the back!" Matt called as he exited, taking in the scene. Jake and Lexi were crouched down by the railing, shooting when it was safe at the fire coming from below them on the beach.

Jake stood with Matt's new information and he looked to him then. "Which direction?" Jake's eyes scanned the beach and he saw a figure moving off towards the pier. Not waiting for an answer, Jake slung his bow up over his shoulder, grabbed his rifle and took off after him, feeling dread settle into his veins. If he got away again...he was not going to let himself think that. He was going to catch him this time.

From the north side of the beach, Matt could see the sparks coming off of rifles and he wondered where the hell it was coming from. As the sounds got closer, he realized that three gunned men were chasing Gibbs and another man up the beach. They were running as fast as they could and taking cover behind the dunes.

"Where the hell were you Jeb?" Matt bit out between rounds.

"Getting some goddamned back-up. This operation is a lot bigger than we first thought. This shack ain't got nothing on the house a few miles up the beach. That's where all the real shit is hidden. This is just a midway point for the operation." Jeb was out of breath and he was dragging his right leg behind him, the front of his pants soaked with blood. There was little time to be had before the gunned men reached the shack, but he had to know what exactly they were dealing with.

They could hear the distant sound of choppers heading their direction and as they continued to fire, the figures that had been chasing Gibbs and the other guy, Brad he thought his name was, were running towards them from the men that were chasing them. The cavalry had arrived; all they could hope was that it wasn't too late.

Lexi sat back against the outer wall of the shack, catching her breath. She finally stood up and started down the ramp, heading towards the pier where Jake had chased Thomas to, hoping like hell Jake would have a good excuse to take him out. Lexi knew if she could get Thomas alone, she would do it herself. There was no way she was going to let him live if she could at all help it. She was wishing fervently now that she had gone against everyone's advice inside that shack and put his sorry life to an end.

Jake ran as fast as he could, gaining a little bit more ground with each pump of the muscles in his thighs, which were screaming at him to slow down, but he didn't listen. The only thing he was listening to now as he made his way towards Thomas was his father's voice bouncing around inside his head.

"No good, little piece of shit. You never were good for nothing. Got yourself distracted by a piece of ass. Now everyone's ass is on the line." His old man's contempt was not even concealed.

Shut the fuck up, he thought. *He's not real,* he told himself.

As if the hounds of hell were on his feet, he quickly waded into the water under the pier and pulled himself up on the under-girding of the structure. At least from this point, he would be able to sneak up onto the pier unobtrusively. He hoisted his body up to the rails and waited for Thomas to run by. He couldn't for the life of him figure out why Thomas was so hell bent on going in what appeared to be a dead-end direction.

As Thomas came creeping past him, his footsteps sure and steady on the worn planks of the boardwalk, Jake hurled himself over the rail just after throwing his weapons to the side. If he had to take him down with his bare hands, so be it.

He went down hard, landing on top of the man. He grabbed hold of Thomas's shirt and pulled him up in time to land a punch to his jaw. Jake ignored the searing pain in his shoulder that the blow cost him.

"That was a pussy hit, Jakey boy." His father's voice, dogging him again. But Jake didn't stop. He pummeled the man again and again, feeling satisfied with each grunt that hissed out of Thomas's mouth.

"She's too *good for you. Because of you, look what's happened to her,"* he continued as Jake rained blow upon blow on Thomas until his face was a bloody mess. Both eyes swollen now, one completely shut. As much as Jake hit him and as satisfying as it felt, it was not enough.

He suspected he could stay on this pier all day and stomp the bastard's ass into the ground and it still would not be enough. Raping women, using them as a possession. This man reminded him so much of his father. The same one inside his head right now, dogging his every action.

"Shut the fuck up." He screamed inside his own head and shut out his father's voice.

He didn't know how long he crouched above Thomas, using his fists everywhere he could hit. He brought his knee down hard on Thomas's groin and felt him try to curl in on himself and Jake smirked.

"Yeah, you sick fuck. You ain't gonna be raping anyone anymore. When you go to prison for life, you'll be somebody else's bitch then!" Jake railed at him as he continued to punch him and then he stood up, wanting to stomp his head into the planks, but a sweet voice stopped him. It stopped everything, all the madness in his head until he was standing there out of breath, blood dripping from his fists.

"Jake?" Lexi said softly, her voice raspy with exertion. Thomas was lying on the pier, not moving, eyes closed and for one moment Lexi thought he was dead. But he was just stunned it appeared. He was still moaning and that meant he was still alive. There were flashing lights on the beach behind them and it looked to Lexi like the cavalry had arrived after all.

She breathed a sigh of relief then and she looked at Jake, realizing that he was still standing over Thomas. "Jake, they're here. It's over," Lexi murmured and he turned to look at her, his expression unreadable.

The next few seconds were over before anyone had a chance to think on them. As Jake turned to face her, Thomas suddenly sat up, grabbed a gun strapped to his leg and held it up, aiming at one or both of them, she was not sure which.

She knew that there was nothing she could do and as the gun went off, once, twice, ears ringing, her breath caught in her chest and she tipped sideways as a force knocked her to the side. She righted herself to see that Thomas had gone down, one shot right between his eyes and he fell backwards onto the pier, lifeless eyes staring up to the night sky.

Lexi turned to Jake in surprise to see Jeb staggering backwards, his hand held over his abdomen where blood was spilling through his fingers at an alarming rate.

Lexi moved fast and Jake was right behind her.

"It's okay, Jeb, you're going to be fine," Lexi crooned as she yelled down the ramp to the pier where figures were approaching. "Get a medic now!" she called.

She looked at Jake then. "Go in the shack. There's a bunch of white towels on top of one of those bins, bring them all." She looked him right in the eye, meeting his gaze as she held both hands over the wound, trying to staunch the flow of thick red blood that was coming out between her fingers.

"He's okay Jake, but I need you to do this for me." Jake nodded at her, his face having gone grey with fear, and ran down the pier, passing two medics as he headed towards the shack.

By the time he got back with the towels, he stood there watching dumbly as they loaded his brother onto a stretcher and he called out then from the edge of the pier.

"He's allergic to Penicillin." He didn't know where it had even come from, that thought seeping out from his memory, but he remembered something from an emergency room visit when they were just kids.

His dad had pushed him down the stairs and he had broken his arm, the bone sticking out at an odd angle and just poking through the skin. Jeb had needed surgery and ended up having a reaction to the antibiotic they had given him. He had almost died and was supposed to wear a medic alert bracelet, but never did. Jake shook his head at the memory. Jacksons could be a stubborn lot.

"We're taking him to county. You can meet us there." The medic said. "You're his brother right? You might need to make some decisions," Jake just nodded at the medic as he looked at his brother, all laid out on the stretcher, oxygen mask on and eyes closed and so very, very pale.

He had never seen his brother like this. Not even in the worst days back when they lived at home, Jeb had always been able to bounce back. He would now too. He had to.

Lexi came up behind him then and put her arms around his waist and resting her chin against his back. He let his head drop forward then, wondering how it had all gone to shit. He had his girl, but had nearly lost his brother. *What kind of fucked up world did they live in anyway,* he thought.

Just as they were about to walk down the pier following after the medics, Jeb's body arched up off the stretcher and shuddered and jolted and Jake just watched in horror as the medics worked on him, trying to bring him back from the brink of death's grip. Jake heard words but they didn't form coherent thoughts or complete sentences.

…seizing….chest compressions….defibrillator….clear!

The jolting whine of the defibrillator pulled Jake from his haze.

Lexi had moved beside him and took his hand in hers, her fingers clasping around him, holding onto him for dear life and he could feel the tears burning his eyes as they traced their way down his face.

Jeb sputtered for a minute and called out Jake's name and Jake slumped in relief. Lexi let go of his hand as he approached the stretcher and the medics just let him. He wondered briefly why they didn't keep rushing him to the waiting helicopter. He heard Lexi sniffling behind him.

"*Jake*. Come 'ere little brother," Jeb called out, his voice barely even a whisper.

Jake looked down at Jeb, his big brother. Sure he was a pain in the ass, but he was his blood. The only blood he had left now.

"You look like shit, Jeb," Jake tried to joke, but the laughter didn't quite reach past his lips and the forced smile definitely didn't reach his eyes. He knew it then. Jeb was dying and it felt like his heart had been ripped from him, the shreds falling to his feet.

"Yeah likewise, Jakey boy," Jeb said and Jake knew that was the last time his brother would ever call him that. "You take care of your girl, you hear." Jeb whispered. "You were always the good one, little brother. Stay good." Jeb reached out and grabbed Jake's hand then. "Love ya," Jeb said.

There were those three words again and he simply couldn't fathom why he and his brother had never uttered them before. He knew, but still; it wasn't right.

"Love ya too Jeb, but you're gonna be fine," he said gruffly, his voice thick with the tears coursing down his cheeks wishing like hell he believed his own words. He knew better. God, *he knew*.

"I'll tell Mom you said hi," he gave him a small smile then and Jake sobbed at his words. "You take care of him, girlie," he looked to Lexi and she nodded at him, unable to speak between her sobs and just reached forward and clasped his hand on the stretcher, so cold and unmoving.

With that, Jebediah Jackson closed his eyes as his body jerked one last time and he was gone. Jake stood there on the pier and let himself feel it. Let himself feel the heartbreak, the pain, let it wash over him like the waves crashing on the pilings of the pier beneath them. He kept waiting for it to knock him down and he could crumble like so much rubble, but he just stood there, in numb disbelief that his brother was gone.

"We're so sorry, Mr. Jackson," the one medic told him and the other nodded his agreement. "Call this number when you can. You all should go be checked out," the medic said and Jake just took the card from him.

Jake just stood there as they wheeled his brother away and Jake looked helplessly to Lexi. She was crying as hard as he was. "I'm so sorry Jake. I know you loved him."

"He was the only blood I had left," Jake sobbed and Lexi's heart broke into a million pieces feeling the pain radiating off of him and she pulled him to her then somewhat awkwardly, being careful to avoid his shoulder.

"He saved your life," he breathed and took a moment to look at her. The look in his eyes pained her.

"I know," Lexi whispered, reaching up to brush his tears away. She realized now that it was Jeb who had knocked her out of harm's way. The bullet he'd taken from Thomas' gun was meant for her.

"I didn't even get to tell him thank you," Jake's voice broke again on those words and it just wrecked Lexi to see him in this much pain.

"Oh honey," Lexi crooned, pulling him to her closer. "He knew," Lexi insisted. "He wouldn't have done it otherwise. He saw how much you loved me. He saved my life. Sacrificed himself so I could live. There's a verse daddy used to say. 'Greater love has no one than this, to lay down one's life for one's friends'. That's what he did. He sacrificed himself so I could be here," Lexi spoke softly, feeling Jake's sobs finally subsiding.

"I'll never be able to repay him." Jake said miserably.

"Some sacrifices we don't have a choice in Jake. They're made for us. And sometimes we don't have to repay every favor done for us in life. This is one of those times," Lexi whispered and he looked at her then.

"I'm going to miss him." Jake said then, meeting her eyes, relieved at the love he found there; at the comfort he always found in looking directly into her eyes.

Lexi looked at him then and saw him, all of him, and knew she had never loved him more. "I know he was your family Jake. He would have been mine too, but-. I can be your family now." Lexi said a little uncertain.

Jake looked at her and he sighed and pulled her more fully into his arms. "Of course you are. You *are* my family. We gotta get you to the hospital. Have you checked over." Jake looked at her worriedly.

"I'm fine, I promise. But, I'll make you a deal. I'll go, if you go," she challenged him.

He smiled softly at her then. "Deal."

He dipped his head down and his lips met hers, his kiss urgent and at the same time, tentative and sweet as his lips trembled.

As her heart beat rapidly in her chest, Lexi knew this kiss was life-affirming; proof that they were still breathing. That they still had this. This thing between them; fleshed out in the middle of chaos and still standing, despite all the odds against them.

Jake rested his head on her chest and wrapped his good arm around her and holding on like he was never going to let go. Lexi finally was back with the love of her life and she didn't intend to let go of him one second sooner than he let go of her. With the way they were both feeling, it would be nothing short of forever.

Chapter 30

Jake stood at the graveside, feeling a whirlwind of emotions. Lexi stood at his side, her hand tucked around his arm and Matt stood on the other, both flanking him like warriors, ready to hold him up should he fall, but he was oddly calm, at peace even.

He tried to listen to the minister as he performed the lengthy Episcopalian ceremony, mouthing the words to the liturgies they were to repeat, but he wasn't there.

Instead he was a teen and his old man had gone into a rage again, this time it was Jeb on the receiving end of their father's fury. Always something, always some minute thing to piss him off and sending him flying off the handle. Jeb had gotten caught stealing some of his old man's vodka for a party. His mom was long gone by then and it was just the three of them. Jake had overheard his brother the day before bragging to his friends that he could get them any amount of liquor they wanted. He just had to wait for their old man to pass out.

Jake had looked out for him, watching the door in case their pops decided to wake up early from his nightly hangover. Jeb had been reaching under the cabinet, just one of the old man's many places that he stashed his booze. His old man had walked in right then, Jake never even having a chance to warn Jeb of him waking up and the impending ass-beating he was about to receive.

"You good for nothin' piece-a-shit thief, I knew you were stealing from me." The oldest Jackson bellowed and Jake fought the urge to go and hide like he normally did when he got in a stir.

But this might be the worst offense ever and as his father unleashed his fury on his brother, taking off his belt and hearing it snap in the air like a whip and hearing the clang of the buckle every time it whipped back as the old man slung it out in wild swings that landed the strop of leather against his back, his neck, the backs of his legs until finally casting it to the side and he was on top of Jeb in an instant. He straddled him and Jeb had only been about 15 or 16 at the time, still too puny to fight off their father with any real results.

As his father wrapped his hands around Jeb's neck, Jake had begun to cry thinking that this would be the night that he finally killed them. Because he knew, when he was done with Jeb, he'd be coming after Jake too. He would never forget the way Jeb's face had gotten red and then had started to turn grey.

He had been pretty young at the time, but he remembered feeling certain that he was going to die. That his father was going to kill him. He didn't think; he just acted. He grabbed the bottle that his father had cast to the side, the one that Jeb had just risked both their lives to steal. And for what, to impress some kids at school and maybe get that girl he'd been chasing for the past two weeks to finally kiss him?

Jake grabbed the bottle, gripped it in his hand by the top and brought it down on his father's head. He collapsed against Jeb, blissfully unconscious. Jeb had run away that night and Jake had gone and hid in his closet, certain that his father was dead and he had killed him, convinced too that he was never going to see Jeb again and he didn't, not until he got back from the military years and years later.

He supposed he had saved Jeb that night and now it had all come full circle. They might not have been the closest as far as family went, but they had their own special way, him and Jeb. He was his brother after all and he had made the ultimate sacrifice in saving Lexi's life.

His life for hers, and Jake would never forget it.

As the priest sprinkled dirt on the casket, Jake gripped the flag that had been given him to his chest, and whispered into the air thinking that Jeb maybe could hear him. "Thanks brother, guess we're even now." He didn't feel the tears coursing down his cheeks until he looked at Lexi, her face blurring in his vision as he wept out his grief.

The priest had stopped speaking and they all looked to the group of men, the honor guard as "Taps" was played by a lone bugler. Tears welled up in his eyes again and as the men hoisted their rifles, Jake tried not to flinch as they fired them, the sound thundering into the clear blue sky, such a stark contrast to the swirl of emotions in his gut.

Jeb had been given a full send-off, buried with high military honors. As the second set of gunfire boomed all around them, Jake was catapulted back to those fields of vanilla orchids, all those years ago when he had loved and lost and vowed to never love again.

As the third set echoed in his ears, he was propelled onto a beach in North Carolina, while a gunshot rang out and his brother fell to the pier, signifying the end of the first part of Jake's life and the beginning of the next.

Life really did come full circle, he thought. It seemed the most important parts of his life were canonized by the sound of gunshots. As he stepped forward as commanded by the priest, he picked up a handful of dirt and sprinkled it on his brother's casket, making the sign of the cross and feeling an odd sense of resolve wash over him.

Jake wanted the rest of his life to be marked by something other than the stark sound of a shot ringing in the dark. He had placed his badge and gun on his nightstand that morning and he didn't plan on picking them back up anytime soon.

No more gunshots for him. No more fighting battles that were not his to fight. From now on, he wanted his life to be punctuated by something different. Soft kisses in the moonlight, afternoon walks and picnics on the beach, Sunday mornings spent in bed in soft silence, the echoes of the past forgotten.

Those were the things in life that he had been missing out on all these years. Those were the things worth fighting for.

Epilogue

Lexi pulled up sharp on the cord, the board flying out of her control, the wave hitting full force as it knocked her to the ground. "Dammit." She sputtered, the saltwater blurring her vision and filling her mouth.

Jake had been patiently giving her instructions all day out on the water. They'd started in the sound again, but finally half way through the day she coaxed him into letting her try out her wings in the ocean. She hadn't had to twist his arm too hard and if she had maybe promised him extra great sex later, well then so be it. He was her husband, now, after all.

They'd finally tied the knot a few weeks ago; just a small ceremony at City Hall with Thad and Laurel present as witnesses.

Now, she saw him waving her over from where he was watching just past the breakers and she shook her head at him emphatically. She loved him dearly but she if he told her to "tuck her knees" one more time to get that "edge", she was going to scream. She'd watched instructional videos all evening last night on Jake's laptop.

They'd decided to go back to the beach house one more time before cooler weather set in. They had settled in to married life just fine. Lexi wasn't pregnant yet, but she figured it would come with time.

Laurel and Thad were now officially dating, taking things slow and Laurel was still in therapy several times a week with Melinda. The two couples had dinner together the week previous and she didn't think she'd ever seen Laurel so happy. She didn't think she'd ever seen either of them this happy.

In addition, they had finally accepted an invitation to Matt and Vivian's end of summer barbecue and it had been great to see everyone together again, healed from all the action that had gone down that fateful night when his brother had given his life. Karen had been found safe and sound, much to Gibbs' and everyone else's relief.

Everything had gone pretty much back to normal, except for them. They were taking time to figure out how they wanted to go forward in life. She had resigned from the U.S. Marshal's office and Jake had done the same from his company. She thought they'd each had enough chaos and danger to last them a lifetime.

Now on the water, Lexi motioned to Jake that she wanted to do this one on her own. She wanted to be able to catch air just one time before they went in for the day. The weather tomorrow would be too dangerous to come out.

Jake had explained it very well what she would need to do and she'd watched enough to know. She looked above her, looking for the zenith, the opening above her head where she needed to get the kite into position.

It had to be timed at just the right moment as well and as Lexi had found out, it was a lot harder than it looked on all those videos. Still, she steadied the cord in her hand, winding it up tight enough to pull the kite into view, right into that frame above her head and it was suddenly as if everything fell into place at once.

It was a cosmic lining up of events, the right wave coming along with the right gust of wind and the right momentum in her body. She shored her feet into place, curling her toes against the board, finding that edge and glancing overhead briefly to be certain the kite was still in the zenith. *It was.*

She watched the wave approach, shifted her body to catch the edge and popped it, the board coming up off the surface of the water as she caught a glide and skimmed over the top of the wave, once, twice, and then like all those other boarders she'd watched, she expertly guided the board back out over the breaker and caught the next one. She nearly lost her balance in her excitement and she couldn't hear anything over the rush of adrenaline in her ears, but she thought she might have heard Jake whoop from across the way.

The next wave took her down, but the feeling she had was exhilarating. She came up sputtering and Jake was right beside her pulling them into safer waters and into his arms.

"You did it, babe!" He said against her ear.

"I did." She put her lips to his and with the wind whipping her hair about her face, she knew nothing could be more perfect than this moment.

A few short weeks ago she'd been driving her car to meet this man to pilot her sister to safety. She had never realized what love could do. Love for her sister. Love for this man.

It was bittersweet of course. She had gotten her sister back, but Jake had lost his brother forever. It was strange the way the universe worked sometimes.

She tucked her head under his chin as his arms came up to envelope her. She thought that their relationship was kind of like that. She had found the love of her life in Jake Jackson and he in her.

She thought now, looking back, that they'd had a cosmic lining up of events of their own. A chain reaction that once it was set in motion, it brought them both together and here on this very beach, they'd found their zenith. That highest place, a place that was almost celestial, where their love could exist forever, together. And that made it all worth it.

The end

About the author

Eliza Payne is a freelance author and poet, born in West Virginia in 1971. She has been writing short stories and novels since the age of 13, but just published her first novel, "Finding Your Zenith", to be released in June of 2016.

She is an alumnus of Winston Salem State University, earning her Bachelor of Science degree in Nursing. However, her true passion has always been literature and theatre and thus, she has spent a lifetime perfecting her craft.

The idea for this book came because of her personal experience, but her experience in working with trauma victims is what gave her the idea for this tale.

She currently resides in Kernersville, North Carolina with her husband, three children and two cats, Jasmine and Mia. She enjoys reading, cooking and Greek mythology. Eliza is presently at work on her next novel to be published late fall of 2016.

Important Notes

The theme of this book is about finding one's true soulmate, but the fiber of this book was written in tribute to all the victims of domestic violence and sexual assault. For all the ones for whom it was too late to save, the ones like me who got away and the ones who are still living under that horrible oppression, this book is a testament that hope can prevail. There is life after trauma and you can come back from it. I am living proof.

I would urge anyone who is currently a victim of domestic violence to call the domestic violence hotline at 1-800-799-7233 or TTY 1-800-787-7224 or visit their website DomesticViolence.org. Please seek help for yourself if you are able.

If you have been a victim of sexual assault, know that there are others out there like you and there is hope beyond what you have experienced. Raiin.org (Rape and Incest International Network) is very well connected in helping victims of rape or incest. Alternatively, you may call them at 1-800-656-HOPE.

As always, if you are in immediate danger, please dial 911.

This is not an easy subject and it is not one that I tackled lightly. My story, Laurel's story, Lexi's story, Jake's story; our stories are just one of many. You are not alone.

Love, light and prayers to you all. xoxoxo

Made in the USA
Middletown, DE
09 January 2023

21043567R00176